COMING NEXT TIME

STORIES! Al
SHERLOCK HOLME

Sherlock Holmes Mystery Magazine ...
is just a few months away...watch for it!

Not a subscriber yet?
Send $59.95 for 6 issues (postage paid in the U.S.) to:

Wildside Press LLC
Attn: Subscription Dept.
9710 Traville Gateway Dr. #234
Rockville MD 20850

You can also subscribe online at
www.wildsidepress.com

FROM WATSON'S NOTEBOOK

As ever, Holmes is pleased that this issue is devoted solely to his adventures. In it are new adventures written from my notes, plus my own recounting of the case of the stockbroker's clerk. In addition—for the first time in nearly a century a new Holmes tale is herein presented. I cannot take credit for it, though, it is of that small company by my literary agent Sir Arthur Conan Doyle that also includes "The Field Bazaar" and "How Watson Learned the Trick," both of which appeared in earlier issues.

And now here is my colleague and co-editor Mr Kaye…

– John H Watson, M D

✗   ✗   ✗   ✗

It's always fun to assemble these all-Holmes issues. As ever, we offer both new authors and pieces by such regulars as Dan Andriacco, Carla Coupe, Jack Grochot, Gary Lovisi, Kim Newman and the good doctor's agent Sir Arthur Conan Doyle in the form of a newly-discovered Holmesian anecdote.

I'm very excited about our next issue. In addition to reappearances by several authors including Dan Andriacco, Laird Long, and Jacqueline Seewald, as well as Dr. Watson's important case, "The Naval Treaty," we will welcome the long overdue appearance of Rex Stout's huge detective Nero Wolfe.

When this magazine was first planned, our publisher thought we should make it the *Nero Wolfe Mystery Magazine*. Though I love that series of novels and stories penned by Wolfe's right-hand man Archie Goodwin, I thought we'd do better with a periodical devoted to Sherlock Holmes and in this the publisher concurred.

But I hoped to bring Mr. Wolfe onto our pages sooner than this. In the next number, this will be accomplished with a new Wolfean anecdote by Archie Goodwin and an article discussing the cast of the series by Robert Goldsborough, who continues the series with his excellent Nero Wolfe novels approved by the Stout Estate.

More details next issue…

Canonically Yours,
Marvin Kaye

✗

ASK MRS HUDSON

by (Mrs) Martha Hudson

I have been planning on such a column as the present one for quite a while. Most of the queries I receive understandably display curiosity over my illustrious tenants Mr Holmes and Dr Watson, whereas I am often asked for new recipes and other "tips," as the Yanks say, about household matters.

But from time to time, affairs both domestic and romantic are raised, and I have been compiling these missives with an eye to devoting an entire essay—this one—to such matters.

✗   ✗   ✗   ✗

Dear Mrs Hudson,

For perhaps a year I have been courted by a gentleman considerably younger than myself. This, as you may imagine, is flattering, but I have not put much stock in his ardent youthful expressions … until now, for you see he has quite amazed me by proposing that we marry.

I daresay his proposal is both legitimate and honourable, for he has ever conducted himself in a gentlemanly fashion and has never presumed to liberties that would be, at best, timely; the furthest he has ventured in this direction is to hold my hand.

Well, I am tempted to say yes to him, but hesitate for a few reasons. Firstly, I have no idea in what manner he is employed, and though I am independently well-off, additional income for the purpose of banking regular sums to guard against health emergencies would surely be prudent. But secondly, you see, I have no idea where he lives, nor has he ever mentioned any member of his family. And third and lastly, whilst I find his company quite pleasant, I am afraid I do not share his professed romantic feelings to the extent that he has declared.

You may wonder that his age—for he is much younger than I—does not constitute a fourth misgiving, but I am generally said to be quite comely, and as stated above, I am sufficiently wealthy to be no man's burden.

But I have never entered into any serious relationship before this, and thus have never married; since you have done both, it is to you I turn with the utmost trust.

Yours faithfully,
Amanda Worthington

✗ ✗ ✗

Dear Miss Worthington,

I do not wish to alarm you, but what you tell me concerning this young man disturbs me considerably. It sounds to me as if he is a confidence trickster who is after your money. However, in the event that he is both genuine and sincere, I should not act precipitately. If you've a mind to wed the gent, tell him your acquiescence depends on knowing more about him. To begin with, he must show you his "digs"… though an adept criminal will manage that convincingly. You should also inquire about his parents and siblings, but above all else, you must know what he does for a living and where he works. I stress most emphatically the importance of this final matter.

It is quite conceivable that these demands may send him away on the instant. Yet even if he provides the answers you seek, there is still the possibility that he is weaving a tissue of falsehood. Since you are a woman of means, I urge you to employ a private investigator to root out the truth. (Of course I cannot recommend Mr Holmes to help you; he does not involve himself in this sort of "case").

Most sincerely,
Mrs (Martha) Hudson

✗ ✗ ✗ ✗

My Good Mrs Hudson–

My wife has just left me for another man. What shall I do? I still love her.

Broken-hearted in Brixton

✗ ✗ ✗

Dear Broken-Hearted,

Let me utter my sincere condolences for your sad plight. I do hope, at least, that there are no children involved in this unfortunate turn of events. Assuming that there are not, you should muster up patience for Dr Watson, who knows much more than Mr Holmes about affairs of the heart (except when they lead to blackmail or murder), once told me that the average affair runs its course in about three months, after which the novelty has worn off and each of the amatory partners suffer deep regret and wish to effect some sort of reconciliation with the person they cheated on. If indeed you do love her as much as you say, accept her return without re-criminations and double your amatory attentions, if at all possible. She will be ever so grateful and unlikely to repeat her indiscre-tion... but if she does cheat on you again, you must steel yourself to get over her somehow!

But if children *are* involved, your first duty must be to protect them, both as their father and as their legal guardian. Whilst I cau-tion you not to say anything derogatory about their mother to them, I strongly advise you to seek the advice of a domestic attorney. Mr Holmes knows an excellent one who will exact a modest fee upon my tenant's say-so.

Sincerely,
Mrs (Martha) Hudson

⚡ ⚡ ⚡ ⚡

Dear Mrs Hudson,
Would you mind telling us something about your late (presum-ably) husband?
Curious in Carfax

⚡ ⚡ ⚡

Dear Curious,
Yes, I would mind.
Mrs Hudson

⚡ ⚡ ⚡ ⚡

Dear Mrs Hudson,
My late husband John Jasper Weems died recently and would have left me penniless but for the generous life insurance payment that my solicitor recently received.

Unfortunately, this worthies's offices have been broken into a few weeks ago and all of the monies stored there have been lifted, even though it was all kept in a state-of-the-art safe.

Have you any advice? I am at a loss as to what I may do, and my bills are accruing at an alarming rate!

Desperately,

Mrs (Elizabeth) Weems

✗　✗　✗

Dear Elizabeth,

I hope you do not mind my addressing you by your first name, but I am touched, troubled—and quite alarmed—at your fiscal predicament. Kindly brace yourself for some shocking news...

Your husband is *not dead!* He is a criminal with whom Mr Holmes is quite familiar. Indeed, he was imprisoned for many years for a crime identical in nature to the one that "Mr Weems" has perpetrated upon you. (I have placed his name in parentheses because his real name is Jacob Moran. He is the younger and estranged brother of the infamous Colonel Moran, who is employed by a man Mr Holmes cautions me not to name).

Rest assured that Moran soon will be brought to justice, at which time what is rightfully yours shall be restored to you. Mr Holmes is about to apprehend him. He says I should tell you that he will not charge for his services, for he was already "on the case." Though if you wish, a small gift would be appreciated; pipe tobacco is always welcome, but if you decide upon this, kindly avoid the more aromatic blends that Mr Holmes enjoys to the discomfort of me and Dr Watson!

I trust your heart shall weather this unexpected turn of events.

Trusting in Your Good Sense

Mrs (Martha) Hudson

✗　✗　✗　✗

In my column in the nineteenth issue of this magazine, I said that I would honour requests to share mixed drink recipes I have concocted for me and my tenants. Here are four of them. Three involve blended scotch, which Dr Watson is fond of, though he generally drinks it neat. Scotch does not mix well with most cocktail ingredients.

For the last recipe, I had to do a bit of research. My church asked me to prepare a libation for a fund-raising party. I came upon Fisherman's Punch though it why it is called that, I have no idea. Do be warned! It goes down ever so easily—and therein lies the danger; it is like the theatrical works of James M Barrie, that dear Scottish playwright, whose compositions are the proverbial iron fist in a velvet glove.

SCOTCH AND DUBONNET

2 oz. of blended scotch
1 oz. of red Dubonnet
3 dashes of orange bitters

1. Ice a cocktail shaker.

2. Strain all liquids into the shaker.

3. Add an orange twist.

✗　✗　✗　✗

ARTHUR'S SWEET

The name of this drink is based on Edinburgh's old mountain Arthur's Seat.

1 oz. of blended scotch
¾ oz. of cherry brandy
1 oz. of fresh orange juice
¾ oz. of sweet vermouth

1. Ice a cocktail shaker.

2. Add all liquids to the shaker.

3. Shake well.

4. Strain into an appropriate glass.

5. Add a cherry.

✗　✗　✗　✗

LOCH NESS BREW

2 oz. of blended scotch
1 bottle of ginger beer
¾ oz. of lime juice

1. Fill a highball glass with ice.

2. Place the lime juice and scotch into the glass.

3. Fill the remainder of the glass with ginger beer.

4. Stir the liquids.

5. Add a slice of lime.

⚹   ⚹   ⚹   ⚹

FISHERMAN'S PUNCH

1 bottle of blended scotch (avoid the peatier ones)
1 bottle of apricot brandy
1 small bottle of armagnac (cognac is also usable)
½ bottle of green ginger wine
1 bottle of champagne

1. In a large punch-bowl place a great quantity of ice.

2. Add apricot brandy, armagnac, scotch and ginger wine

3. Fill to half the bowl's capacity with plain soda.

4. Chill the mixture till just before serving.

5. Add champagne and stir.

⚹

SCREEN OF THE CRIME

By Kim Newman

SHERLOCK HOLMES

After Arthur Conan Doyle and Sidney Paget, the most important figure in the rise of Sherlock Holmes from one-shot detective novel hero to global icon was actor-author William Gillette. Though Doyle had killed off Holmes in "The Final Problem" in 1893, the character remained popular—and Doyle, among others, made several attempts to transfer Holmes (and Watson) to the stage. However, Gillette pulled off the trick—combining elements from several stories ("A Scandal in Bohemia," "The Final Problem," "The Greek Interpreter") along with new-made plot-licks and supporting characters in a script which debuted in 1899. Remembered for his trend-setting performance as Sherlock Holmes, Gillette is often overlooked in his capacity as a major writer involved with the character. Gillette didn't include Mrs. Hudson in his *Sherlock Holmes*, replacing her with "Billy the Page" (a role once played by a young Charlie Chaplin). Billy become so much a part of the show (he has more to do than Watson) that Doyle—in what now seems an astonishing admission the franchise had got away from him—later wrote the character into "The Adventure of the Mazarin Stone." In an exchange of cables, which later pasticheurs have used to justify all manner of mischief, Gillette asked Doyle "may I marry Holmes?" and received the reply "you may marry him or murder him or do anything you like with him."

Gillette achieved great success in the star role of Holmes, which he played in New York and London. H.A. Saintsbury took over the part when Gillette moved on (and was identified with the role enough to appear in a 1916 film of *The Valley of Fear*). Gillette returned to the deerstalker and dressing gown for revivals of the play throughout the rest of his life—and even appeared in a radio version. In 1916, Gillette reprised the part in a movie directed by Arthur Berthelet at the Esssanay Company's Chicago Studios, making his only feature film appearance. A major hit in its day, but also old-fashioned even by the standards of 1916, the film was long thought lost… until the Cinematheque Française discovered a print of the 1919 French release version. This divided the film into four chapters suitable for exhibition run as a serial in the manner of Louis Feuillade's popular homegrown *Fantômas* and *Judex* adventures (in contrast to which, it must have seemed even more mannered). Restored, the film has been screened at festivals around the world with a live musical accompaniment by the pianist Neil Brand (who adds an enormous amount of value to the work). I caught it at the London Film Festival, where it was supported by the very lively short *Canine Sherlock Holmes* (1912), which involves a couple of other once-famous characters—Hawkshaw the Detective (from Tom Taylor's *The Ticket of Leave Man*, 1863) and E.W. Hornung's arch-thief Raffles (who is a lot less gentlemanly in this outing)—along with Hawkshaw's intrepid dog Spot. A BluRay/DVD release is available from Flicker Alley.

Sixty-three-year-old Gillette, returning to a role he'd created in his forties, wisely underplays Sherlock Holmes while everyone around him overacts. Coming to this legendary performance after seeing every other surviving Sherlock is a strange experience: whenever Gillette makes a gesture or pulls a face which evokes what Clive Brook, Eille Norwood, Arthur Wontner or Basil Rathbone did with the role, there's a little spark of realisation that subsequent actors were following conventions this man invented. Brook, in particular, seems to have been cast in a remake of *Sherlock Holmes* simply because he resembled Gillette—and several of Rathbone's ever-changing Holmes hairstyles evoke Gillette's look. There's even an early instance of deliberately modifying an established image—Holmes plays with his pipe, but later takes up cigarettes instead. A whole sequence involves his glowing cigar-end in a darkened cellar; the most famous theatrical effect in the play, this gambit is reproduced crudely on film. Despite the clutter of incidents, characters and plots, the thrust of Gillette's play is that the stiff Holmes falls in love with leading lady Alice Faulkner (Marjorie Kay). Gillette exaggerates Holmes's upright posture and resolute jaw in the early stretches so there's more contrast when he unbends a little and begins to pitch woo.

Purists still find this Holmes-in-love angle makes the play a hard-sell revival, and pasticheurs have mostly preferred to have the detective seethe with unexpressed or thwarted passions rather than earn a happy ending. However, Gillette had canny commercial instincts and may have sensed that Holmes would only become a universally popular character if he turned Doyle's calculating celibate into a deeply repressed romantic whose remoteness might intrigue and excite female audiences (in the 1960s, the unsmiling likes of Ilya Kuryakin and Mr. Spock had the same appeal). Gillette, picking up on one or two moments in Doyle, also senses Holmes's potential as a comic character. Some of his best bits of business come in moments when he is awkward or embarrassed by his emotions and for once Watson (Edward Fielding) gets to patronise him. The curtain of the play, with Holmes giving up detection for marriage, is as final in its way as falling over a waterfall— which, as we know, wasn't that final at all—in putting an end to the saga. The Holmes we meet in *Sherlock Holmes* is an established detective, Watson has moved on from Baker Street and the feud with Moriarty (black-eyed Ernest Maupin) is ongoing. Gillette saw the play as a one-off and wrote a finish which mitigated against sequels—showing how different the Victorian stage was from even the early cinema.

Made in the middle of World War One, if before American entry into the conflict, the 1916 *Sherlock Holmes* is the only Holmes film made before 1939 to have a period setting. Doyle was still publishing Holmes stories, but outside of the topical "His Last Bow" had opted to stick by Holmes's retirement in 1903 and set them in the late Victorian period. Filmmakers didn't cotton to this nostalgic element as quickly as Holmes's creator did. Note how the recent TV series based on Thomas Harris's Hannibal Lecter novels has a contemporary setting rather than stick with the 1980s of the books (longer ago now than the 1890s were in 1916) and no one complained that Will Graham was a man out of time (though a key plot point about home movies had to be dropped). Purely because of the war, the London of the film is explicitly identified as a bygone era, with hansom cabs, fussy diplomats out to squelch scandal among the ruling houses of Europe (Bohemia had a lot more to worry about in 1916 than a philandering king), and outdated clothes (including Holmes's tweed overcoat and deerstalker). In an alteration to get past the Lord Chamberlain, no-better-than-she-should-be cast-off mistress and blackmailer Irene Adler is dropped—the equivalent character is the deceased sister of irreproachable heroine Alice Faulkner, who has inherited incriminating letters after her sister has been driven to suicide. Alice is so noble she wouldn't dream of blackmailing the rotter, though she's not above holding the evidence over his head.

Like the play, the film lurches somewhat from act to act. It probably works better as a serial. Part One involves Alice falling in with a couple of scoundrels, James Larrabee (Mario Majeroni) and his sister Madge (Grace Reals). Part Two has the Larrabees enlist Moriarty to get back at Holmes and includes the Professor's famous visit to Baker Street. Part Three is the cigar-in-the-cellars escape from a gas trap (which Gillette might have borrowed from Arthur Morrison's *The Dorrington Deed Box*—Doyle's own gas trap came in "The Retired Colourman," written in 1926). Part Four tidies up the plot ends and sets up the happy coupledom curtain. Outside of Gillette, only Maupin makes much of an impression—and here Moriarty is meekly led off by the police rather than getting a spectacular death scene. It has glimpses of muddy streets but (unsurprisingly) no sense of London, while most of the drama takes place indoors with plentiful title cards and stark poses. Nearly a hundred years on, it's an important find and of more than academic interest—thanks to the lively music and careful restoration, it's even an entertaining evening's cultural archaeology and proof that what entertained our great-grandparents still works. Now, if only someone could turn up that H.A. Saintsbury movie…

THE ABOMINABLE BRIDE

In the past five years, the media image of Sherlock Holmes—taking in the detective himself, his supporting cast and extended world—has changed more than in over a century of stage, screen, illustration, and radio adaptations. Four separate Holmes franchises—the cinema films directed by Guy Ritchie with Robert Downey, Jr., the British television series *Sherlock* with Benedict Cumberbatch, the American television series *Elementary* with Jonny Lee Miller, and the Russian television series *Sherlok Kholms* with Igor Petrenko (more on that next issue)—abjure the Gillette-Norwood-Wontner-Rathbone-Cushing-Wilmer-Brett image of a straight-backed, authoritative, incisive, dryly good-humored, heroic genius to present the sleuth as a scruffy, bipolar, tragic-absurd, callous, troubled, high-functioning autistic/recovering drug addict. Even the one-off *Mr Holmes*, with a more traditional-seeming Ian McKellen, is concerned with the shortfall between the man Holmes seems to be and the person he actually is.

As radical is the way these takes on Doyle focus on Holmes (and Watson) almost to the exclusion of their cases. Mysteries sometimes seem like distractions from storylines more concerned with Holmes's psychological state and his thorny relationship with the version of him popularised by Watson (which is to say, Doyle). The shift in the direction began as early as Billy Wilder's film *The Private Life of Sherlock Holmes* (1970) and Nicholas Meyer's novel *The Seven-per-Cent Solution* (1974)—outliers for the 21st century Sherlock—though William Gillette probably kicked it off in 1899 by having Holmes fall in love. Typically, contemporary Holmes franchises stay away from "faithful" adaptations of the original stories—fair enough, since they've all been done so often that yet another straight Red-Headed League or Baskerville Hound is scarcely worth the effort. Instead, scripts braid together clues, characters, bits of business, the skeletons of Doyle's plots, fan fiction-like speculations about secondary characters like Mrs. Hudson and Irene Adler, increasingly complicated layers of meta-fiction, and kinetic displays of illustrated deduction or steampunk action-adventure. The upshot is a series of plot mazes which allow Holmes and Watson to explore themselves rather than simply find out who did it and how.

So we come to *The Abominable Bride*—perhaps the most convoluted essay in post-modern Holmesiana imaginable. Debuting on New Year's Day, it's a feature-length episode of Stephen Moffat and Mark Gatiss's BBC *Sherlock*, intended as a stopgap between limited-run series which are getting harder to fit into the actors' busy schedules. In three sets of three adventures (beginning in 2010), *Sherlock* has presented Holmes (Cumberbatch) and Watson (Martin Freeman) in contemporary London, ingeniously fitting the consulting detective into a world of mobile phones, the internet, 24-hour surveillance, forensic science, and selfies. Here, Watson is still just back from Afghanistan but with post-traumatic stress disorder and a thrill-seeking danger junkie streak. He chronicles his adventures with Sherlock on a blog. Moriarty (Andrew Scott) is a Joker-like giggling nemesis/dark doppelganger/putative slash fiction love interest. Mary Morstan (Amanda Abbington) is an ex-secret agent. Irene Adler (Lara Pulver) has a website for sexual services. Crucially, it's all about Sherlock, as the mercurial Cumberbatch misreads social cues disastrously, turns up naked at Buckingham Palace, squabbles childishly with his spymaster brother (Mark Gatiss), fakes his death and is shocked people are upset by the jape and—at the end of *His Last Vow*, the series three closer—shoots dead the master blackmailer Charles Augustus Magnusson and is sent on a suicide mission to make up for it.

All this is rushed through in a "previously…" montage at the outset of *The Abominable Bride* before a timer rolls back and we meet an alternative version of this Holmes and Watson in a Victorian setting. There's a brief remake of the first episode (*A Study in Pink*) with a setting more closely approximating Doyle's, populated by people who are Victorian versions of the modernised versions of Victorian characters. Gatiss is buried in a Robert Morleyish fat suit as a Mycroft intent on eating himself to death for a bet, Una Stubbs's Mrs. Hudson is sulking that Watson never gives her anything to say in his *Strand* magazine stories, Mary Watson is a simmering suffragette who resents being neglected by her adventure-seeking husband and Lestrade (Rupert Graves) is back to being a grumpy plodder. Only after all this do we get a story nugget—spun out of Doyle's throwaway mention of Ricoletti and his Abominable Bride (the aluminium crutch has gone missing)—about the veiled and painted Emilia Ricoletti (Natasha O'Keeffe) who publically shoots herself *before* murdering her abusive husband. Though Emilia is demonstrably now as dead as Jacob Marley, her spectre keeps popping up to kill a series of unlikeable men, which tips the viewer off as to which big issue is going to be raised and then dropped before the show takes another direction and reverts to its usual business of getting under Holmes's skin.

With the widespread acceptance of the series' take on Holmes, it was a clever notion to put all the characters into Doylean dress. Even forensic bods Molly (Louise Brealey) and Anderson (Jonathan Aris), essentially inventions of Moffat and Gatiss, show up with false whiskers and starched collars. Some moments of *The Private Life of Sherlock Holmes* are paraphrased as Holmes complains about the way Watson has misrepresented him in his stories—with the stinging comeback from his biographer that he has had to work hard to depict "an unprincipled drug addict as some sort of gentleman hero." In common with Moffat's tenure as the showrunner of *Doctor Who*, there's a strange insistence on having characters usually depicted as altruistic good guys taken off their pedestal as their best friends repeatedly—in long dialogue scenes—tell them what shits they are. Maybe so, but the way modern culture is uncomfortable with the notion of friendship is oddly disturbing. In recent years, many characters traditionally thought of as fast friends have been shown as dysfunctional couples at best and arch-enemies at worst: Batman and Superman, Napoleon and Ilya, the Lone Ranger and Tonto, Iron Man and Captain America.

For an hour or so, *The Abominable Bride* is dazzling. Like its manic-depressive hero, it has great highs as writers and cast seize opportunities to enjoy themselves and lows as they have to get back to a story no one cares much about and which (spoiler) *turns out not to be happening at all*. It offers more in-jokes than a generation of scholars will be able to catalogue—note the way Holmes assumes a Paget-like ruminative pose which also evokes the way Steve Ditko drew Dr. Strange, the character Cumberbatch is currently playing. Five orange pips pop out of an envelope, and a monstrous regiment of women manifests (Lily Clarke is a great new addition as the Watsons' know-all maid). The goings get gothic with black Klan hoods and Latin chants and creeping through Hammer Films sets. It's as much comforting fun as a BBC holiday ghost story of yore. But it can't last.

A few anachronisms ("a virus in the data") hint this isn't a straight historical adventure after all, and the penny drops that all this has been Cumberbatch/Sherlock high on a cocktail of many drugs retreating into his "memory palace" (a feature of the *Hannibal* franchise too) to explore an unsolved case from the 1880s that bears on the quandary raised in the last minutes of *His Last Vow* (how can someone blow their brains out and survive to commit more crimes?). So, not only has Sherlock been puzzling out the solution to the abominable bride business while zonked out in a private jet but has masochistically imagined versions of all his friends being horrid to him (and each other), exposing all his failings as a human being and as a detective (he takes the case of a threatened husband in his imagination and then stands back while the odious client is murdered). He even realises this was irrelevant to the Moriarty case too, which means this runaround won't impact on the ongoing story.

Back in the memory palace/dreamworld/holodeck, Holmes has his imagined versions of Watson and Moriarty join him at an (impressive) waterfall for another group therapy session which will end with someone (or everyone) taking the plunge. Here, the writers acknowledge we've been here before—in *Sherlock* and in every other incarnation of the stories all the way back to "The Final Problem" and "The Empty House"—and that we will be here again as endless variations on the conflict and the outcome play out over and over. Like so much else in *The Abominable Bride*, it's brilliant, clever and funny—but feels like a cheat if you tuned in expecting a story.

✗

Kim Newman is a prolific, award-winning English writer and editor, who also acts, is a film critic, and a London broadcaster. Of his many novels and stories, one of the most famous is *Anno Dracula*.

SHERLOCK HOLMES FOR CROWN AND COUNTRY

The Great Detective in Public Service

by Dan Andriacco

A slightly different form of "Sherlock Holmes for Crown and Country: The Great Detective in Public Service" was originally delivered as a talk at the inaugural meeting of the Diogenes Club of Washington, D.C., on September 20, 2014. Author Dan Andriacco had always been fascinated by the number of spy stories in the Canon. As a boy he fantasized about putting them together into a small anthology. Instead, he wrote about them.

When Sherlock Holmes hung out his shingle as the world's first consulting detective, his original clients were what he called "government detectives" and private ones who needed his unique help. But over the years he also served crown and country on numerous occasions—although not always both at the same time. This should not be surprising in one whose patriotism was reflected in the V.R. design of the bullet holes on the wall at 221B.

Leaving aside the sometimes contentious issue of chronology, the first *published* case in which Holmes's client is a government official is "The Naval Treaty." Watson's old school fellow Percy "Tadpole" Phelps, working at the Foreign Office through the influence of his mother's brother, appeals to the doctor to get Holmes on the case of a secret naval treaty which had been stolen on his watch.

This treaty between Italy and Great Britain is of enormous importance, says Percy's uncle, Lord Holdhurst: "The French or the Russian embassy would pay an immense sum to learn the contents of these papers." Alfred Hitchcock would have called that a McGuffin, his name for the goal or valuable object that the protagonist pursues in a story. Think "The Purloined Letter" or *The Maltese Falcon.* The Bruce-Partington Plans, the Mazarin Stone, the Beryl Coronet, Baron Gruner's diary, and the provocative letter at the heart of "The Adventure of the Second Stain"—all of which Holmes sought for Crown or country—are also McGuffins.

Watson's description of Lord Holdhurst, the foreign secretary and "future premier of England," is quite telling: "Standing on the rug between us, with his slight, tall figure, his sharp features, thoughtful face, and curling hair prematurely tinged with grey, he seemed to represent that not too common type, a nobleman who is in truth noble." As Watson hints here, not all noblemen—and not all cabinet ministers—are portrayed so positively in the pages of the Canon.

The dramatic high point of "The Naval Treaty" comes when Holmes has Mrs. Hudson serve up the missing treaty on a breakfast plate. Some commentators have called this cruel, but Watson describes Holmes as having at this point "a mischievous twinkle." It's all in good fun for Holmes. But Phelps, just recently recovered from nine weeks of brain fever, is only saved from fainting dead away by having brandy poured down his throat. Fortunately for him, Watson was always equipped with medicinal liquor for just such emergencies.

When he sufficiently recovers, Phelps kisses Holmes's hand (surely an odd way to show appreciation) and then blesses the detective for saving his honour. Holmes responds: "Well, my own was at stake, you know. I assure you it is just as hateful to me to fail in a case as it can be to you to blunder over a commission."

In other words, Holmes claims self-interest. But I think he doth protest too much. For later on he says that if Scotland Yard finds the bird has flown, "all the better for the government. I fancy that Lord Holdhurst, for one, and Mr. Percy Phelps for another, would very much rather that the affair never got as far as a police-court." By implication, the patriotic Holmes puts the good of the state over enhancing his professional reputation by notching up another case he solved.

In the opening paragraph of "The Naval Treaty," Watson refers to "The Adventure of the Second Stain," which he said "deals with interests of such importance and implicates so many of the first families in the kingdom that for many years it will be impossible to make it public."

And in fact he never did, most scholars agree. "The Adventure of the Second Stain" that Watson wrote later takes place during some autumn while he is still or again living in Baker Street, not the July after his marriage to Mary Morstan as did the one mentioned in "The Naval Treaty." It is clearly a different case with the same name.

Watson calls it "the most important international case which he (Holmes) has ever been called upon to handle." Appropriately, the client is no minor Foreign Office official out of Watson's past. The Prime Minister himself, to whom Watson assigns the pseudonym of Lord Bellinger, calls on Holmes at Baker Street, along with the Right Honourable Trelawney Hope, Secretary for European Affairs. A saber-rattling letter from a foreign potentate—often identified by commentators as Kaiser Wilhelm II—has disappeared. If the letter becomes public, war almost certainly will result. The Prime Minister appeals to Holmes and Watson's honour—there's that word again!—and to their patriotism, "for I could not imagine a greater misfortune for the country than that this affair should come out."

Critics have noted the parallels between this affair and that of "The Naval Treaty." In each case a document of international consequence—the McGuffin—has been lost. And in each case the document was hidden beneath a carpet, although not permanently in "The Adventure of the Second Stain."

If Holmes experienced *déjà vu*, he did not say so. Rather, he emphasized how difficult the case was: "Every man's hand is against us and yet the interests at stake are colossal. Should I bring it to a successful conclusion, it will certainly represent the crowning glory of my career." He did, and it did, and yet Holmes attempted to hide the achievement from his client in order to protect the *honour* of a lady. But Lord Bellinger was no fool, which leads to a marvelous closing scene:

> The Premier looked at Holmes with twinkling eyes.
> "Come, sir," said he. "There is more in this than meets the eye. How came the letter back in the box?"
> Holmes turned away smiling from the keen scrutiny of those wonderful eyes.

"We also have our diplomatic secrets," said he and, picking up his hat, he turned to the door.

One suspects that Holmes had secrets from Watson as well. Surely—as commentators have speculated—his older brother Mycroft must have sent the Prime Minister to Baker Street on that occasion. But only in "The Adventure of the Bruce-Partington Plans" does the indolent co-founder of the Diogenes Club himself appear at 221B. Sherlock Holmes decides then that it is finally time to tell Watson the truth about Mycroft's unique role at Whitehall.

> "You told me that he had some small office under the British government."
> Holmes chuckled.
> "I did not know you quite so well in those days. One has to be discreet when one talks of high matters of state. You are right in thinking that he is under the British government. You would also be right in a sense if you said that occasionally he *is* the British government."

Mycroft arrives in a state of high agitation. His normal bored demeanour gone, he strives to impress upon his sibling the importance of the case: "You must drop everything, Sherlock. Never mind your usual petty puzzles of the police-court. It's a vital international problem that you have to solve." Mycroft even tries a carrot, "If you have a fancy to see your name in the next honours list—" But only after he assures Mycroft that "I play the game for the game's sake" does the great detective agree to look into the matter.

Mycroft's last push is an appeal to patriotism: "In all your career you have never had so great a chance of serving your country." The response? "Well, well!" says Holmes, shrugging his shoulders. Perhaps that was a pose, an attempt to appear blasé before his big brother. As the case nears its end, Holmes strikes a much different note to Watson: "If time hangs heavy, get foolscap and a pen and begin your narrative of how we saved the State."

Before they can do that, however, Holmes suborns Watson into burglary. At first the good doctor resists—which he did *not* do in "A Scandal in Bohemia."

"I don't like it, Holmes."

"My dear fellow, you shall keep watch in the street. I'll do the criminal part. It's not a time to stick at trifles. Think of Mycroft's note, of the Admiralty, the Cabinet and the exalted person who waits for news. We are bound to go."

My answer was to rise from the table.

"You are right, Holmes. We are bound to go."

He sprang up and shook me by the hand.

"I knew you would not shrink at the last," said he and for a moment I saw something in his eyes which was nearer to tenderness than I had ever seen.

Apparently Holmes chokes up when he is about to commit a felony. Later, he confesses his law-breaking to his brother and to Inspector Lestrade. The Scotland Yarder warns him that some day his penchant for burglary will get him and Watson into trouble. "For England, home and beauty—eh, Watson?" Holmes responds in the words of a Royal Navy toast. "Martyrs on the altar of our country."

Instead of suffering martyrdom, though, Holmes eventually is called to Windsor where he receives a remarkably fine tie-pin "from a certain gracious lady." Watson, pushing his own deductive talents to their limits, tells us, "I fancy that I could guess that lady's august name and I have little doubt that the emerald pin will forever recall to my friend's memory the adventure of the Bruce-Partington plans."

That was in that hallowed year of 1895. In 1902, Holmes refused a knighthood ("The Adventure of the Three Garridebs"). Why refuse, given that he accepted the French Legion of Honour ("The Adventure of the Golden Pince-Nez")? I suspect that Holmes thought that service to crown and country was its own reward. But why was that knighthood-worthy adventure never told? Perhaps it was too sensitive, the same reason that we have been deprived the story of "the lighthouse, the politician and the trained cormorant"—which was surely another affair of state.

The last recorded meeting of Sherlock Holmes and Dr. Watson took place on the evening of August 2, 1914, "the most terrible August in the history of the world." We know about it from the account originally published in *The Strand* under title of "His Last Bow: The War Service of Sherlock Holmes."

In this fourth espionage story in the Canon, it is Holmes who is the spy. During two years of undercover work in America and Ireland, he has supplied the master spy Von Bork with false plans and arranged for some of the German's best men to be arrested. Posing as an Irish-American named Altamont, Holmes has disguised his rather public face by adopting what Watson calls "that horrible goatee." "These are the sacrifices one makes for one's country," says Holmes, pulling at his little tuft. "To-morrow it will be but a dreadful memory."

Watson asks him how he got lured away from his bees. "Ah, I have often marveled at it myself. The Foreign Minister alone I could have withstood, but when the Premier also deigned to visit my humble roof—" One can't help but think that Altamont is engaging in a bit of blarney here. That was at least the third Prime Minister to visit Holmes at home; the old sleuth-hound should have been used to it by then. But he goes on:

> "It has cost me two years, Watson, but they have not been devoid of excitement. When I say that I started my pilgrimage at Chicago, graduated in an Irish secret society at Buffalo, gave serious trouble to the constabulary at Skibbareen and so eventually caught the eye of a subordinate agent of Von Bork, who recommended me as a likely man, you will realize that the matter was complex."

No doubt the great detective's well-honed burglary skills came in handy at Skibbareen! Anthony Boucher suggested with great plausibility that Holmes learned about being an undercover agent from Birdy Edwards (*The Valley of Fear*). Perhaps some day the Irish and American adventures that Holmes merely sketches out in this story could receive a more complete treatment, similar to the second half of *The Valley of Fear*.

After two solitary years of acting a part, Holmes brings in Watson for the end-game. Surely this was not merely because he valued the doctor's skills as a chauffeur. No, it was a tribute to their friendship, their many years as comrades in arms. And at the end they stand on the terrace for perhaps their last quiet talk together, and some of the most memorable lines in the entire Canon:

> "There's an east wind coming, Watson."
> "I think not, Holmes. It is very warm."

"Good old Watson! You are the one fixed point in a changing age. There's an east wind coming all the same, such a wind as never blew on England yet. It will be cold and bitter, Watson, and a good many of us may wither before its blast. But it's God's own wind none the less and a cleaner, better, stronger land will lie in the sunshine when the storm has cleared. Start her up, Watson, for it's time that we were on our way. I have a check for five hundred pounds which should be cashed early, for the drawer is quite capable of stopping it if he can."

The Basil Rathbone film *Sherlock Holmes and the Voice of Terror* ends with this quote up to "when the storm has cleared." It also features Von Bork as a Nazi agent. After the great critical success of Rathbone and Nigel Bruce in 20th Century Fox's *The Hound of the Baskervilles* and *The Adventures of Sherlock Holmes*, Universal acquired the franchise and in 1942 brought it into the 20th century. Bluntly stated, the first three Universal pictures—*The Voice of Terror, Sherlock Holmes and the Secret Weapon*, and *Sherlock Holmes in Washington*, are World War II propaganda films. In *The Voice of Terror*, for example, a young woman named Kitty, reminiscent of Kitty Winter, gives a rousing appeal for help to a pub full of ruffians: "England's at stake. Your England as much as anyone else's! No time to think about what side we're on—there's only one side, England, no matter how high or how low we are." The film was immediately followed by a pitch to buy war bonds.

David Marcum, writing in the winter 2013 issue of *The Baker Street Journal*, made the ingenious suggestion that these films were actually adventures of Solar Pons, the latter-day Holmes clone, and his Watsonian associate Dr. Parker. "Pons's and Parker's names were changed to Holmes and Watson for easier familiarity to the 1940s movie-going public." Well, that would at least explain Rathbone's bizarre hair-do in those three movies, the reason for which has been a Sherlockian mystery for more than seventy years!

Ouida Rathbone, Basil's wife, in 1953 combined elements of all four canonical spy stories, plus "A Scandal in Bohemia," "The Final Problem," and "The Adventure of the Empty House" into a play called "Sherlock Holmes: A Drama in Three Acts." It closed after just two evening performances and one matinee. This stitched-together Frankenstein of a work demonstrates that great source material—dialogue ripped from the stories—doesn't necessarily make for a great play. You still need a plot. Mrs. Rathbone seems to have missed that[1].

Spy stuff involving international intrigue and foreign agents was not the only opportunity Holmes had to serve the crown.

In "The Adventure of the Beryl Coronet" and "The Adventure of the Illustrious Client," Holmes indirectly serves the interests of the same exalted personage. The clue to that connection, if you need one, is that Alexander Holder—the unhappy custodian of the Beryl Coronet—refers to "my illustrious client." Surely the gentleman in question was then the Prince of Wales, later King Edward VII.

In both of these cases, as in the spy stories, Holmes's task is to retrieve a McGuffin. The Beryl Coronet, a magnificent piece of jewelry, is "one of the most precious public possessions of the empire"—and yet the playboy prince pawns it to get ready cash! In "The Illustrious Client," the object of the quest is the dirty diary of another playboy, Baron Gruner, which Holmes sees as the only way to tear Violet De Merville's affections away from the scoundrel.

Unsurprisingly, Holmes turns to burglary *once again* to get his hands on the diary. And *once again* he gets away with it. The story closes with these words: "Sherlock Holmes was threatened with a prosecution for burglary, but when an object is good and a client is sufficiently illustrious, even the rigid British law becomes human and elastic. My friend has not yet stood in the dock."

How illustrious? When Sir James Damery refuses to reveal the name, Holmes demurs: "I am accustomed to have mystery at one end of my cases, but to have it at both ends is too confusing. I fear, Sir James, that I must decline to act." And yet, he does act—even though Sir James never gives up the name. But at the end of the case, Watson glimpses the armorial bearings of their ultimate client on the brougham that picks up Sir James. He tries to blurt out the name to Holmes, but the latter stops him. "It is a loyal friend and a chivalrous gentleman," says Holmes. "Let that now and forever be enough for us." We can be sure, though, that Miss De Merville's friend was *royal* as well as *loyal*.

"The Adventure of the Illustrious Client" is a favorite story of many Sherlockians. "The Adventure of the Mazarin Stone," by contrast, ranks dead last on most lists. Its plot is onion-skin thin and much of the dialogue wooden. However, it is within the topic at hand because the case again involves royal jewelry. For a change, someone other than Holmes has committed a burglary—the hundred-thousand-pound burglary of the Crown Diamond, also called the Mazarin Stone. The Prime Minister, the Foreign Secretary, and a reluctant Lord Cantlemere hire Holmes to get it back by any means necessary.

Billy the page can get along with the Prime Minister and has nothing against the Foreign Secretary, but he can't stand Lord Cantlemere. "Neither can Mr. Holmes, sir," Billy tells Watson. "You see, he don't believe in Mr. Holmes and was against employing him." Holmes gets his revenge in the end by slipping the recovered Mazarin Stone into the politician's own overcoat and pretending to find it there. Like a certain monarch, Cantlemere is not amused. In fact, he lives up to Billy's description of him as "a stiff 'un." But ultimately he is forced to acknowledge the nation's debt to Holmes and to withdraw his skepticism about the sleuth's professional powers. Holmes, not entirely mollified, twists the knife a bit as he dismissively refuses to explain how he got the diamond back:

> "This case is but half-finished; the details can wait. No doubt, Lord Cantlemere, your pleasure in telling of this successful result in the exalted circle to which you return will be some small atonement for my practical joke. Billy, you will show his Lordship out, and tell Mrs. Hudson that I should be glad if she would send up dinner for two as soon as possible."

Why did Holmes even take the Mazarin Stone case in the face of Cantlemere's skepticism and their clear mutual dislike? Possibly an ego-driven desire to prove the skeptic wrong was a factor. But, surely, so was patriotism. For Sherlock Holmes was not a man to let "the folly of a monarch or the blundering of a minister" ("The Adventure of the Noble Bachelor") keep him from answering the call of duty. For no matter the personalities involved, he always stood ready to be of service... to crown and country.

✗

Dan Andriacco, a long-time Sherlockian, is the author of *Baker Street Beat: An Eclectic Collection of Sherlockian Scribblings* and nine Holmes-themed mystery novels and collections. His amateur sleuth, Sebastian McCabe, and brother-in-law Jeff Cody appear most recently in

Bookmarked for Murder. A frequent contributor to *SHMM*, Dan blogs at www.DanAndriacco.com.

1   This is the author's opinion. I have a copy of her play and mean to anthologize it; I find it rather charming. By the way, not only was Nigel Bruce too ill to play Watson but he died on the show's opening night. –Marvin Kaye

THE CASE OF THE BURNT SONG

by Martin Rosenstock

The case I am about to relate occurred some years ago, but not until today have I found the strength to take pen in hand so as to put the events to paper. Over the long years of my life, I have witnessed many a times the consequences of violent actions, first on the battlefields of Afghanistan and later at the side of my friend Sherlock Holmes. As a rule, I am little bothered when beholding the wounds people inflict on each other, nor am I unduly troubled by the effects on others who must bear witness to such calamities. My medical training inculcated a certain stoicism within me, perhaps even coldness, I am sometimes afraid.

Matters are different, however, when I think of young Ben Connolly, whose chalky features appear frequently before my mental eye at night as if conjured by the darkness. I know then that I will chase after sleep fretfully until light seeps through the curtains and I am tempted to steal over to the medicine cabinet with the flask of laudanum. A few times I have succumbed and have swallowed a spoonful of the ghastly brown liquid and then unconsciousness thankfully came and blotted out my memories. Inevitably, though, they would return, more vivid than before, pulsating with a sickening energy all their own.

Ben Connolly counted amongst the Baker Street Irregulars. He was a lad of eight or nine and like most of the Irregulars had probably never been inside a school. He was possessed of a native intelligence, however, and somehow had learned to read. On occasion, I would see him in our parlour with a penny dreadful on his knees, eagerly perusing some improbable adventure story. Every few seconds his dirty little hand would reach out and without looking up he would take a biscuit from the saucer that Mrs Hudson had placed before him on the table. Holmes meanwhile would be in his study assembling a package he wanted delivered or compiling a list of items to be picked up at the chemist's. My companion thought much of this particular street urchin: "None of them are angels, Watson, but you can rely on Ben and he has a quick mind."

Little in Ben's appearance suggested the remarkable. He was of average height for his age, round faced, a little stocky and usually clad in a grey jacket and brown trousers. In recollection, his attire seems a little better than that of the other Irregulars. Unlike theirs, his clothes would occasionally change so that the arms of his jacket generally extended all the way to his wrists and did not end close to his elbows. Two creases that we usually develop in later years and which betoken our struggles with life's disappointments ran from his nose to the corners of his mouth.

✗   ✗   ✗   ✗

One autumn night, I was woken by peremptory knocks on the door of my room and Holmes's voice, clipped and urgent as I had rarely heard it: "Watson. Watson, get up and dress. Rush! There is no time to spare."

Before going to sleep, I had been reading one of Joseph Conrad's sea tales and my dreams had taken me far away to windswept tropical isles by the Strait of Malacca.

"One minute," I groaned, struggling to find my bearings. "I will be out presently." I turned on the gas and looked at my watch on the bedside table. The hands showed almost two o'clock. All this boded ill. I dressed as fast as I could, my loudly beating heart and the coldness of the room dispelling my drowsiness.

I heard a child's voice through the door, but when I opened it and stepped into the parlour, I was not a little surprised to see Ben Connolly standing next to Mrs Hudson in the gaslight. The good woman, dressed in her nightgown and with a bonnet over her hair, was bending at the hip and holding out a glass of milk to the boy. He, however, seemed not even to notice her but instead was staring at me with an intensity of expression as if he had been willing me to emerge from my room.

"Dr Watson," he blurted out. "Please come, me mother... me mother, she needs 'elp!"

I nodded, and at this moment Holmes entered from his room, looking no different than if it had been two in the afternoon. He gave me a curt nod, we donned our coats, and I took my bag of instruments and drugs from the cupboard.

As we rushed down the stairs, Ben in the lead, I glanced over my shoulder to see Mrs Hudson at the door of our flat, her right hand pressed to her lips and an expression of anguish on her face. We stepped into the street, and I shuddered in the dank air. By the curb a four-wheeler stood waiting. Ben must have secured it on the way. The driver huddled on the box, a cap pulled over his ears. We all three climbed aboard and the smack of the whip set the vehicle clattering on its way.

"Well, Ben," I said. "Now tell us what happened."

Ben sat next to Holmes across from me. The boy's pale features seemed to be working but in the darkness I could not be certain. Finally, there came a sob and in a little voice he said: "Someone… me mother… someone 'urt me mother!"

There was no point in pressing him for details. I would have to see for myself. I felt strangely at a loss for words. Ben had never mentioned his mother, at least not to me. Had I been asked to guess, I would have surmised him to be one of the many orphans or abandoned children who live on the streets of the metropolis. Now all I could say was: "We will do what we can, Ben."

I glanced out of the window. We were close to the river and moving eastward at a fast pace through empty streets. Patches of fog lay over the pavement, shimmering in the moonlight. Every once in a while I would catch sight of a shadowy figure, collar raised and hands crammed into his pockets, stomping along the sidewalk or disappearing into a house door. What could bring any-one out at this time of such a miserable night, I wondered.

Suddenly, Holmes spoke up: "Ben, when did this occur?"

At first, the lad did not seem to have heard. He had begun to sway rhythmically back and forth, as if in trance. But then he re-plied: "I don't know, Mr 'olmes. I found her 'alf an 'our ago." He paused for a moment. "In 'er… place. She wasn't at 'ome, not in the pub, neither. Mary was there, though, and she told me she was there not long ago, but that she left. She said she thought she'd gone to… the place. So I looked in the place, Mr 'olmes. And there she was! I ran to fetch Dr Watson right away. But before, I ran to fetch Mary. So someone would look after 'er."

I do not know if this outburst made more sense to Holmes than it did to me but the great detective had no more questions.

I, however, did. "Ben," I said. "It is two in the morning. What were you doing up so late?"

"I… I was out with the lads, Dr Watson…."

"Engaged in what sort of enterprise?" I wanted to continue. "A child of your age!" But since the issue did not seem pertinent to the case in hand, I held my tongue.

✗ ✗ ✗ ✗

As our cab drew closer to Whitechapel, Ben's impatience increased by the second. He moved forward to the edge of the seat, his eyes glued to the window. Occasionally he would mutter something under his breath that sounded almost like an imprecation directed at our driver to make haste. The scent of the East End, composed of fish, rotting seaweed, and the offal of the tightly crammed inhabitants, began to permeate our little rolling compartment. Finally we heard the sound of the driver reigning in his horse and before the cab had come to a stop, Ben had already torn open the door and jumped onto the pavement.

"Come, Dr Watson! Please, 'urry!" And he was scampering towards a door in what I could barely make out to be a three-storey building. I followed, medicine bag in hand, while Holmes stepped up to the box to pay the driver.

"Dr Watson, 'ere."

Ben was waiting for me in a hallway that led past a narrow staircase to the back of the building. At the far end of the hallway, a ray of light fell through a gap in a door. There came a creaking sound as the door opened and I beheld a female silhouette. Ben tugged at my sleeve and we made our way along the uneven boards of the hallway. The woman's face emerged in the half light. Her features were quite remarkable. She had high cheekbones and a narrow chin, giving the lower half of her face a triangular shape. The whites of her large grey eyes were reddened from crying. Her complexion was flushed, her lips full while at the same time oddly pale. I immediately recognized a consumptive. Lush auburn hair fell back onto her shoulders. I guessed her to be in her mid-twenties.

Before we could do so much as exchange greetings, Ben pulled me past her into the room and towards a large, lavishly cushioned bed. On this lay a woman illumined by a gaslight in the corner. The bodice of her greenish dress had been opened to help her breathing, around her head was wrapped a cotton cloth soaked with blood. Ben knelt down beside her and gingerly touched her shoulder.

"Mum, mum, can you 'ear me? Dr Watson is 'ere."

I sat on the bedside and felt for the woman's pulse at her carotid artery. I could sense her heart beating, irregular and as if far away at the bottom of a well. Her breathing was a hoarse and shallow whistle. I searched her face for signs of animation. There were none.

The age of Ben's mother was hard to guess. Life had certainly left its marks. Silver strands gleamed in those of her brown curls not covered by the cloth and thin lines rose steeply from her upper lip. At the same time, though, I could still discern her youthful self, a memory of a wilful and high-spirited girl, generous, perhaps careless with her emotions, and strong.

I reached for the cloth. The blood in it was half-coagulated and the fabric clung to her hair. When the cloth came loose, what must have been a half pint of blood and *liquor cerebrospinalis* spilled onto the cushion. In an instant I realized that there was nothing I could do. She would be dead before sunrise. In fact the end could come any minute. I had seen similar cases in the field. An explosion, say, had flung a soldier against a boulder or a metal case and his skull was stove in. The woman's blood was flooding her brain. Inevitably it would fail. One day, I am sure, surgeons will be able to treat these horrible injuries. A great man will develop a method to snatch such victims from death's doorstep. In moments like these I wish the Almighty had been more abundant in His gifts to me.

I staunched the blood with gauze and then applied fresh bandages. The woman who had opened the door and whom I surmised to be the Mary of Ben's disjointed narrative handed me a cushion and I settled the patient's head back as comfortably as I could. As I glanced sideways, I saw that Ben's eyes were riveted to my every move. I did not have the heart to tell him the inevitable fate of his mother. Instead I reached into my bag again, brought out my stethoscope and pressed it to his mother's skin next to her sternum. My intention was to gain some time in which to compose my thoughts. I was convinced that the procedure would not tell me anything I did not already know, but I was mistaken. Under the metal of the chest piece I felt an unevenness, as if of cartilage where none was supposed to be. I pushed the hem of the dress a little more to the side and discovered the unmistakable outline of a huge tumour. I must have drawn breath or given some other sign of dismay for Ben grabbed my arm.

"Dr Watson, what is it?"

"Nothing, Ben... it's, it's... nothing."

The poor woman must have been in agony. The tumour appeared close to breaking through her skin, and I was certain that were I to examine her entire body I would find other manifestations of this cursed disease. I looked at her face, placid now in what seemed a deep exhaustion, and could not help but reflect that her assailant had not robbed her of much time. Perhaps she would have had a few more months on this earth, perhaps only weeks. Sometimes the malignancy wreaks its destructive work with horrific speed.

"Will you be able to make 'er well again, Dr Watson?"

And this time, to my own surprise, I found the courage to speak the truth. "No, Ben," I said, shaking my head. "I cannot help your mother. No one can, not the best doctor in the world."

The color drained from the boy's face. There is the well-worn expression that someone turned pale as a ghost. Ben, I had the impression, turned translucent. His features appeared to lose all materiality and to become little more than a mirage through which I could see the burgundy wallpaper behind him. This is the image that has been seared into my brain and which haunts me during some nights. Many times have I had to tell a person that there was no hope, either for him or the person he loved, yet never had I had to speak such words to a child. Ben's trials, however, were not nearly over.

Thankfully, at this moment Mary laid a hand on the boy's shoulder and I could see her slender fingers trying to exert some comforting pressure. The hold of her hand seemed to prevent the boy from simply disappearing. She then bent down and whispered in his ear and when he finally began to sob she pulled him against her and cradled him in her arms.

I looked around and saw Holmes at the opposite side of the room engaged in the scrutiny of a mantelpiece on which stood a number of knick-knacks. My companion seemed particularly interested in the mantelpiece's left corner, over which he now passed a forefinger. He then lifted it to his eyes before rubbing it clean against the surface of his thumb.

I looked to his feet and saw on the fake marble base of the mantelpiece a maroon circle of dried blood. Tracing my eyes over a thin carpet in my direction, I discerned some blotches of the identical substance. I scanned the room. Some effort had been expended to create the illusion of a space far removed from London's East End. Chintz curtains closed off a window. In a corner stood a worn *empire* sofa, a lacquered Oriental-looking table to the side, on it a decanter half-filled with what appeared to be sherry. A brass chandelier with empty candle-holders hung from the ceiling. Cheap oil paintings of questionable taste adorned the walls.

The light suddenly flickered as a draft of cold air entered the room and a loud male voice could be heard from the hallway, pausing at brief moments for quiet responses. I looked to Mary and saw her closing her eyes in fatigue. "Our landlord, Mr Thompson," she whispered. "He lives upstairs. I asked him to fetch the priest." The boards of the hallway creaked under heavy boots and then the door flung open.

In stepped a lanky man in brown corduroys. His thinning grey hair stood in all angles from his bony head. Clearly he had been in bed not a long while ago. Two or three steps behind him followed the priest, a gentleman in early middle age with well-groomed dark whiskers and a florid complexion. He was in a tattered coat that had a patch on the elbow. In his hand he carried a black breviary. Mr Thompson made an expansive gesture, taking in the room, and said in what I can only describe as a loud hiss: "The results of my efforts, Father!"

The priest laid a hand on Mr Thompson's forearm in an effort at conciliation but the landlord would not be dissuaded from making his views known.

"I'm only a businessman, a decent businessman. My rent is reasonable. I am lenient when it is a day or two late. I turn a blind eye to many things." He lifted his large hands in histrionic exasperation. "One must make allowances for the state of the world. You know this, Father. All I ask for is a quiet demeanour. And what do I get in return?! Rows and more rows! And ingratitude!"

I rose from the bedside. Cleaning my hands with a cloth soaked in rubbing alcohol, I approached the two men. I could now clearly read dismay in the priest's features. His lips were pressed together and a vertical line creased his forehead. We shook hands, and he introduced himself: "Father Ryan."

"Watson," I said, and turned to exchange greetings with Mr Thompson. He towered half a foot above me and glancing down while squeezing my hand, he apparently read my profession in my appearance: "Well, Father, the doctor is already here, so your presence is not even necessary."

"Oh, yes, it is," I interjected quickly. "Very much so, in fact."

The priest had been looking over my shoulder towards the victim and now raised his eyebrows to me. I shook my head.

"She is not… conscious?" he asked.

"No," I said. "And I doubt that she will regain consciousness."

He cleared his throat and moved past me towards the bed. He and Mary exchanged nods and after a moment's hesitation he ruffled the boy's hair. "You have to be strong now, Ben," he mumbled, as if uncomfortable with the platitude. "Your mother would want it so." There was a hint of brogue in the priest's voice, but I guessed that he had left Ireland many years ago to minister to the spiritual needs of the Catholics living in the East End.

"Yes, Father," whispered Ben.

The priest knelt by the bedside and folded the dying woman's hands on her abdomen, carefully placing a rosary between her fingers. We all watched in silence as he proceeded to voice the Latin rite of absolution. I noticed that Holmes had taken up station beside me. Father Ryan next extracted a small golden flask from his coat pocket, dipped some oil onto his fingertips and made the sign of the cross on the forehead of Ben's mother and on her lips. He then opened his breviary and began quietly reading psalm twenty-three.

When, at one point, Mary turned to look around, Holmes caught her eye. She took a step towards us. Holmes can lack tact when his curiosity has been aroused, but I could tell from the constricted tone of his voice that he was aware of the indelicate moment of his question. He looked towards the bed. "Where did you find her?"

"Agnes?" Mary turned up her hands. "Right there, sir." She indicated the prostrate figure and then wiped tears from her lids with the back of her index finger.

Holmes looked thoughtfully at Ben, who now stood alone observing the priest.

Mr Thompson spoke up, his voice, barely lowered, still his customary hiss: "The ruffian was probably some sailor. You gentlemen should see the street outside during the day. Thronging with those types. It will be hard to catch him. His ship might weigh anchor with the morning tide, it could be past Gravesend in a few hours."

Much as I disliked to, I had to agree with the man. There was no time to lose if we wanted to preserve a chance of apprehending the villain. I looked to Holmes who was standing impassively, his chin resting on his right fist, to all intents lost to the world.

The final crisis came suddenly. It was precipitated by a drop in blood pressure. The features of Ben's mother turned white. I rushed to her side as a violent spasm passed through her frame. Her eyelids fluttered, then snapped open with mechanical suddenness. I am not sure that her eyes still had sight as they stared ahead to the foot of the bed. Her back arched and her arms began flailing and then reached out as if groping towards something in the distance. The rosary flew against the curtain and fell to the floor.

Things had become too much for Father Ryan, who took a few steps back in horror at the spectacle of mortality. I reached for the dying woman's hands and her fingers closed around mine like a vice. Her lips were quivering and a strangled wheeze emanated from her throat. For a moment I thought she might regain command of her voice, but then, just as abruptly as the crisis had begun, it came to an end. Her mouth went slack and the strength seeped from her fingers. As I watched, the sheen that marks the eyes of the living turned dull and her pupils dilated. It was over.

I laid her hands back on her body and reached up to close her eyes. As I rose, my thorax felt as if it had shrunk and was preventing the expansion of my lungs, a feeling that always besets me in these moments. This time, however, the sensation was particularly strong and I believe I may in fact have gasped for breath.

I looked around at immobile features. Father Ryan and the land-lord both showed the appearance of men who had encountered a power so fearsome it had chilled the very core of their existence. Mary's lips were curled inward, as if holding back a scream. Her hands clutched the boy's chest and pressed him to her legs. Even Holmes seemed a little shaken.

I nodded to the priest, indicating that whatever remained to be done fell into his realm alone. Then I went down on my haunches to look into Ben's face and in a sorry attempt at encouragement lifted the corners of my mouth. His features remained impassive. He was on the verge of catatonia and I wondered if he would ever again become the carefree boy I had known.

As I stood up again, Holmes was saying: "Miss Mary, I should like to see where Ben and Miss Connolly lived. Is it far from here?"

"No," she replied. "Just a five-minute walk."

I nodded in approval. "It would do the child good to leave this place."

Father Ryan was absorbed in prayer and Mr Thompson declared that he would stay behind and see to it that the authorities were informed. To this Holmes assented, and we set about to depart. My companion lit a paraffin lantern that stood on a sideboard. I made a motion towards the door through which we had entered, but Holmes pointed to a curtained alcove at the opposite side of the room.

"I believe that is another exit. Let us leave through there."

We crossed the room and I pulled back the curtain. Indeed, it concealed another door and also a wash basin with a jug of water standing on the rim. I pressed down the door handle and noticed that the brass surface was not quite smooth. When I looked closer, I discovered a brownish smear.

"Some dried blood here," I announced.

Holmes held up the lantern and produced a murmur of assent.

He opened the door. It gave onto a dingy alleyway. Holmes shone the light along the wall to our right, then stopped. About three feet from the ground two maroon smears were visible on the brickwork. The killer had wiped his hands on the wall in an attempt to remove the shameful marks of his deed.

✗   ✗   ✗   ✗

Mary took the lead, holding Ben by the hand, who trudged mechanically by her side. Holmes and I followed. We passed through the alleyway into a side street that ran parallel to the one by which we had arrived. As we walked along a row of shuttered shop fronts, I whispered to Holmes what I had discovered during my examination of Ben's mother, that she had in fact been a dying woman for many months. After a moment my companion nodded at this piece of information, as if it fit into his view of the case. We turned a corner and entered a street of what appeared to be in the thin light of the lantern modest, yet clean whitewashed houses. A church bell began to chime in the vicinity. It was four o'clock in the morning.

After a hundred yards, Mary stopped in front of one of the houses and made a motion for Ben to unlock the door. Obediently the lad dug a key ring from his trouser pocket. He opened the door and we all ascended a staircase. On the first floor landing, he changed keys and inserted the one selected into the lock. Holmes stood right behind him, ready to fend off an attack should our arrival disturb the villain.

The door swung open and we peered into a dark room, in which it was possible to make out the appurtenances of a kitchen. A draft of cold air was coming our way. Mary pointed to the gaslight above a table. Holmes cautiously stepped into the flat, turned up the light and set the lantern aside. A small kitchen lay before us that gave onto a parlour with a sofa and two easy chairs. To the right, a door to another room was visible. Holmes went to investigate and then waved us to enter. There was no one in the flat. However, someone had been there very recently. Perpendicular to the entrance was another door and next to it a window. One pane of this had been smashed from the outside. Glass lay on the floor below. The draft was issuing from the rectangular hole.

We all stepped up to the window. The door next to it had a key in the lock. Outside lay a courtyard. I could make out a thin patch of grass, some clothes-lines and to the side, next to a scrawny tree, three rubbish cans. A narrow metal staircase led from the door to the courtyard. Clearly, whoever we were looking for had used this back entrance to force his way into the flat.

I turned and surveyed the room. It had been subject to a hasty search. The drawers of a cupboard had been yanked open, some of the contents lay scattered on the floor. The books on a shelf had been removed and stacked on the floor. Even some newspapers and magazines had been pulled from a rack and thrown onto a table.

Holmes's eyes darted from one item to the other. Then he emitted a grunt as if struck by an obvious notion and swiftly walked to a metal stove, a sturdy contraption, perhaps two feet in width, three in height, with a dirty white enamel coating that stood against the wall and marked the border between parlour and kitchen. He grabbed a poker from the surface of the stove and lifted first one lid, then another. Here he whistled silently, then reached into the stove and, with a grimace of pain, pulled out something that looked like a charcoal briquette and hastily laid it on the kitchen table.

As Mary, the boy, and I approached, I recognized the thing for what it was. We were looking at a thick packet of burnt letters. Curls of smoke were rising from it. Odd individual sheets could be discerned, ashen ghosts of their former selves that would disintegrate into fragments upon an injudicious touch. However, the fire appeared not to have consumed the packet fully. The string that held the letters together was blackened but had mostly survived. The villain had probably dropped the packet into the stove and then fled by the way he had come, without ascertaining that a strong fire was burning and that they had fallen into the center of the flames. As I looked closer, I could discern a slim margin of the sheets on the right side of the packet, singed to a yellowish brown, but not yet turned to ashes.

Holmes pulled out his penknife, seated himself, and with extreme care began to separate the individual sheaths, salvaging the sections that remained somewhat whole.

I could tell that he would be absorbed in this task for some time and therefore nodded to Mary. "I shall make some tea. Maybe you should take the boy to bed."

"Yes, Dr Watson. I would love a cup," she replied, and pulled on Ben's hand.

They disappeared into the adjoining room and I filled a kettle from a pitcher of water. From a steel bucket, I poured coal into the stove and set the kettle upon it. While waiting for the water to boil, I busied myself with fixing a wooden board, which from the crumbs upon it I guessed to have been used for cutting bread in front of the broken pane of glass. Then I searched for the tea, but finally realized that it was in front of me on the counter in a tin box. Mary returned as I was pouring the boiling water into an earthenware teapot. She stood next to the stove and stretched out her hands over its surface.

"It's beginning to get a little warmer in here," she observed.

I nodded and then looked towards the door through which she had just come. "Did Ben fall asleep?"

"Yes, two or three minutes and he was sound asleep."

She took three cups and saucers from a cupboard and the same number of spoons from a drawer and set the table. Holmes did not look up. He had separated some of the singed edges from the briquette and placed them in front of himself on the table. I noticed that he had also removed his magnifying glass, which he always carries with him, from his coat pocket. Currently, the little device lay unused by his elbow as he slowly pulled another brownish-yellow sliver from the wreckage.

Mary and I sat across from each other and let the tea draw. Neither of us, I believe, was quite sure what to say. Finally, Mary spoke up.

"I always liked coming here. I have a room three streets over, not this large…." Her voice trailed off.

"It is a nice flat." Then I asked: "What was she like? Miss Connolly? Agnes?"

Mary reflected for a moment, her eyes looking past me. "She was a good person," she then said. "She would cook, and we would all have dinner, Ben, Agnes, and me. Sometimes we would play cards. She was a good player…. She was a headstrong woman, quick. She cared for Ben a lot, she drank a bit much sometimes…."

The image Mary evoked in halting phrases exacerbated my sense of failure. I had been unable to preserve a life and other lives were now the poorer for it. I took the pot and poured tea, first for Mary, then for Holmes, who would let it go cold, I knew, then for myself.

Mary and I drank silently. The hot liquid revived us both. Mary, I noticed, had a light West Country accent and I wondered by what paths she had arrived in London and at her present station in life. Yet I did not venture to make enquiries in this regard. Instead, I gestured towards the cup she was holding between both her hands and remarked upon something that had struck me.

"That appears to be real china, quite expensive…."

Mary gave the cup an appraising glance. "You might well be right, Dr Watson. Agnes could afford nice things."

We looked at each other and she read the question on my mind. "I do not know," she said, shaking her head, and then brushed a strand of auburn hair behind her ear. "Agnes had a gentleman who gave her money every month, I believe. But I do not know who he is, she never told me. We haven't known each other that long."

"How long have you known each other?"

"Since summer, when I arrived. We met in a pub. Not far from here, the Red Lion. She could tell I was lost, and she helped me out. I will always be grateful for that. Who knows what would have happened to me otherwise."

Then Mary added as if in afterthought: "That's where Ben found me tonight, when he was done gallivanting, in the Red Lion. I was chatting with a friend. That's why I was there so late. The publican locks the door and lets some of us stay after closing time…."

"I see. And the room where Agnes and you… you share it, I take it…?"

"Yes. We each pay half the rent to Mr Thompson. He's not a nice man, but he does help if a gentleman becomes unpleasant." And then she continued with a measure of confidence that I attributed to my profession: "But I'm not… I can't see anyone at the current time. I'm… I'm on the rag."

I nodded. "But why was Mr Thompson not there to help Agnes tonight?"

"He was in bed, his rooms are on the top floor. He came to the door in his night gown when I ran to fetch him. He hadn't heard a thing. It was very unusual for Agnes to bring a man to the room so late."

For a minute we both fell silent, drinking our tea and pursuing the trains of our private thoughts. Finally, I motioned towards my chest by way of indicating hers and lifted my eyebrows. She shook her head and then said, hesitatingly: "There is only a little blood…."

"Please come and see me when you can." I reached for one of my cards and held it out to her. When she took it, our fingers touched briefly.

Mary studied the card, then looked up at me. "Dr Watson, I know… there is nothing to be done."

"We will have to see. Please…."

At this moment, there came from the head of the table a satisfied "Ahhh," and we both spun around. Holmes was leaning over a piece of paper, his right eye to his magnifying glass, his nose almost touching the surface of the table. Without raising his head, he motioned for us to approach.

As Mary and I rose, I noticed faint natural light entering through the window. The night was almost over. My companion set down the glass and gestured towards the piece of paper. I took the glass and leaned down.

The piece was of an irregular crescent shape on its left side, straight on its right, and perhaps a little over an inch in width. I deduced that this section, which had escaped the fire, came from the right margin of a page. As I peered through the glass, I could make out a few letters and words in a strong, rightward-sloping hand. They ran as follows:

> …………………………oth
> …………………..ight believe:
> ………………........lful workman.
> …………........et about with lilies
> …..........ung roes that are twins.
> …………………......ing together.
> ………………………………..ad.

I straightened my back and with a shrug handed the glass to Mary. She took it and leaned down to have a look for herself.

"Well?" said Holmes before Mary had completed her investigation, a tone of expectation in his voice.

I opened my eyes wide, expressing puzzlement.

"It is rather part of a gentleman's education, you know, Watson."

"Is that so?" I said, maybe a tad peevishly, with Mary standing there.

She was now mumbling under her breath: "That must be an s. Set about with lilies. And young, I guess. So, young roes that are twins…." She looked up at us both. "Some kind of poetry, perhaps?"

"Brava!" exclaimed Holmes. "Some kind of poetry it is."

Taking the piece of paper, he stood up and went over to a hook in the wall on which Mary had hung his coat. From the inside pocket he took his notebook, placed the piece of paper inside, then donned the coat.

He looked at his watch. "We should go. I believe we now know all that we need to know."

Mary and I regarded each other in amazement. I then shrugged, crossed the room and took my coat. Mary, however, shook her head.

"I will stay with Ben. I am quite tired. You gentleman can find me here if need be."

Holmes nodded. "That should be just fine."

On the threshold, as Holmes was already walking down the stairs, I looked back. Mary had taken her cup of tea in both her hands again and her eyes appeared to be looking inward. Then they focused on me and she smiled. For a moment, the sadness that enveloped her seemed to shift and grow weaker and I saw something else in her features, something that may have been mischievousness. I am not sure. It disappeared before I was able to ascertain whether my imagination was playing tricks on me. I raised my hand in a good-bye, closed the door and followed my friend out into the early morning street.

✗   ✗   ✗   ✗

Holmes turned his steps in the direction from which we had come and I surmised that his intention was to return to the main road and to hail a cab there. However, as we reached a side street, he abruptly made a left turn. We walked past narrow redbrick buildings and I noticed light in some windows. Then a few figures became visible ahead of us in the mist. The East End was readying itself for another day of toil, while only a mile or two away other men and women were still in deep slumber.

"Where are we going, Holmes?"

"We are going…." He paused, as if momentarily not quite sure of himself. I knew that he had memorized the map of the city, but perhaps a detail had slipped his mind. Then, however, we reached another side street and he pointed: "There."

A church steeple rose into the grey morning sky like some ancient monument from Britain's prehistory.

"That must be it," said my companion. "It's the only Catholic church in the area."

Questions were racing through my mind, but in the long years of my acquaintance with Holmes I have learnt to await the unfolding of events. We approached the church. It was set back from the road in a little park. We entered through a gate and then mounted the few steps to a side entrance. The door swung open when Holmes pulled on the knob. We stepped into a nave and then passed into the transept. A scent of frankincense hung in the cold air. In the apse, an elderly man in black was lighting candles. I took him to be the sexton preparing the church for morning mass.

As we walked past the pews, the sexton made a motion to approach us but Holmes raised his hand: "Please, good sir, do not inconvenience yourself. We only need to have a few words with Father Ryan. Is he in the vestry?"

"Yes, sir," replied the old man. "He should be there."

We ascended the steps to the altar, passed it and turned into a corridor that branched off from the apse. In a side room we found the priest. He was sitting at a table already wearing his chasuble. Before him lay an open book. As we entered, he rose and a strange expression took shape on his face. Perhaps this expression signified consternation, perhaps shock, perhaps relief. He did look exhausted to the point of illness. His eyes were bloodshot and his erstwhile ruddy complexion had turned the jaundiced colour of nausea.

"Good morning, Father," said Holmes.

The priest nodded, mutely, before replying: "Good morning, gentlemen."

"It appears you had no chance to go to bed," said Holmes.

"Yes, I only returned an hour ago."

Holmes motioned towards the book on the table: "Are you preparing today's lection?"

"Merely reading a passage…."

Holmes angled his head. "Ahh, Peter 3:7," he said and then, looking at the priest, continued: "'Likewise, ye husbands, dwell with them according to knowledge, giving honour unto the wife, as unto the weaker vessel, and as being heirs to the grace of life; that your prayers may not be hindered.'"

"I see you are familiar with the gospel, Mr Holmes," said the priest. "Are you a religious man?"

"Alas, no," replied my companion. "My interests lie almost exclusively in this world."

"Yet you can quote the Holy Writ, chapter and verse...."

"It is part of life. Hence, one must study it. Don't you agree?"

"I suppose that is a good enough reason," replied Father Ryan.

Holmes reached into his coat pocket and retrieved his notebook. He opened it and laid the singed fragment on the table. "And occasionally one stands surprised at the Word's richness."

Father Ryan followed Holmes's motion with a sideways glance but chose to ignore the piece of paper. Holmes made an inviting gesture: "Please, do have a look."

After a moment's hesitation, the priest bent over the fragment and made a show of studying it. I could see his features working. His teeth pressed down on his lower lip and his eyelids twitched. A blotchy redness began to colour his cheeks.

Holmes said, "I believe the first two and the last two lines are the writer's own and I would not want to hazard a guess as to the words that the fire destroyed. But the three middle lines, I am quite confident, complete as follows:" And he intoned, rather flatly: "'The joints of thy thighs are like jewels, that are made by the hand of a skilful workman. Thy navel is like a round bowl never wanting cups. Thy belly is like a heap of wheat, set about with lilies. Thy two breasts are like to young roes that are twins.'"

"The Song of Songs...." said the priest in a voice cracking under the strain. His fists were clenched and a gleam shone in his reddened eyes. The man had a temper and it was on the point of erupting. Holmes stood quietly, his long arms dangling by his side. Yet I knew his outward appearance belied the inner tension. He was readying himself for an attack. The two men stared at each other for what must have been half a minute, taking each other's measure.

The priest exhaled. "I sinned. There is no excuse," he said with tired sadness, then added: "But the child, the boy...." A note of incomprehension lay in his voice, as if for a long time he had been pondering an equation, yet could not solve it.

"Agnes wanted you to take care of him," my companion stated.

"How could I do that?! All I could do was to provide her with money and that I did!" Father Ryan's jaw momentarily clenched in vexation. "I could not be a father to Ben! We had discussed this! Many times." He took a step backwards as if to steady himself against the table. "She flew at me the moment I came into the room. I needed to take the boy. He was mine! I told her to be reasonable. I pushed her away, and she slipped... she slipped, and she struck her head against the mantelpiece."

I realized at this moment that the priest did not know of the condition in which Agnes had been. Presumably she had intended to tell him, tell him that she was dying and that he needed to assume his responsibilities, finally. Yet the events unfolded in a manner that did not allow her to carry out her plan.

"You had not seen each other in a while, I assume," said Holmes.

"No. Yes," replied the priest, incongruously. "I would see her in mass, every Sunday. But we did not talk. I would leave some money for her under a flowerpot by the rectory on the first of a month. We haven't been... been seeing each other for almost a year now."

"And recently she summoned you."

"Yesterday. I received a letter from her telling me, imploring me to come to her room, late at night, around one in the morning. It was urgent, we needed to discuss matters. We had only met there once a long time ago. It was too dangerous. We used to meet in a small hotel in Lambeth. Be that as it may, after much hesitation, I went."

He passed a palm over his mouth in a grasping gesture as if to catch something invisible that was escaping from between his lips. Clearly he did not wish to relate his final encounter with the woman he had once loved, perhaps had never ceased to love. My companion remained silent. An exact recounting of the events was unnecessary.

Father Ryan continued: "When that landlord, Mr Thompson or whatever his name is, came to fetch me, I was in my parlour. I believe I was waiting. Part of me knew I would be called. I felt that judgment had arrived," he said. "I felt certain that she would be conscious when we returned, that she would point to me as the man who had pushed her. That everything would be revealed. But then she died without uttering my name. And I felt that I had been spared. Maybe for a reason, I thought. But now you are here. How did you find me so fast?"

"It was really quite simple," replied Holmes. "In cases like these, one is initially drawn to the hypothesis that the malefactor is of a violent disposition, or worse, that he is animated by hatred of the female sex. You will remember the so-called Jack the Ripper murders of a few years ago when this was presumably the motive of the killings. It quickly became clear to me, however, that such could not be the nature of the case at hand. Quite the contrary, in fact. The room in which Agnes lay showed no evidence of a struggle. Nothing was disturbed, not even the decanter on the table. There was blood on the floor, though, and on the edge of the mantelpiece…."

"I told you, I pushed her. She slipped!" Father Ryan interjected. "It happened so fast, I could not hold her!"

Holmes continued evenly: "Who carried Miss Connolly to the bed and bandaged her head? This was the obvious question. Ben could hardly have done so, but I did not want to presume. His recollection of finding his mother was haphazard and occasionally we will develop strength far beyond our normal capacity in moments of crisis. I surmised though that only a grown man could have carried Miss Connolly. A grown man who was not callous. Yet he had not come forward but had fled the scene. This could point to guilt or to fear of exposure and shame, given the circumstances."

He looked the priest in the face. "And that was when you and Mr Thompson arrived. What I noticed immediately, if you will forgive me, was the rather shoddy appearance of your coat. It even had a patch or two. Watson noticed this, too, I daresay, like he notices many things. However, one must draw conclusions from what one notices. Therein lies the art of reading the world. Now I am aware that the clergy in this country do not receive remuneration according to their deserts. A new coat every few years, however, is well within their means. This led me to think that this coat you were presently wearing was a cast-off, an old coat you kept in case of emergency, say for times when your current one was dirtied."

The priest was looking at the floor. "It was covered in blood from when I carried Agnes to the bed."

"What also struck me," Holmes proceeded, "was your general appearance, in particular in contrast with Mr Thompson's. He had clearly been in bed recently. He looked dishevelled. You, however, appeared quite presentable, beard combed, no traces of tiredness in your face. How could one explain the fact that you had been up in the middle of the night when Mr Thompson came to fetch you? Many innocuous explanations were possible, of course, but you will understand that I began to consider you with a suspicious eye."

The priest nodded glumly.

"After you carried Miss Connolly to the bed, you stayed with her as long as you could," Holmes said. "In fact, you only left at the last possible moment. When you heard your son in the hallway, coming to find his mother…."

"He was calling for her."

"You escaped by the back entrance, past the wash basin…."

"In the nick of time."

"But you realized that within a few hours a murder investigation would be underway. You reflected on what linked you with the dying woman in the room…."

The priest's voice had been growing more animated. He threw up his hands. "I wasn't sure she was dying! I hoped she was only unconscious! Though all that blood was horrible. I hoped Ben would do exactly as he did, fetch a doctor." There were tears in his eyes, which he blinked away. "But yes, I knew she might die. She had mentioned our old letters at some point, that she had kept them. Not to blackmail me. She kept them as tokens of memory of… what we once had."

He hesitated and then continued in a rush as if to forestall any misunderstanding on our part. "I never gave her money to buy her silence. Agnes would never have betrayed me. I gave her money because I wanted her to live decently and I wanted to do right by the boy." The priest paused. "The Song of Songs was a piece of drollery between us. Agnes once said that the Holy Writ lacked something of life's fullness and I proved her wrong by quoting the Song of Songs. And from then on I would quote it every once in a while… as a lark, you might say…."

"And so you rushed to her flat, found the letters and dropped them in the stove. Then you returned to the rectory in time for Mr Thompson to come calling for you."

There was no response.

After a few moments my companion did something he rarely does: he exhibited a gesture of kindness. At least he tried to do so. Laying his right hand against the priest's shoulder, Holmes turned to me: "Watson, perhaps you would like to inform Father Ryan of Miss Connolly's condition."

I nodded and then proceeded to give the priest a synopsis of my discovery on examining Agnes's chest. I told him that her disease had been far advanced and that death for her had been both close and certain. Father Ryan shrank back from me, and by the time I concluded he had sat down again on the chair on which we had found him on entering the vestry.

"That is why she called for me," he spoke between sobs. "But how was I supposed to know? Why didn't she just tell me…."

All that had to be said had been said and while I waited with the sad figure of Father Ryan, Holmes went back into the church to instruct the sexton to fetch a constable. He arrived a few minutes later and took the priest into custody. Father Ryan did not look up as he walked past us out of his church, stooped and with heavy steps.

Tiredness suddenly struck me, less, I suppose, the result of my foreshortened hours of sleep than of the events that had unfolded. My spirits were drained. As Holmes and I returned to the main road to fetch a cab to our quarters at 221 Baker Street, I kept reflecting on the events of the night. Finally I turned to Holmes and remarked: "An unfortunate accident, really. He merely pushed her. He did not intend to do her harm."

Holmes took a long time to reply. "Perhaps," he said after lighting his pipe and taking a puff. "But intentions are not the only source of man's actions. Father Ryan believes that he only intended to push Miss Connolly away, but why did he push so hard? For that matter, why did she fly at him so violently?" He shrugged and flicked the match into the gutter.

All this seemed cryptic to me but I did not ask the great detective to clarify his words. I had my own dilemmas to ponder.

The court, if I remember correctly, saw the case my way. Father Ryan did not go to the gallows. The jury gave credence to his statement that he had caused his former lover's death inadvertently. I am sure his frock also had a part in preserving his life. He could, of course, not reclaim his profession and I believe he left for the New World shortly after being acquitted, whether in the hope of finding a new flock or to enter a different walk of life, I do not know.

Mary came to see me a week after the events related. My examination revealed that her disease had not yet entered the critical phase in which there can no longer be any redress. I advised her sternly to leave the unhealthy environs of the city for a warmer and drier climate. She had saved a little money and I believe I gave her a small sum myself. We saw each other for the last time on the morning she sailed for Lisbon. We shook hands and then, before she walked up the gangway, she leaned forward and kissed me on the cheek. We waved to each other as the ship pulled away from its moorings and headed down the Thames. For many months thereafter we exchanged letters, but then, as is common between human beings whose lives have been parted by larger forces, we lost touch. In one of her last letters I think she mentioned encountering a baker in a village on the Algarve coast and I like to imagine her standing on the threshold of a cottage watching over a few young children playing in a garden. The warm southern wind is pulling strands of her auburn hair across her face and there is a smile on her lips, the smile of a person who against all odds has succeeded in finding a small parcel of safety and happiness in the dismal chaos of human life.

As for Ben, after a few months he rejoined the Baker Street Irregulars and every once in a while he would come to our flat to read his penny dreadfuls and eat Mrs Hudson's biscuits and wait for Holmes's instructions. Yet he was silent and withdrawn despite Mrs Hudson's best efforts to cheer him up. A few times, I tried to engage him in conversation, but I could tell that he did not look upon me as someone in whom he wished to confide. As he grew older, he drifted away from the Irregulars and eventually ceased membership altogether. I would see him now and then standing with a group of boys on a street corner, usually somewhat to the side, smoking and perhaps looking into a newspaper. And then he disappeared. My guess is that he went to sea like so many young men of his class, as a deckhand on a merchant sailor or as an ordinary seaman on a ship of the line. This is a hard and dangerous life. Great Britain demands much of her sons. She does acknowledge them, however.

✗

Martin Rosenstock studied Comparative Literature at UC Santa Barbara. After job-hopping around the colder latitudes of the US for three years, he decided to return to a warmer climate. In 2011, he took a job at Gulf University for Science and Technology in Kuwait, where he currently teaches.

SHERLOCK HOLMES: DISCOVERING THE BORDER BURGHS AND, BY DEDUCTION, THE BRIG BAZAAR

In the style of Sir Arthur Conan Doyle

In February 2015, the Holmesian world was electrified by a report in The Telegraph *that a new Sherlock Holmes story had been discovered in a fund-raising booklet published in Scotland in December 1903. Further analysis revealed it to be an early pastiche and not the work of Sir Arthur Conan Doyle. A disappointment, to be sure, but the story's resurfacing did allow many Holmesian scholars to stretch their research wings and, like Holmes himself, discover the truth of the matter. For a more detailed discussion of the story and its reason for being, as well as its connection with Sir Arthur Conan Doyle, consult the February 20, 2015 post in* I Hear of Sherlock Everywhere *(ihearofsherlock.com), by noted scholar Mattias Boström.* SHMM *is pleased to reprint the story in its entirety.*

"We've had enough of old romancists and the men of travel," said the Editor, as he blue-pencilled his copy and made arrangements for the great Saturday edition of the *Bazaar Book*. "We want something up-to-date. Why not have a word from Sherlock Holmes?"

Editors have only to speak and it is done, at least, they think so. "Sherlock Holmes!" As well talk of interviewing the Man in the Moon. But it does not do to tell Editors all that you think. I had no objections whatever, I assured the Editor, to buttonhole Sherlock Holmes, but to do so I should have to go to London.

"London!" scornfully sniffed the Great Man. "And you profess to be a journalist? Have you never heard of the telegraph, the telephone, or the phonograph? Go to London!

"And are you not aware that all journalists are supposed to be qualified members of the Institute of Fiction, and to be qualified to make use of the Faculty of Imagination? By the use of the latter men have been interviewed, who were hundreds of miles away; some have been "interviewed" without either knowledge or consent. See that you have a topical article ready for the press for Saturday. Good day."

I was dismissed and had to find copy by hook or by crook. Well, the Faculty of Imagination might be worth a trial.

The familiar house in Sloan Street met my bewildered gaze. The door was shut, the blinds drawn. I entered; doors are no barrier to one who uses the Faculty of Imagination. The soft light from an electric bulb flooded the room. Sherlock Holmes sits by the side of the table; Dr. Watson is on his feet about to leave for the night. Sherlock Holmes, as has lately been shown by a prominent journal, is a pronounced Free Trader. Dr. Watson is a mild Protectionist, who would take his gruelling behind a Martello tower, as Lord Goschen wittily put it, but not lying down! The twain had just finished a stiff argument on Fiscal policy. Holmes asked, "And when shall I see you again, Watson? The inquiry into the "Mysteries of the Secret Cabinet" will be continued in Edinburgh on Saturday. Do you mind a run down to Scotland? You would get some capital data which you might turn to good account later."

"I am very sorry," replied Dr. Watson, "I should have liked to have gone with you, but a prior engagement prevents me. I will, however, have the pleasure of being in kindly Scottish company that day. I, also, am going to Scotland."

"Ah! Then you are going to the Border country at that time?"

"How do you know that?"

"My dear Watson, it's all a matter of deduction."

"Will you explain?"

"Well, when a man becomes absorbed in a certain theme, the murder will out some day. In many discussions you and I have on the fiscal question from time to time I have not failed to notice that you have taken up an attitude antagonistic to a certain school of thought, and on several occasions you have commented on the passing of "so-called" reforms, as you describe them, which you say were not the result of a spontaneous movement from or by the people, but solely due to the pressure of the Manchester School of politicians appealing to the mob. One of these allusions you made a peculiar reference to "Huz an' Mainchester" who had "turned the world upside down." The word "Huz" stuck to me, but after consulting many authors without learning anything as to the source of the word, I one day in reading a provincial paper noticed the same expression, which the writer said was descriptive of the way Hawick people looked at the progress of Reform. "Huz an Mainchester" led the way. So, thought I, Watson has a knowledge of Hawick. I was still further confirmed in this idea by hearing you in several absent moments crooning a weird song of the Norwegian God Thor. Again I made enquires, and writing to a friend in the South country I procured a copy of "Teribus." So, I reasoned, so—there's something in the air! What attraction has Hawick for Watson?"

"Wonderful," Watson said, "and—"

"Yes, and when you characterized the action of the German Government in seeking to hamper Canadian trade by raising her tariff wall against her, as a case of "Sour Plums," and again in a drawing room asked a mutual lady friend to sing you that fine old song, "Braw, braw lads," I was curious enough to look up the old ballad, and finding it had reference to a small town near to Hawick, I began to see a ray of daylight. Hawick had a place in your mind; likewise so had Galashiels—so much was apparent. The question to be decided was why?"

"So far so good. And—"

"Later still the plot deepened. Why, when I was retailing to you the steps that led up to the arrest of the Norwood builder by the impression of his thumb, I found a very great surprise that you were not listening at all to my reasoning, but were lilting a very sweet— a very sweet tune, Watson—"The Flowers of the Forest;" then I in turn consulted an authority on the subject, and found that that lovely if tragic song had a special reference to Selkirk. And you remember, Watson, how very enthusiastic you grew all of a sudden on the subject of Common-Ridings, and how much you studied the history of James IV, with special reference to Flodden Field. All these things speak, Watson, to the orderly brain of a thinker. Hawick, Galashiels, and Selkirk. What did the combination mean? I felt I must solve the problem, Watson; so that night when you left me, after we had discussed the "Tragedy of a Divided House," I ordered in a ton of tobacco, wrapped my cloak about me, and spent the night in thought. When you came round in the morning the problem was solved. I could not on the accumulative evidence but come to the conclusion that you contemplated another Parliamentary contest. Watson, you have the Border Burghs in your eye!"

"In my heart, Holmes," said Watson.

"And where do you travel to on Saturday, Watson?"

"I am going to Selkirk; I have an engagement there to open a Bazaar."

"Is it in aid of a Bridge, Watson?"

"Yes," replied Watson in surprise; "but how do you know? I have never mentioned the matter to you."

"By word, no; but by your action you have revealed the bent of your mind."

"Impossible!"

"Let me explain. A week ago you came round to my rooms and asked for a look at Macaulay's *Lays of Ancient Rome*. (You know I admire Macaulay's works, and have a full set.) That volume, after a casual look at, you took with you. When you returned it a day or two later I noticed it was marked with a slip of paper at the "Lay of Horatius," and I detected a faint pencil mark on the slip noting that the closing stanza was very appropriate. As you know, Watson, the lay is all descriptive of the keeping of a bridge. Let me remind you how nicely you would perorate—

> When the goodman mends his armour
> And trims his helmet's plume,
> When the goodwife's shuttle merrily
> Goes flashing through the loom,
> With weeping and with laughter.
> Still the story told—
> How well Horatius kept the bridge,
> In the brave days of old.

Could I, being mortal, help thinking you were bent on some such exploit yourself?"

"Very true!"

"Well, goodbye, Watson; shall be glad of your company after Saturday. Remember Horatius's words when you go to Border Burghs:—"How can man die better than facing fearful odds." But there, these words are only illustrations. Safe journey, and success to the Brig!"

✗

THE SINGULAR AFFAIR AT SISSINGHURST CASTLE

by David Marcum

FX:	WAGON WHEELS AND HORSE WALKING STEADILY
WATSON:	Holmes, I appreciate the chance to get out of London for the day, and Kent is certainly lovely in the spring, but you don't always have to be so mysterious.
	Why are we here?
HOLMES:	We are going to Sissinghurst. Do you know of it?
WATSON:	Not at all, I'm afraid.
HOLMES:	I received a letter several days ago from the owner of Sissinghurst Castle and the surrounding farm, a Mr. Stanley Cornwallis.
WATSON:	And what does Mr. Cornwallis require from Mr. Sherlock Holmes?
HOLMES:	He is being bothered by a treasure hunter.
WATSON:	Treasure? In Kent? I might believe that about some of the areas along the coast with their centuries of smuggling and the occasional shipwreck. But deep in the heart of the county? Not likely.
HOLMES:	There is more than one kind of treasure, Watson. It was only a few months ago that I told you about Reginald Musgrave at Hurlstone, and the recovery there of the lost crown of the former King of England.

WATSON: As I recall, King Charles's crown was hidden at Hurlstone during the reign of Cromwell and the Commonwealth. Does Cornwallis suspect something similar is hidden at Sissinghurst?

HOLMES: No, he believes exactly the opposite. He is certain that there is *nothing* hidden at the house. The estate apparently has some connection with events relating to those muddled times of transition between Mary and Elizabeth. It is a common story in that area, but there has never been any hint of treasure.

WATSON: Then why is there a treasure hunter?

HOLMES: Several weeks ago, an American arrived in Sissinghurst who has repeatedly insisted on searching the buildings and grounds for something of value. So far, Mr. Cornwallis has denied him any access. However, it seems that in spite of his initial disbelief, Mr. Cornwallis did become more interested in whether there is any truth to the American's claims.

WATSON: And so he communicated with you?

HOLMES: He wrote, asking if I would be interested in doing some research to determine if there was any possibility of truth in the matter. I replied, and then I devoted part of a day in the reading room at the British Museum. Although there is some local historical significance to Mr. Cornwallis's farm, I found no evidence of anything relevant to a treasure at Sissinghurst.

WATSON: They why have we traveled down here?

HOLMES: I was ready to relay my results to Mr. Cornwallis when this morning's wire arrived. Something seems to have happened that made our presence

	necessary. As you can see, the message is rather vague as to details.
WATSON:	*(Reading)* Come at once. Situation becoming intolerable. Please wire details of arrival. Cornwallis. *(Normal voice)* Vague, indeed. It could be anything from an unpleasant encounter with the American, to murder.
HOLMES:	Well, perhaps not murder. If it was that, Cornwallis might have used stronger language than to simply call the situation "intolerable." *(Louder)* Driver, what can you tell us about this area?
DRIVER:	Not much to tell, sir. There's the village, and the main farm. It's well run, it is. The farmhouse is very nice. And then there's the old house beside it. Hundreds of years old, it is, but it's mostly fallen down now. Some calls it a castle, maybe because it has something of a tower, but it's really naught but an old house.
HOLMES:	Did anything interesting ever happen there?
DRIVER:	Not much. Of course there was "Bloody" Baker.
HOLMES:	I learned something of the fellow during my researches. A fellow with the appellation "Bloody" certainly sounds somewhat interesting, eh, Watson?
	Driver, what can you tell us of this man?
DRIVER:	Not much, sir. Baker were a Catholic man, back during the reign of Mary. He was the owner of Sissinghurst then, and he made it his business to make life hell for the Protestants living around here. That's about all I know for sure, but I've heard about him all my life.

FX:	WAGON WHEELS SLOW TO A STOP; THE HORSE NICKERS
DRIVER:	There's Sissinghurst. We're nearly there now, sirs.
MUSIC	SHORT BRIDGE
CORNWALLIS:	Mr. Holmes? I am Stanley Cornwallis. Thank you for coming. I apologize for not sending a carriage to the station. I have been too distracted by today's events.
HOLMES:	It is quite all right, Mr. Cornwallis. We arranged for transportation. I have brought Dr. John Watson with me. He is an experienced investigator as well and often accompanies me.
	(Ad lib general greetings:Nice to meet you, etc.)
HOLMES:	What are the events today to which you referred?
CORNWALLIS:	Come this way, gentlemen, around to the back of the house.
FX:	FOOTSTEPS THROUGH GRASS OR ALONG WALKWAYS
CORNWALLIS:	*(Slightly winded)* Is Dr. Watson aware of the reason I originally wrote to you?
HOLMES:	Somewhat. However, I have not revealed to him as yet the little bit of information that my researches revealed.
CORNWALLIS:	*(Irate)* I have not received a report from you, either, Mr. Holmes. Did you find any indication whatsoever that there might be some sort of rare artifact or treasure at Sissinghurst?
HOLMES:	None whatsoever. While there appears to be a long history to the place, there is nothing

	monumentally outstanding and certainly nothing that makes this small byway any more interesting than countless other villages across Britain.
CORNWALLIS:	*(Agitated)* Then why would that insane American do *that*?
FX:	FOOTSTEPS STOP
WATSON:	Oh… my.
HOLMES:	Is this what you meant, Mr. Cornwallis, when you wired that the situation was becoming 'intolerable'?
CORNWALLIS:	Of course that's what I meant. This situation! That American! It's all intolerable. And I want you to gather evidence to stop it. I will prosecute him, sir. I will! I wired for you as soon as we found this and I have sent for the law as well. The man will pay!
WATSON:	Your stone terrace, Mr. Cornwallis. It's… it's been nearly destroyed. Almost all of the stones are overturned—
HOLMES:	What indication do you have that the American is responsible for this? Did you perhaps catch him in the act?
CORNWALLIS:	No, no. It was this way when we came out this morning. He did it during the night. I'm sure he did it. He has been pestering me for weeks to dig on the grounds for his ridiculous treasure. When I said no, he obviously came back on his own and did this.
WATSON:	And you say that you have called for the police?
CORNWALLIS:	Actually, I did not notify them immediately. My first thought was to send for you, Mr. Holmes.

	I sent one of the farm hands into the village to send a wire. He waited for your reply and then returned here. Later, I thought to send my man back for the constable, but I neglected to tell him to meet your train.
WATSON:	*(To himself)* That explains why there was no one to meet us at the station.
HOLMES:	Perhaps we could go inside while we wait for the constable to arrive and you can tell us about this American. We can discuss the history of this estate and why there might—or might not—be any treasure at Sissinghurst.
MUSIC	SHORT BRIDGE
WATSON:	Have you ever seen any indication of anything that might be considered treasure here?
CORNWALLIS:	No, Dr. Watson. The property has been in my family for many generations and there has never been anything like that here.
WATSON:	Was there ever any evidence of visits here by royalty? Did anyone in your family ever travel or have adventures in foreign lands which might have given them an opportunity to obtain a treasure?
CORNWALLIS:	There is a rumor that Edward I stayed here in the village in the early 1300s, but if so, he would certainly not have hidden a treasure here.
WATSON:	No, that can't be it.
CORNWALLIS:	And, of course, there was Sir John Baker, who owned the house in the early 1500s and was left two hundred pounds by Henry VIII, in spite of Baker's noted pro-Catholic beliefs.

HOLMES: Ah, yes, "Bloody" Baker. He is the center of your American's treasure theories. What can you tell us of him?

CORNWALLIS: Why, that is Sir John, over there in that painting over the fireplace.

WATSON: *(Muttering)* Grim looking fellow. *(Louder)* But overall he does not seem very threatening. Certainly not worth the name "Bloody" Baker.

HOLMES: Hmm. *(Reading)* "Sir John Baker. 1488 to 1558." *(Normal voice)* Long-lived for his time. As I understand it, he was quite a successful man in this region.

CORNWALLIS: Yes, he was. Although he was fiercely pro-Catholic, Sir John enjoyed an excellent relationship with King Henry VIII, in spite of Henry's strong anti-Catholic beliefs.

HOLMES: In fact, I learned that during the time King Henry was taking so many estates, churches and monasteries from pro-Catholic citizens and redistributing them to his friends and cronies, he actually gave many properties to Sir John, who ended up owning a number of manors and farms scattered around this area of Kent.

CORNWALLIS: Peacefully, I might add.

WATSON: But there was nothing bloody about any of that! Was there ever any indication of Baker showing excessive violence toward the local Protestants?

CORNWALLIS: None, Doctor. He questioned them and often they had their property taken from them, but I have never heard anything that would lead to the name "Bloody" Baker.

HOLMES: As I understand it from your original letter, it is the claim of the American treasure hunter...

I'm sorry, what was his name again, Mr. Cornwallis?

CORNWALLIS: Burke. Philo T. Burke.

HOLMES: Ah, yes. Peculiar name, isn't it, Watson? It is the claim of Mr. Burke that during this time, Sir John Baker took something of great value from one of the local families and hid it here at Sissinghurst. During the confusion following Queen Mary's death, the item was never recovered. And soon after, Sir John died and his secret with him.

CORNWALLIS: That is Burke's assertion, yes. However, there is no basis for such a fabrication. The local families have never mentioned any lost treasure, nor have they ever listed the theft of a treasure amongst their grievances against Sir John.

HOLMES: This location has spent the better part of the last thousand years in relative ease and peace. Even the tensions between Catholics and Protestants in the area never achieved any great level of bloodshed.

CORNWALLIS: Would you be willing to present your evidence to Burke? Excellent!

FX: CARRIAGES ARRIVING OUTSIDE (MUTED)

CORNWALLIS: That will be the constable. Will you relate to him as well what you have told me?

HOLMES: Of course.

FX: CURTAINS PULLING BACK AND WINDOW OPENING

CORNWALLS: Look out there! That's not the constable! It's Burke with several carriages of rough-looking men with him!

MUSIC   SHORT BRIDGE

FX: QUICK FOOTSTEPS ACROSS GRAVEL

CORNWALLIS: Burke! What is the meaning of this? I have told you that you are not allowed on my property!

BURKE: *(American accent)* Good morning to you, Mr. Cornwallis. I realize that we have had some disagreements in the past, but we cannot let something like that stand in the way of the historical find of the century! Just think, sir, when the truth is revealed, your little castle here will be the destination point of visitors from both Europe and America!

CORNWALLIS: Leave! Leave now! The law will be here soon and then I will have you arrested! Do you think you can get away with vandalizing my property and trespassing? I will have you arrested and then deported!

BURKE: I don't think we've had the pleasure, gentleman. My name is Philo Burke, late of Cleveland, Ohio. I'm sure Mr. Cornwallis has told you about me.

CORNWALLIS: Yes, I have. They are here because of you. They can debunk your whole treasure theory. This is—

HOLMES: *(Interrupting)* We have been doing some research for Mr. Cornwallis in London. Mr. Cornwallis is correct. There is no evidence of any historical event here that would indicate the presence of treasure.

BURKE: Of course, that is what the official records would say. If there was a conspiracy to conceal the fact that "Bloody" Baker had hidden a treasure here, he would have covered his tracks well.

(Ad lib:The men of the press muttering to themselves)

BURKE: *(Louder)* Boys, I've looked at the same papers in London that this gentleman is referring to and I can tell you that there is more to it than he thinks. In fact, *(Lowering voice)* I was even able to find a coded message contained in the papers, which is what led me to search under the flagstone terrace behind the house!

CORNWALLIS: You destroyed that terrace! It has only been there for thirty years, since the current house was built. It wasn't even there when Sir John lived here!

BURKE: Mr. Cornwallis, I do not know if you are truly ignorant of the historical nature of what is hidden here or if you yourself are part of the conspiracy to keep the truth hidden. But I tell you that the truth must come out and you cannot stop it! I have brought these fine men of the press with me today, to assure that the truth will be told. For too long the secret has been kept! Come with me, boys!

FX: MULTIPLE FOOTSTEPS ACROSS GRAVEL (FADING)

BURKE: *(Fading)* Follow me behind the house. Whatever it is, it's been buried for over three hundred years. It's time to bring it out into the sunshine!

HOLMES: *(Low voice, but still nearby)* What do you say to a day in Kent, Watson?

WATSON: *(Low voice)* Kent sounds wonderful. If we don't get killed in the crossfire. I assume you didn't want Burke to know you are a detective.

HOLMES: *(Low voice)* Exactly. Burke may or may not have heard of me, but I want to see what his game is for a while and the best way to do that is to let him play it out. The terrace is already damaged. A little more destruction cannot hurt it too badly. Let us see what Mr. Burke has planned for us.

MUSIC   SHORT BRIDGE

HOLMES: Hurry, Watson, let us hear what Mr. Burke is saying to the press.

BURKE: *(Voice becoming louder; Speaking to the press)* As you can see, I was unable to finish my search of the terrace last night. I was interrupted and forced to flee when I thought I was about to be discovered. Of course, I will recompense Mr. Cornwallis for the cost of repairs to his terrace.

CORNWALLIS: You certainly will!

BURKE: However, I feel that once the treasure is recovered, he will be so grateful that he will understand why this was necessary, and he may not even ask for any compensation.

REPORTER #1:   And what is your deal in all this, Mr. Burke? If they find a treasure, you don't get to keep it.

BURKE: Certainly not. My only interest is in the advancement of historical knowledge.

REPORTER #2:   How did you get onto it? Being from Ohio and all?

BURKE: I came across some old documents which made references to other documents. I followed the trail, using the specialized knowledge I have acquired from a lifetime of study, until I found conclusive proof of the Sissinghurst Treasure.

FX: FLAGSTONE STONE OVERTURNING (FADING)

REPORTER #3: *(Slightly in the distance)* Oi! What's this?

HOLMES: *(Softly)* I believe we are about to see Mr. Burke's surprise, Watson.

REPORTER #2: It's a skeleton! Down in the hole underneath this terrace stone!

REPORTER #3: This stone wasn't flipped like all the others. I was just looking to see what was underneath. And—oh my God! The back of his bloody head's been knocked in!

REPORTER #1: Let me see!

REPORTER #2: Get out of the way, you!

BURKE: Well, I had not expected this. No, sir. Had you, Mr. Cornwallis? Did you perhaps know what we would find?

CORNWALLIS: *(Stunned, quiet)* No. No, of course not.

HOLMES: And what did you expect, Mr. Burke?

BURKE: Well, sir, to be honest, I did not rightly know. Treasure of some sort, of course, perhaps a chest, but I never expected to find a murder.

WAGNER: *(Fading in)* Murder? What's this about a murder? How was this found, sir?

CORNWALLIS: Constable Wagner! It's about time you arrived.

REPORTER #2: It's a skeleton. Underneath this paving stone.

WAGNER: Any idea who this might be?

CORNWALLIS:	None. This terrace is only thirty or so years old. There is no indication that there has ever been a treasure here, contrary to Mr. Burke's wild claims. Let alone a skeleton. This gentleman will tell you. He has researched the matter.
WAGNER:	And your name sir? You look familiar to me. Wait, aren't you—
HOLMES:	Might I speak with you in private for a moment?
WAGNER:	Why, um, certainly.
FX:	FOOTSTEPS ACROSS GRAVEL (FADING)
REPORTER #1:	*(Yelling)* Mr. Cornwallis! Do you care to give a statement about this gruesome discovery?
REPORTER #2:	*(Abrasive)* Mr. Cornwallis, sir! Do you know which member of your family killed this man and hid his body under the terrace?
REPORTER #3:	Do you feel that it is now the right time to reveal the location of the treasure?
CORNWALLIS:	Burke! This is all your fault! I'll—
FX:	FOOTSTEPS ACROSS GRAVEL (RETURNING)
WAGNER:	*(Loud)* You people. I want your names and which paper you are with. Then I want you to clear off out of here. Return to the village and don't leave until I tell you so. *(Normal tone)* Mr. Cornwallis, I am going to leave the remains here under your responsibility until I can return. Mr. Burke, you will return to the village with me.
BURKE:	*(Angry)* Wait! You cannot simply go off and leave this find unprotected. We don't know how

it got here. His family may have something to do with it.

You may get back and the treasure may be gone! Or the bones!

WAGNER: Sir, there are a number of witnesses who have seen the skeleton, most of them reporters that you brought here yourself. Too many people have seen this. I do not think that anything will happen here while I'm gone, and I trust these men to watch over things until I return. Gentlemen, until I return, good day.

FX: FOOTSTEPS ACROSS GRAVEL (FADING)

CORNWALLIS: Mr. Holmes, what does it all mean? Is it possible that "Bloody" Baker was not the innocent man your researches showed?

HOLMES: Perhaps you should go inside and rest, Mr. Cornwallis. Dr. Watson and I will be responsible for the skeleton until the return of Constable Wagner.

CORNWALLIS: Yes, of course. Thank you, Mr. Holmes.

FX: FOOTSTEPS ACROSS GRAVEL (FADING)

HOLMES: What do you make of it, Watson?

WATSON: This is certainly no murder, is it?

HOLMES: As I'm sure you can see, the bones are clean and white. More importantly, they were obviously once *wired together*. What does this suggest?

WATSON: This fellow has, until recently, been the resident of some sort of teaching facility, perhaps a hospital. I imagine, from his excellent condition, that he has not been dead and preserved for too many years and that he certainly has not been in this hole for very long.

HOLMES: No, not for more than twelve hours or so, I would say. The bones are extremely clean and there is no sign of discoloration from exposure to the soil or the ground-water. In addition, the sides of the hole are still quite vertical, and there has been no creep or collapse of the walls.

WATSON: But why was he placed here? I assume that Burke is behind this.

HOLMES: Oh, of course he is. Obviously, he came out here last night and buried the bones under a flagstone large enough to cover a skeleton before he replaced that stone and proceeded to disrupt a number of others. Then, as we saw a few minutes ago, he let someone else make the discovery, creating the shocking effect that he was attempting.

WATSON: But surely he realizes that a cursory examination would show that this skeleton is of very recent origin?

HOLMES: Possibly. It may be that he has such a low opinion of the country constabulary that he believes the skeleton's condition would not be noticed. Or more probably, he does not care. He intentionally made sure there were reporters here and he seemed pleased that they were writing down everything they saw and heard.

WATSON: When you referred to this as Burke's surprise, did you know exactly what was going to be found?

HOLMES: Not at all. But when Burke arrived with the reporters, I realized that he had probably hidden something that he wanted to be found in front of witnesses. However, I did not know what form the item would take.

WATSON: But what about the hole in the skull?

HOLMES: It simply adds to the effect. I'm sure the hole was knocked there by Burke to give the initial impression that the fellow had been murdered. If you look, you can see that the exposed cracked edges around the hole are clean and white, even cleaner than the surface of the skull, indicating that the wound is of recent origin.

WATSON: So all this has been arranged for some reason as a show for those reporters brought down by Burke.

HOLMES: Exactly. Although I am not quite certain of his motive at this point, I believe that we shall have to give Mr. Burke a little more line in order to set the hook before we can reel him in.

WATSON: And the constable? Did you make him aware of all this?

HOLMES: I did. He appeared to recognize me and was in fact about to identify me when I stopped him. I quickly explained to him what we have seen about the age and provenance of the skeleton, as well as Burke's apparent actions in the matter. He immediately picked up on what I was telling him and he agreed that we should allow Mr. Burke to act out his little drama for a while.

WATSON: I see. In that way, we might have something more against him than a simple charge of terrace vandalism. As it stands now, Burke could simply claim it was a joke, make restitution or pay a small fine and disappear without the real reasons behind this ever becoming known.

HOLMES:	And now let us go inside, where you can check on Mr. Cornwallis and I can smoke a pipe or two until Constable Wagner returns.
MUSIC	SHORT BRIDGE
WATSON:	Cornwallis finally dropped off to sleep. The poor man is a nervous wreck. I am afraid that if this continues, he'll suffer a case of brain fever.
HOLMES:	And what news do you have for us, Constable Wagner?
WAGNER:	The village doctor is outside, loading the skeleton. He has confirmed that is it is simply a medical exhibit, and not a murder victim.
HOLMES:	And the laborers you brought with you? Can they be discreet?
WAGNER:	I've sworn these men to secrecy. Burke is being watched by one of my men at the local inn. He's been holding court with those reporters, spinning one wild theory after another.
WATSON:	I can just imagine.
WAGNER:	By the time I left, he had one going where "Bloody" Baker kidnapped half the countryside at one time or another during Queen Mary's reign, holding them for ransoms until the families gave him their valuables.
WATSON:	Oh, my Lord.
WAGNER:	He's even saying that Mr. Cornwallis will be putting this place up for sale soon in order to get away from the horrible reputation that this place has acquired.
WATSON:	You can't be serious.

WAGNER:	He's hinting darkly that the place is haunted. The reporters are eating it up. They're already clogging up the local telegraph office, passing on these stories to their newspapers.
HOLMES:	I am sorry that we must let Burke continue to play out this nonsense until we can discover his true motives. It is going to cause a certain amount of distress for Mr. Cornwallis before it is all over.
WATSON:	*(Softly)* That is for certain.
HOLMES:	However, as I told Watson, it will be better if we can arrest Burke for more than simple vandalism. Do you suppose that you could get a few wires off for me without alerting the reporters?
WAGNER:	Of course. The telegraph agent is my brother-in-law.
HOLMES:	Stress the urgency of these. The longer this goes on, the more mess Mr. Cornwallis will have to deal with.
WAGNER:	Certainly, sir. I'll let you know if I hear anything. I'll be back out first thing in the morning.
FX:	FOOTSTEPS ACROSS ROOM (FADING); DOOR SHUTS
WATSON:	What now, Holmes?
HOLMES:	Now, old friend, we wait.
MUSIC	SHORT BRIDGE
WATSON:	*(Narrating)* The next morning, the sun was quite high in the sky and still there was no word from Constable Wagner, either of news regarding Burke's activities in the village the night before, or answers to Holmes's telegrams. And as for Holmes? He was becoming quite impatient.

HOLMES:	Blast! Wagner seemed quite intelligent, Watson. I cannot understand why we have heard nothing!
WATSON:	Perhaps he has nothing yet to tell. And if that gaggle of reporters is still in the village, he has no doubt had other matters to deal with.
HOLMES:	Possibly, possibly. Ah, Mr. Cornwallis. How are you feeling this morning?
CORNWALLIS:	Not well, Mr. Holmes. Not well at all. All night I tossed and turned, wondering what that man Burke will come up with next. What can be his purpose in all this?
HOLMES:	I hope to have an answer for you soon. Ah, I perceive that Constable Wagner has arrived. Hopefully, he has some news.
FX:	FOOTSTEPS ENTERING THE ROOM
WAGNER:	The story is in all the papers, I'm afraid, sir. Have a look at these, the latest editions down on the London train this morning.
FX:	NEWSPAPERS RUSTLING
HOLMES:	What of the replies to my telegrams, constable?
WAGNER:	I have them right here, sir.
CORNWALLIS:	*(Groans)* Treasure! They all have stories about the estate being filled with buried treasure. We shall be overrun!
WATSON:	Secreted fortunes, bloody murders. There are speculations enough here to fire any boy's wildest dreams. This paper even hints that there are lost entrances to a vast underground cavern on the estate filled with hoards of gold and jewels.

WAGNER: And what of this one? It speaks of the tower, which it says was designed with hidden passages and booby traps for the unwary.

WATSON: Look here! This reporter speculates that Mr. Cornwallis intends to sell the estate and leave the country, due to the fact that the *foully-murdered victim* found under the *ancient flagstone terrace* was such an embarrassment to the family that he can no longer stand to remain in England.

CORNWALLIS: This states that I was aware of the murdered victim, as well as many others hidden around the estate and that I will flee from the authorities before I can be questioned or jailed!

WAGNER: Mr. Burke has spread it around that he will be exposing another surprise here today at eleven a.m. Mr. Cornwallis, I'm afraid that the reporters will be coming back here then. It appears that half the village will be joining them.

CORNWALLIS: Oh my.

WAGNER: My men and I will be here, but I'm afraid there aren't enough of us to stop them. We will arrest as many as we can, if you'd like, but I cannot do anything until they actually trespass on the property.

CORNWALLIS: Of course, of course. Thank you.

HOLMES: Based on the information in these wires from America, you *can* arrest Burke, however.

WAGNER: Yes, sir. Anytime you say. And a good thing, too. I simply wanted to speak with you about it first.

HOLMES: Excellent. Watson, will you hand me that Bradshaw from that shelf behind you? Thank you.

	Would you care to examine the telegrams while I ascertain today's train schedule?
FX:	BOOK PAGES RUSTLING
HOLMES:	There is a train at eleven a.m, departing for London. An amazing coincidence, wouldn't you say? Exactly the time everyone will be gathering here at the Sissinghurst house.
WATSON:	Perhaps we should be at the station, then.
HOLMES:	Quite.
CORNWALLIS:	What? Won't you be here at eleven when Burke and the reporters come back? I don't understand.
HOLMES:	I believe that the reporters will be here without Mr. Burke and without him to provide any entertainment, I feel that they will soon become disinterested and leave. In the meantime, Mr. Burke will probably be attempting to slip out of town on the first train of the morning.
CORNWALLIS:	What?
HOLMES:	I am still not entirely certain as to Mr. Burke's reasons for creating this entire production, although certain aspects of the matter are becoming clear. However, yesterday, through the kindness of Constable Wagner and his brother-in-law, I cabled several acquaintances of mine in the United States, particularly a police officer in Cleveland, Ohio. What he replied about Mr. Philo T. Burke was of some interest, indeed.
WATSON:	These cables make interesting reading. Confidence man. Thief. Forger. Murderer. A very wanted man in America. It was rather careless of Mr. Burke to reveal his true name and place of origin, wasn't it?

WAGNER:	Once they found out where he was, the Americans then wired me as well as Mr. Holmes here to hold Burke until they can send someone after him. Should be here in about a week.
HOLMES:	Do you have enough men to keep an eye on the reporters, as well as making sure that Burke cannot slip away?
WAGNER:	As soon as I got this information, I quietly sent to surrounding areas, requesting some additional constables. Burke's under observation in the village by my men, but right now it's not a problem. He's still sitting around, feeding whatever crazy stories that he can think of to those reporters.
HOLMES:	When the time comes to travel out here from the village, he will certainly arrange for the reporters to go on ahead of him. Then he will quietly slip away to the train station and head back to London.
WAGNER:	That's the way I see it. Of course, we will prevent him.
HOLMES:	Mr. Cornwallis, we must leave you now to stop Mr. Burke. Rest assured that this matter will soon be concluded.
MUSIC	SHORT BRIDGE
FX:	TRAIN STATION. A TRAIN IS PREPARING TO DEPART
WATSON:	*(Softly)* There he is. On that bench on the upside of the platform.
WAGNER:	*(Softly)* I see him.
HOLMES:	*(Normal tone)* Mr. Burke? A moment, if you please?

BURKE:	*(Nervous)* Hmm? Is there a problem, gentle-men?
WAGNER:	There doesn't need to be. Mr. Philo T. Burke, of Cleveland, Ohio, I place you under arrest.
BURKE:	Oh, no you don't!
	(Ad-lib:Scuffle)
BURKE:	*(Angrily, out of breath)* What are you, anyway? One of those Scotland Yarders?"
HOLMES:	I am Sherlock Holmes.
BURKE:	*(A beat)* Heard about you. In fact, someone I met over here, never mind who, warned me not to get tangled up with you. I thought this far out in the country I would be safe. Never had a chance, did I?
WAGNER:	Come on, get him to the station.
MUSIC	SHORT BRIDGE
BURKE:	Search my bag all you like, gentlemen. There's nothing criminal in there.
HOLMES:	Nothing but these handwritten papers, Burke.
BURKE:	Those? They're nothing. Just some harmless scribbling. Certainly nothing illegal about them.
WATSON:	What are they, Holmes?
HOLMES:	See for yourself.
FX:	PAGES RUSTLING
WATSON:	Why, each one of these is a handwritten draft, describing the upcoming sale of the Sissing-hurst farm and castle.
WAGNER:	Sale? How can he plan a sale of something that he does not own?

HOLMES:	They are all very similar, having only slight variations from one another. Obviously, the sheets were rough drafts of some sort of prospectus. Notice the numerous scratched-out words, as if Mr. Burke tried differing combinations before settling on phrasing that pleased him.
WAGNER:	But what is the purpose, Mr. Holmes?
HOLMES:	I am not completely certain, but I believe that I have a reasonable understanding of Burke's plan. It fits his background as a confidence man and trickster. Correct me if I'm wrong, Mr. Burke.
BURKE:	I've done nothing wrong here.
HOLMES:	Burke researched and found a likely spot in Sissinghurst. The place was old, but there never was any reason to think that treasure had been hidden there. However, there was enough history to the place that stories of treasure could be fabricated, at least long enough to serve Burke's purpose. And of course, there was the association with the fascinating "Bloody" Baker.
WAGNER:	But where's the crime? If it hadn't been for those telegrams, we wouldn't have had reason to arrest him except for a petty charge of vandalism. What did he gain from all of this?
HOLMES:	After picking Sissinghurst, Burke showed up and began to make himself a nuisance to Mr. Cornwallis. His plan was to continue that for a few weeks until he could stage the incident with the reporters, the terrace, and the skeleton. I expect that when you got here, Mr. Burke, you did not know exactly where or how the incident would take place, but I'm sure you had the skeleton with you, as you looked for a likely spot.

	Did you buy the skeleton, Mr. Burke, or did you steal it from a medical school or hospital?
BURKE:	This is your tale, Mr. Holmes. I'm simply an innocent victim.
WATSON:	So it was his intent all along to create a story that would grab the imaginations of the reporters. He made it seem as mysterious and exciting as possible, throwing in hidden treasure, an unexpected dead man and hints of hauntings and conspiracy.
HOLMES:	What he was after, of course, was to have numerous stories about the incident in as many different newspapers as he could find. He never intended that the story should hold up to any kind of close scrutiny. He planned to be gone as soon as possible and he didn't care if the exact origins of the skeleton were quickly discovered.
WATSON:	Of course. As long as he had the newspapers containing the stories of treasure and a possible sale of the estate, he would be able to carry out the rest of his plan.
WAGNER:	So after he left for London on this morning's train—
HOLMES:	He would wait there for a few days, seeing if any other useful newspaper articles were printed that might add to the recently fabricated treasure legends of Sissinghurst Castle. He would buy up as many old copies of today's newspapers as he could reasonably carry for future use.
WATSON:	Then, after returning to America—
HOLMES:	After returning, he would have printed a series of brochures, false deeds and other bogus documents, each implying that he was the agent responsible for selling the Sissinghurst estate.

He would let on that people in England were reluctant to buy the estate, possibly afraid of ghosts.

WATSON: By showing a number of legitimate British newspapers, each with stories verifying Burke's claim that the estate was for sale and why, he could sell the estate over and over again to gullible American investors.

HOLMES: Exactly.

WATSON: Each would think they were getting the place at a bargain and not only acquiring an actual English estate with a castle, but also a property fairly loaded with hidden treasure and an interesting ghostly history.

HOLMES: Of course, after each false sale, he would simply move on and try the same thing in a different town. Is that substantially correct, Mr. Burke?

BURKE: You're the one telling it. I'm just listening. So far, all you can charge me with is vandalism of Cornwallis's terrace and you'd have to prove that. What difference does it make if I decided to leave town? And maybe I just bought all those newspapers because I thought it was an interesting story.

FX: CHAIR MOVING BACK AS BURKE STANDS UP

BURKE: So unless you can do better than that, gentleman, I am going to depart.

HOLMES: I don't think so, Mr. Burke. You were a little careless in telling me that you were from Cleveland, Ohio. I wired to some professional acquaintances there about you. Your history is an interesting one. Apparently your violent attack on one of the city's most prominent citizens, which caused you to flee America late last year, is still the subject of much discussion there.

BURKE: It's a lie!

HOLMES: The man later died. The Cleveland police were quite pleased to know that you are here and they are sending someone to retrieve you, even as we speak.

(Ad lib:Scuffle)

WAGNER: *(Winded)* Put him in a cell. He's the guest of Her Majesty now until his own people come to fetch him.

MUSIC SHORT BRIDGE

FX: TRAIN TRAVELING AT A STEADY SPEED, OCCASIONAL WHISTLE

WATSON: Poor Mr. Cornwallis. I fear that he will be bothered by the aftermath of this affair for years to come.

HOLMES: Perhaps. He is certainly fearful that people will be trespassing on the estate, digging and looking for treasure and then bringing suit against him if they somehow fall and hurt themselves in the process.

WATSON: Well, I hope it doesn't turn out that way. And, after all, you were able to give the reporters most of the facts and Constable Wagner will be telling them the rest of the story.

HOLMES: Hopefully, the whole matter will die a quick death. *(A beat)* Watson, would you enjoy attending a concert tonight when we arrive back in London? They are playing German music, which I find especially appealing.

WATSON: Certainly.

HOLMES: Good. Then I believe we shall just have time for
              me to tell you of an investigation I conducted
              not long after I entered private practice in Lon-
              don. It was on an estate similar to Sissinghurst
              in central Norfolk.

WATSON: Really?

HOLMES: Unlike Sissinghurst, however, this estate did
              indeed reveal a singular treasure, which we
              might, if you are interested and not too busy, go
              to see tomorrow at the British Museum.

                                                            ✗

David Marcum is the author of *The Papers of Sherlock Holmes, Volumes
I & II*; *Sherlock Holmes and A Quantity of Debt*; and *Sherlock Holmes
– Tangled Skeins*, and he is the editor of the three-volume set *Sherlock
Holmes in Montague Street*, and the massive ongoing four-volume (so
far) *The MX Book of New Sherlock Holmes Stories*, available from MX
Publishing. This play was first performed by Jim French's "Imagination
Theatre" and broadcast nationwide on November 23, 2014. John Patrick
Lowrie played Sherlock Holmes and Lawrence Albert was Dr. Watson.

THE CASE OF THE SWINDLED CANDIDATE

by Jack Grochot

Politics was a topic in which my friend Sherlock Holmes displayed very little interest, but when a politician acted scandalously or violated the public's trust, an outraged Holmes screeched to the high heavens about the infraction, usually at mealtime when I was his only audience.

The object of his most recent castigation was Alistair McBroom, a Member of Parliament whose malfeasance and wickedness brought disgrace upon the House of Commons as well as caused great upheaval in our system of government.

"Will they never learn to behave like representatives of the people, Watson?" Holmes protested loudly over a bowl of piping-hot chicken and dumplings soup at lunch. "The courts must guarantee that the punishment fits the crime, rather than promote leniency and mercy in egregious situations like this one. McBroom is a corrupt official who deserves no more respect than an ordinary thief!"

Holmes puckered, blew his breath over a spoonful of steaming broth and swallowed it as more angry words crossed his lips. "I am livid enough to change my mind and take up the case of Humphrey Ecklin, after all."

"Humphrey Ecklin?" I interjected. "The candidate for Parliament who was defeated handily in the recent election? I cast my vote for him, but, as usual, chose the losing contender."

"Yes, the reformer," Holmes confirmed. "He appealed to me in correspondence after the loss, complaining that the election was illegitimate. He accused the incumbent, Noah Hammer, of manipulating the results. I initially rejected Ecklin's plea for my intervention because I considered it then to be a matter of sour grapes. But if his allegation is verifiable, it could produce the resignation of another dishonest public servant. I think I shall invite Mr Ecklin to our flat in a letter today to see what he knows about the situation and whether his accusation contains substance."

Several days later, one Humphrey Ecklin was waiting at the bottom of our staircase as Mrs Hudson, our landlady, appeared in our doorway to announce the gentleman's arrival with the comment that he was polite and punctual, as Holmes had predicted when telling Mrs Hudson about the appointment. "It is exactly two o'clock, your visitor is downstairs, and he flattered me with a compliment about my beauty," she stated without a hint of humility. "Shall I send him up?"

"By all means, Mrs Hudson, and forgive me for not having remarked in the past about your pretty, young face," Holmes laughed.

"Oh, Mr Holmes, not you, too," she giggled.

Holmes went to the threshold to greet Ecklin, extending a hand and introducing me as a trusted associate in areas of tremendous importance. Ecklin belied the image of a hard-charging challenger that the press had depicted. He was a thin, tiny man, a head and shoulders shorter than I, with a soft-spoken manner, making him seem a tad bashful, in fact. He wore a Norfolk jacket and knickerbockers over trousers of heather tweed, a lucent top-hat, accented by a glistening white shirt with a starched collar and a scarlet bow tie. His demeanour was subdued, and his personality amiable with not an inkling of the firebrand I had pictured in my mind prior to our acquaintance.

"I must say that I anticipated a much more animated character, based upon your portrayal in the newspapers," I observed when he praised my writings about Holmes's adventures.

"Oh, I can be quite the agitator when I make a speech," he volunteered, "but in the company of refined professionals such as yourselves, I revert to my natural posture. Mr Holmes, I come here today to humbly implore you again to investigate the fraudulent actions of Noah Hammer. No official in London will give me attention and I have exhausted my efforts to persuade the authorities to question the conditions of my trouncing at the polls."

"What evidence do you possess that the election was unfair?" Holmes wanted to know.

"Only this, sir," Ecklin answered. "Over the three weeks of voting, I led in the tallies, but in the final few days, Hammer surged ahead with five votes to my one, all of his coming from the West

End. It stands to reason that the population could hardly have experienced such a drastic change of opinion in one section of the city."

"I grant you it is suspicious," Holmes surmised, "although it is possible Hammer's followers and campaign staff focused their work on the West End and counted on a heavy turnout to reverse the tide."

"Except for one consideration, Mr Holmes," countered Ecklin. "I hail from the West End and that is the territory where I drew my most fervent support."

"Curious," Holmes acknowledged. "It merits scrutiny. Yet I hesitate to commit my time to a problem involving a subject I abhor, politics."

"This is more than political, Mr Holmes," Ecklin argued. "Our society is rooted in the concept of an untainted electoral process."

"I am acutely aware of our precious liberties, Mr Ecklin," Holmes contended, "and it is precisely because those rights might have been jeopardized that I shall mull over pursuing this issue."

Just then, another ring at our doorbell unexpectedly interrupted the conversation and a familiar male voice could be heard downstairs insisting to Mrs Hudson it was urgent that he see Holmes and Ecklin. The voice belonged to Inspector Lestrade of Scotland Yard and he came through our doorway with a worried expression on his narrow face.

"Sorry to break in on your discussion, gentlemen," he began, "but I have notice from our intelligence squad that Mr Ecklin is in danger. We have kept Mr Ecklin under surveillance ever since we came across the scuttlebutt off the street and we assumed he came here to drag you into the election controversy, Mr Holmes. You both need to take precautions."

"Who would want to harm Mr Ecklin and why would I fear for my own safety?" Holmes queried.

Lestrade frowned, lifted the brim of his hat, scratched his forehead and sighed. "You both are dealing with a treacherous power broker in Mr Hammer. He will do anything to retain his position and all this noise about stealing votes has him on guard and preparing for war," Lestrade advised. "Any attempt to deny him his seat in Parliament is going to be regarded as a threat and an act of aggression."

"I doubt he would be so foolish as to injure an opponent because the finger of suspicion would point directly at him," Holmes conjectured. "Hammer is an astute politician, not a hoodlum. Where did your intelligence squad pick up such information?"

"A member of a street gang in the neighborhood of Mr Ecklin was arrested for a robbery and offered a tidbit to trade for a lighter sentence. He said the gang's leader was paid to instruct his thugs to rough up Mr Ecklin to within a centimeter of his life. The robbery suspect didn't know who handed over the money, but the lieutenant in charge of the intelligence squad deduced it was Hammer or one of his goons."

"It is all a little too far-fetched for me to fathom," Holmes observed, "but on the off-chance it is true, I recommend you maintain your surveillance on Mr Ecklin, at least for the time being."

"We intend to do just that," Lestrade disclosed. "If you start asking questions about the election, though, I can't guarantee you will be protected, Mr Holmes."

"I am not concerned, Inspector. I can adequately defend myself against a few felons," Holmes boasted. "Besides, I have Dr Watson and his old service revolver for added security."

"Let me contribute my sentiments to this conversation, gentlemen," Ecklin broke in. "I am convinced Hammer is capable of violence when his empire is threatened, but I don't expect to be escorted by bodyguards when I make my rounds in the city. My travels sometimes bring me to places where confidentiality is the password, such as today when I came to meet privately with Mr Holmes. I shun the thought of the police knowing my every move. It is disruptive to my methods."

"Have it your way, then," Lestrade growled. "But don't come griping to the police when you are recovering from a thrashing. Consider this a forewarning."

Lestrade stomped out of the apartment, his beady eyes glaring and his pace quickened by the abrupt rejection of his designs.

"Not a wise decision, Mr Ecklin," Holmes calculated. "You are vulnerable to attack without support from the law."

"I have been without support from the law ever since the rigged election and I can manage my affairs cautiously as long as you are on my side, Mr Holmes," Ecklin claimed defiantly. "I suggest you begin your inquiry with no more worry than you demonstrated for your own well-being."

With that, our courageous visitor withdrew from our chambers after bidding us adieu, convinced Holmes would prove him exact in his allegation against Hammer.

"Watson, that man is determined to be vindicated but at what cost to his good health?" Holmes wondered after Ecklin went out onto Baker Street.

✗　✗　✗　✗

Noah Hammer inhaled the smoke from his expensive imported cigar from behind an uncluttered mahogany desk in a corner office at the House of Parliament, ordering one of his several aides to place Sherlock Holmes under the watchful eyes of the informants who had been following Humphrey Ecklin.

"This nosey detective cannot make a move without my knowing every person he contacts, understand?" Hammer barked. "Holmes is a dangerous adversary, more so than that irritating sore loser who called on him this afternoon. I want reports every day about the comings and goings of my newest enemy."

Uncorking a bottle of claret, Hammer poured half a glass and gulped down two swallows before summoning a second aide for another assignment. "Sharpen your claws, Lester, because I want you to bring in that pipsqueak of a party boss Marvin Kilgore. He deserves a tongue-lashing from me for not delivering the ten thousand votes he promised from the East End. After I finish with him, he'll wish he had been struck dumb by the hand of God. And he can forget about my sponsoring his son as a page in the House of Commons."

Impressed by his own words and the influence he wielded, Hammer began to concoct measures to punish the party workers who defected to support Ecklin, as well as to reward the loyalists who gave the entrenched incumbent yet another victory.

Hammer rose from his high-back leather chair, took one stride toward the corner of his desk, felt spasms in his head, throat, arms and legs, then a tremendous sharp pain in his chest. He struck his fist against his sternum, collapsed, convulsed, heaved, and died, his face and hands purple from lack of oxygen.

One of his assistants was entering the room at that moment and witnessed the fall, immediately rushing to his chieftain's prostrate body, turning Hammer onto his side and fruitlessly trying to find a pulse in the carotid artery. "Lord! Someone help!" he shrieked, bringing the rest of the staff into the smoky room. "I'm afraid Mr Hammer has suffered a fatal episode," he announced, and instructed a secretary to notify the House medical personnel along with the police.

The officials who arrived on the scene at first erroneously attributed the death to a heart attack, but they qualified their opinion by referring their analysis to the coroner. Two days later, the coroner ruled the death a murder after finding a substantial trace of strychnine in the victim's blood during the post-mortem examination.

⚹   ⚹   ⚹   ⚹

Seated in an armchair with the evening *Standard* on my knees, I read aloud the news about the autopsy to Holmes, who was stretched out on the sofa in his stocking feet and mouse-colored dressing-gown eagerly awaiting a reaction in a beaker of chemicals suspended over a Bunsen lamp.

Shocking as the information was to me, Holmes embraced it matter-of-factly. "I suspected as much from the description of his seizure in the press, Watson," my fellow-lodger remarked. "He was relatively young and fit, virtually precluding a cardiac malfunction. I deduced that a lethal dose of poison had been dissolved in the wine bottle."

"I suppose he had a host of people who hated him enough to want to kill him," I surmised.

"And counted among them would be my latest client, Mr Ecklin," Holmes intoned. "With that in mind, I expect a visit from Lestrade before long."

Unmistaken, at breakfast the next morning, Holmes and I heard through the open bay window a carriage approach our address. Glancing outside, we saw the determined-looking police inspector with two others alight from the vehicle to ring our doorbell.

Once upstairs, Lestrade apologized for interrupting our meal, but said his arrival at such an early hour with the pair of partners from Division B was necessary. "We are en route to another location in the West End to take Ecklin to headquarters for questioning," he apprised. "We came here to interrogate you first, Mr Holmes, about the details of the conversation you had with our suspect yesterday afternoon."

"The subject of the talk I had with my client is a secret matter, Lestrade, you should know that," Holmes quarreled. "Do what you must without my cooperation."

The impertinent inspector and his comrades departed in haste while Holmes fumed at the intrusion, saying with agitation that the attempt to intimidate him into revealing the particulars of his and Ecklin's rendezvous had failed miserably.

"What you learn today at the Bureau of Elections and elsewhere could actually help Lestrade establish a motive for the murder," I speculated.

"I daresay if I find facts that point to a bogus election, Ecklin could be treading in deeper waters than he imagined when he made his appeal to me," Holmes commented. "Be that as it may, I'd best get started."

Humming a tune we heard several nights earlier at Covent Gardens, Holmes bounded down the stairs and darted out onto Baker Street, not returning until dinner time. Meanwhile, I spent the day writing of our encounters at Baskerville Hall, napping once when my eyes grew so weary that I couldn't concentrate on the task.

"Success, Watson!" Holmes shouted as he crossed our threshold and glared at me in the wicker basket-chair. "Ecklin is on the mark! The election of Hammer was a sham!"

"What led you to that conclusion?" I demanded, no longer absorbed in the paragraph I was penning.

"The ghost of a dearly-departed friend gave me the initial clue," he began. "Join me in a hearty supper at Simpson's and I'll tell you all about it. The special tonight is crab cakes—I saw it advertised on the chalkboard out front when I rode by on my way home."

Seated at our usual table and sharing a carafe of sauterne, Holmes jabbered on about the steps he had taken in his investigation. "I first obtained a list of registered voters in the West End from the Bureau of Elections and I found on it the name Abner McCutcheon, the friend I mentioned who passed away three years ago after a long battle with consumption. The address on the list, 425 Hatfield Road, was the same address for at least one hundred other electors. Thinking it was a large apartment complex, I took a cab there, only to determine that the place was Calvary Cemetery. I compared the names on the tombstones to the list of registered voters, and, voila, they matched! Persons unknown, more than likely Hammer's allies, impersonated the deceased and cast ballots for the incumbent.

"There were two other addresses, one on Tecumseh Street and the other on Mulberry Lane that were specified for many more voters and those addresses, too, were cemeteries. Again, the names on the tombstones matched the names on the list. A case of election fraud, Watson, pure and simple. It is elementary."

"Holmes, you have sufficient evidence to invalidate the outcome of the contest, then," I blurted.

"Perhaps," Holmes quibbled. "All that remains is to persuade someone in authority to verify my findings and declare the election faulty. Possibly a special election would follow or the Prime Minister might appoint a successor to Hammer."

"Whichever occurs, Ecklin has another chance of winning," I added.

"If he is not arrested for the murder," Holmes reminded me.

✗ ✗ ✗ ✗

While we dined on the special, Inspector Lestrade was surrounded by reporters in the lobby of the Metropolitan Police Service headquarters explaining the circumstances of what prompted Scotland Yard to take Ecklin into custody and lodge a charge of willful homicide against him.

"Under questioning, the defendant denied ever handling the bottle of claret, but we took impressions of his fingerprints and found his latent thumb print on the neck, just below the cork," Lestrade proclaimed. "It was then that he admitted giving the wine to Hammer as a peace offering after the election, a drink laced with the deadly toxin. Besides the victim's fingerprints, there were no others on the bottle except Ecklin's. This is proof beyond a doubt that Ecklin dispensed the strychnine and intended for Mr Hammer to die."

Reading the inspector's pronouncements in the *Times* the next morning, Holmes flew down the stairs en route to Scotland Yard, bellowing over his shoulder on his way out the door that if the wine bottle were nearly full, Lestrade probably was correct.

The bottle, half empty, sat atop Lestrade's desk as if it were a trophy for his solving the crime. "Your suspect is more than likely innocent, Inspector, a fact that you should recognize from the contents of that jug," Holmes criticized, to which Lestrade replied: "Mr Holmes, the case is open and shut and I'll not accept any of your hare-brained theories."

"You leave me no alternative but to humiliate you once more in the presence of a jury," Holmes cautioned. "The least you could do is let me consult with my client while you listen out of sight in a secluded corner of the cellblock."

"Your wish is granted, but I must warn you that anything incriminating he says in confidence that I overhear will be used in court," Lestrade agreed and escorted his rival to the lockup.

"Oh, Mr Holmes, I am being made the object of a terrible injustice," Ecklin squawked when he saw the consulting detective approach the bars. "Please prove them wrong before I am dangling from the end of a rope."

"I shall do my best, Mr Ecklin, but the evidence is not trifling," Holmes responded. "You can assist me in my effort if you answer truthfully my questions."

"Anything you want to know I shall tell you honestly," Ecklin promised.

"Excellent. When were you last in the office section of Parliament?" Holmes quizzed.

"Never—never in the office section, only in the gallery of the House of Commons and the House of Lords," Ecklin insisted.

"Then where did you give Mr Hammer the wine bottle?" Holmes wanted to learn.

"It was at his home on Lower Burke Street between Notting Hill and Kensington," came the rejoinder. "Why is that so important?"

"That will become clear when I complete my inquiry," Holmes retorted. "Was anyone at his house at the same time?"

"Yes, his wife and his campaign strategist, Willard Farmer," Ecklin remembered.

"Did they drink any of the wine while you were there?" Holmes asked him to recall.

"All three of them did," Ecklin revealed. "They offered me some but I declined because I don't imbibe."

"Then if you had poisoned the wine, all three of them would be dead," Holmes noted loudly to make certain Lestrade overheard.

"I am done with you for now, Mr Ecklin. Bear up, all is not hopeless," said Holmes to conclude the interview.

"A likely story—he had all night to dream that one up," Lestrade gloated after he and Holmes returned to the inspector's desk.

"The fact of the matter is that the bottle is half empty—hardly a contrived alibi," Holmes contradicted. "If Mr Ecklin's account were not true, then Mr Hammer would have been the first to drink from the bottle and it would be nearly full. Someone added the poison when the untainted wine was already halfway consumed. My hare-brained theory is sufficient to cause a jury to pause before rendering a quick verdict."

"Maybe so, but it is not enough to cause me to dismiss the charge," Lestrade barked. "The newspapers would crucify me!"

"You should have thought of that before you made such a bold statement that you cannot now retract," Holmes admonished. "I must be off to refute your allegation or to find it *bona fide*."

✗   ✗   ✗   ✗

Holmes's first move was to pay his respects to Hammer's widow and to locate his campaign advisor to corroborate Ecklin's version of events. Holmes walked briskly to the Underground station at Whitehall Place and boarded a train to Lower Burke Street, an avenue where the well-to-do lived in brick or stone houses with entrances for their servants and impeccably manicured lawns and shrubs. At the address furnished by Ecklin, Holmes approached a gardener to see if the lady of the house was at home.

"She is, but she's not in the mood for company, gov'nor, because she buried her husband Wednesday last," the man informed Holmes. "Still in mourning, y'see."

"My presence here is official—it's about her late husband that I wish to speak with her," Holmes advised.

"You the police, then?" the gardener wondered.

"I am a detective in private practice, not one of the authorities," Holmes acknowledged.

"Well, then, you'd best postpone your plans until sometime next week," the gardener contended. "Sorry, but Mrs Hammer wishes to be left alone in her bereavement."

"Here is my calling card," Holmes said compliantly, "would you make sure she gets it?"

"Rap on the servants' door and hand it to the butler—he'll give it to her, gov'nor," the groundskeeper instructed.

The butler, an elderly lanky gentleman in a brown herring-bone suit with emerald cufflinks on his shirt, told Holmes to wait in a chair at the kitchen table until Mrs Hammer learned of his coming. "I believe she will want to be brought up to date on news of the murder," he guessed. "Scotland Yard has kept her in the dark for the most part."

The butler re-appeared momentarily with the wife of the late Noah Hammer in tow. She wore a black dress with a dark veil over her face, a woman at least twenty years younger than Hammer and remarkably shapely, as well as beautiful with shoulder-length, wavy black hair and soft features. Sherlock Holmes rose to express his condolences and hold her dainty right hand in his, charming her in his singular way with the opposite sex.

"Mr Holmes, your reputation precedes you," she said with a mellow voice. "Did you bring any information that would help ease the pain in my heart?"

"Only that the police seem to have arrested the wrong person," he disclosed.

"Do you mean Mr Ecklin is innocent?" she went on, startled.

"You can confirm his story with your answer to my question," Holmes continued.

"Please ask it, then," she begged.

"When Mr Ecklin came here after the election with a bottle of claret, did you and your husband and Mr Hammer's campaign strategist take a drink of it?" Holmes quizzed.

"Why, yes, we did. Of course! I see your point! If the wine had been poisoned by Mr Ecklin, we all would have succumbed. I should have emphasized that to Inspector Lestrade. He might have looked for the killer in another direction if I had mentioned we all three drank a toast to my dear Noah's triumph."

"Pity you hadn't, Mrs Hammer. It could have spared Mr Ecklin a horrendous ordeal," Holmes grumbled. "I won't trouble you any further in your time of grief. I'll be getting along now, unless you would indulge me in a matter of curiosity."

"Certainly, Mr Holmes. What is it?" the widow acquiesced.

"You dabble with chemicals, do you not?" Holmes prodded.

"In a manner of speaking, I do—I am an experimental chemist for a pharmaceutical firm, Boscomb International," she revealed. "What on earth made you ask?"

"I couldn't help notice the pale green stain on the tip of your left forefinger, a sign of someone engaged in science," Holmes said to enlighten her. "The hands often expose an occupation."

"Sometimes I am a little clumsy," she quipped, awestruck by Holmes's ability to observe an extraordinarily minute detail.

Holmes excused himself once again and set out to locate Willard Farmer, the erstwhile campaign strategist. Finding him at party headquarters teaching a class of volunteers the tactics of electioneering, Holmes joined the group, which was preparing for the mayoral primary. When calling for questions from the audience, Farmer recognized Holmes first.

"Was it your bright idea to have the dead vote in the Hammer-Ecklin contest?" Holmes spouted.

"W-w-hat is the meaning of this? Who *a-a-re* you?" Farmer stammered indignantly.

"I am an outraged subject of the Crown who has investigated the rigged election of Noah Hammer," Holmes shouted. "If you please, answer my question."

"This class is dismissed. I'll entertain no more questions," Farmer declared and started to exit the room.

"Before you rush out, be aware that Scotland Yard wishes to ask the same question in the office of Inspector Lestrade," Holmes foretold. "Perhaps you would rather discuss it with me in the privacy of your office."

"I'll not tolerate this badgering," Farmer asserted loudly. "Once more, who *are* you?"

"I am Sherlock Holmes, your nemesis," the renowned detective boomed.

"Holmes! The famous name doesn't frighten me. I am as clean as a hound's tooth!" Farmer hooted.

"Then whose strategy was it for the deceased to vote?" Holmes persisted.

"I have no knowledge of that, Holmes. Go poke your long nose into someone else's business," Farmer commanded and stomped down the hallway with Holmes at his heels. "Tell me this, then," Holmes said to change the subject, "did you drink from the wine bottle that Ecklin brought with him to Hammer's dwelling?"

"What if I did? How would that change anything?" Farmer answered with frustration in his voice. "He is as guilty as sin in my book."

"Come now, Mr Farmer, you know as well as I do that if Ecklin doused the wine with strychnine, you wouldn't be here to deny wrong-doing," Holmes debated angrily. "It was your obligation to advise Scotland Yard that you drank from the bottle without ill effects."

"Kindly leave me alone, or I'll," Farmer started to say when Holmes interrupted.

"Or you'll what—summon the police? I gravely doubt it," Holmes scoffed, then turned abruptly, departing and returning to Baker Street.

"It was useless trying to drag the truth out of Farmer," Holmes groused after filling me in on his activities. "The scoundrel is a slithering snake in the grass, a perfect companion for an unscrupulous politician with no limits. I shall abandon Farmer for Lestrade to deal with once I introduce him to the alternatives in my case."

"You have solved it, then?" I exclaimed

"It is practically complete, but before I can pronounce it at an end I must gather more facts to take into court," he allowed. "Come along with me tomorrow, Watson, when I contact the chief chemist at Boscomb International's research laboratory."

"I'd be delighted, Holmes," I concurred. "Conceivably, I could make a contribution to your chat with the chap."

"Excellent! Your familiarity with remedies and ailments would surely be beneficial," he stated gratefully. "In the meantime, I shall commence my surveillance."

With that, Holmes constructed a sandwich with a slab of leftover ham and a tablespoon of horseradish, wrapped it in newspaper, poured some stale hot coffee into a flask and scurried off to places unknown to me.

Passing him in the hall, Mrs Hudson delivered a warm cherry pie she had baked, our favourite, saying that when she set it on the table Holmes had "gone out on one of his tangents. He'll never make someone a decent mate."

Late afternoon turned into evening and evening became night-fall before Holmes came back to our diggings with a glint of satisfaction in his expression. He fumbled with a plate and spatula to serve himself a slice of the pie, not mentioning his adventure until I coaxed.

"Well, are you going to keep it to yourself or will you divulge what you learned to your biographer?" I pleaded. "My readers will be up in arms if I fail to include the consequences of your surveillance."

"Always eager to report the dramatic, eh, Watson?" Holmes shot back. "You can engross your readers with this tidbit: the lady is a two-timer, to be sure, and Willard Farmer is her paramour. This I discovered while hiding in the bushes at Mrs Hammer's residence, then later listening to their palaver at the open parlour window. It seems they carried on an affair during the campaign and Hammer grew jealous of their spending so much time together. He warned his unfaithful wife that he would divorce her, send her back to the edge of poverty from whence she came and create a terrible scandal if he found out she and Farmer were romantically linked. That was inevitable, because she is pregnant with Farmer's child and her abdomen is beginning to swell. Hammer would have known the child was not his because his wife had forbidden him to touch her for more than a year. Apparently Hammer was an ogre and the marriage was doomed."

"Good gracious, a motive to kill the rogue," I chimed in.

"Precisely," Holmes assented, grinning. "Now the question is whether she alone or both of them were responsible for Hammer's untimely demise. We shall determine the answer to one part of that puzzle tomorrow at Boscomb International."

The significance of an interview with the chief chemist became clear to me; therefore I slept restlessly while Holmes was awake until after midnight, pacing the floor of our sitting-room, his old and oily clay pipe clenched between his teeth.

Early in the morning, I smelled the aroma of fresh-brewed coffee and stumbled down to the stove to pour a cup as Holmes sipped his and chewed the last bite of his toast. "There is a news article in the *Times* saying that Ecklin's trial date has been set for the week after next," he informed me. "I presume his barrister is counting on my testimony to sway the jury, so we'd best hustle to Wordsworth Road to obtain the data I need from the chief chemist. I'll resist the temptation to predict what he has to offer."

I took a sponge bath and shaved hurriedly, nicking myself on the chin twice. Soon we were in a hansom on our way to the laboratory, Holmes with his fingertips drumming against his thighs and the toes of his boots tapping against the floorboard.

Boscomb's headquarters was far smaller than I imagined, a square two-story brownstone building no more than forty paces in length and width, situated on a gravel lot. Offices for the company's hierarchy occupied the second floor and the research laboratory only half the first floor with a production facility in the remaining half. A sourpuss seated at a reception desk just inside the entrance asked in a bitter tone what we wanted. "We don't allow soliciting," she snarled.

"We are probing a murder, not selling anything," Holmes bristled. "We are here to see the chief chemist."

"Oh," the woman responded curtly. "That would be Leonard Caruso. He's in the lab, but you can't go in there, not even the police. Security regulations."

"Then please bring him here or we'll come back with a writ to take him with us," Holmes bluffed, taking advantage of her incorrect assumption.

"Wait right there," the woman ordered and she disappeared behind the swinging double doors of the laboratory.

A minute later, a pudgy, middle-aged gentleman in a white frock emerged to greet us, identifying himself as Mr Caruso and bemoaning, "What is all this about a writ?"

"That is neither here nor there, Mr Caruso, we'd prefer this to be a casual interview," Holmes assured him. "We are investigating the murder of Noah Hammer, whose widow works for you, does she not?"

"Yes, Ophelia is employed in my lab," Caruso answered. "She is an exemplary employee, in fact."

"What are her duties?" Holmes continued.

"Is she in trouble? I thought Scotland Yard arrested the person who killed her husband," Caruso maintained.

"This is merely routine," Holmes said to carry on the charade. "What are her duties?"

"She is developing a cure for influenza, actually," Caruso disclosed.

"And does the formula involve strychnine?" Holmes queried.

"The formula is proprietary, sir," Caruso resisted. "I cannot reveal the ingredients."

"A man's life is at stake, Mr Caruso, so I need not relate to you the measures we can take to determine if the formula calls for strychnine," Holmes pressed.

"A very small measure of it, yes," Caruso acknowledged.

"And Mrs Hammer has access to a supply of it?" Holmes wanted to establish.

"Yes, we have a supply of many dangerous substances that are used in the manufacture of medicines and strychnine is one of them," Caruso advised.

"That is all I needed to know, Mr Caruso, we have disrupted your work long enough," Holmes said apologetically. "We shall relay your information to Inspector Lestrade, who is in charge of this investigation."

"Where is this all leading, if I may ask?" Caruso wondered in conclusion.

"In the end, it is leading us to the truth," Holmes contended. "Wait for word from Inspector Lestrade."

Once we were outside, Holmes patted me on the back sympathetically. "It is unfortunate that you didn't have the opportunity to make the contribution to the conversation you thought you might," he said to ease my obvious disappointment.

"I was going to ask him if one cubic centimeter of strychnine per thousand parts was a reasonable estimate of the amount in the formula," I remarked, "but the dialogue was so intense that I dared not interfere."

"Your discretion was appreciated, Watson, be certain," Holmes commented and thanked me again. "The thrust of the interview with Caruso will raise sufficient doubt in the jury's mind to render a verdict of not guilty at Ecklin's trial, do you not agree?"

"It is sufficient to raise doubt in my own mind," I consented.

⚔ ⚔ ⚔ ⚔

Two weeks later, Holmes ascended the witness stand and enthralled the jurors with his findings, all of the twelve decision-makers in rapt attention with their eyes shifting from Ecklin to a shocked and dismayed Mrs Hammer in the balcony. She buried her lovely countenance in her hands as Holmes testified about the secret life she was living, then she shook her head no when he came to the revelation from the chief chemist. The pale green stain on her left forefinger was residue from strychnine, Holmes disclosed, demonstrating with his own finger the result of an experiment he conducted with the same poison at the deal-top table in our apartment.

The jury's deliberations lasted less than an hour and the foreman stood erect to announce the acquittal, causing Humphrey Ecklin to jump to his feet and grasp the right hand of his lawyer, then turn to Holmes in the gallery and smile at him broadly.

Set free by the constables in the courtroom, Ecklin posed in the foyer for a photograph and to make a speech to the crowd of reporters who clamoured for a statement. "I kept faith in the justice system and justice has been served," he beamed. "Now it is the duty of the police to search in another direction to solve the crime."

Inspector Lestrade watched in the background, his arms folded and his expression icy.

Afterward, when the commotion ceased, Holmes shared a private moment with Ecklin on the marble steps outside the courthouse.

"I am bursting with pride—I cannot contain myself," Ecklin sputtered. "If I understand the law of double jeopardy accurately, a defendant is prohibited from standing trial a second time for the same offense. I have outwitted the authorities and the great Sherlock Holmes! I killed that monster! I waited until the bottle of claret was half gone and slipped two tablets of strychnine into it when no one in the room was watching. I'm to become the next Member of Parliament and not a living soul can deny me that honour."

Before a stunned Holmes could react to this most haughty confession, Ecklin strutted off into the busy thoroughfare below.

✗

Jack Grochot is a retired investigative newspaper journalist and a former federal law enforcement agent specializing in mail fraud cases. He lives on a small farm in southwestern Pennsylvania, where he writes and cares for five boarded horses. His fiction work includes the book *Come, Watson! Quickly!*, a collection of five Sherlock Holmes pastiches. The author is an active member of Mystery Writers of America.

THE LATE CONSTABLE AVERY

by G C Rosenquist

As I sit here in the sunny parlour of 221B Baker Street taking my afternoon tea, I'm suddenly struck with the urge to tell you about a most interesting case my good friend Sherlock Holmes and I tackled together early on in our friendship. It was a rather unexpected affair.

The constables of Scotland Yard hold their annual benefit to raise funds for the *London Constables Retirement Fund* on the last Friday of every October and this particular year they'd asked Holmes to give a short speech about his recent wildly successful partnerships with Scotland Yard. But getting Holmes to appear at any public function has always been comparative to putting a collar on a feral cat. His blade-sharp mind considered public appearances and speeches utter faff; pretentious strokes of the ego. It took a fortnight of prodding by me, thickly printed flattery from various editorial columnists of local news sheets and a personal request from Commissioner of Scotland Yard Yancy Carruthers to convince him to take a night off from his mental ruminations and violin practice.

As our cabriolet rode up to the marble stepped entrance of the London Central Event Hall on Belgrave Street, I asked Holmes if he had his speech with him. He shot me a confident glare and tapped his fingertip to his temple. "It's all in here, Watson," he said.

"Quite, quite, of course," I agreed, sincerely embarrassed at my error. Holmes had the memory of a hundred pachyderms.

When we entered the event hall, we found it full of formally dressed constables and their wives. A five-piece brass band played "*Oh, Tallulah*" on a large stage at the rear of the hall, but I could barely hear them over the din of countless voices and jovial laughter. Immediately, Holmes and I were beset by one constable after another, all eager to shake Holmes's hand. Some of them remembered working with Holmes on this case or that. A well-timed glance at my friend told me that he was enjoying every minute of his new-found fame.

Finally, like a ghost, silver-haired Commissioner Carruthers appeared out of the crowd and led us up to the stage. I was seated at a table in front with three other constables and their wives as the Commissioner quieted the band and told people to take their seats. Then he introduced Holmes and the hall erupted in exuberant cheers and applause lasting sixty whole ticks. There was complete silence during his speech except for the moment when a tardy constable rushed into the hall and seated himself at a table in back. Holmes hesitated a moment, took notice of the interruption so quickly I doubt anyone except me noticed, then he finished his speech with kudos to Commissioner Carruthers and the good constables of London proper. That brought the roof of the event hall down with applause, cheers and whistles, this time lasting ninety whole ticks.

The five-piece brass band started up again as Commissioner Carruthers, knowing Holmes preferred to make his exit, again led us through the crowd of hand-shakers and back-patters. Near the doors, that tardy constable greeted us, his hand outstretched. Holmes took the young man's hand and shook it briskly. But what struck me about the man was the pale and glossy tint his face held and there was a small purple bruise on the left side of his chin. I'd seen this paleness on the faces of many fever victims over the years. It concerned me so much that I asked him about it.

"I was caught in the rain last night during my rounds and feel only a little under the weather, it's the reason I arrived late. I do apologize," he said in a forced jubilant tone.

"Is that a bruise on your chin?"

"The bruise? Oh…yes, I had a run in with a drunken labourer last night just before it began raining. It doesn't hurt as bad now. I'm fine, really, Dr Watson."

"You know me, then?" I asked, not recalling the man's features at all.

"Of course he does, Watson," Holmes interrupted matter-of-factly, still grasping the constable's hand. It seemed to me a prolonged hand shake. Then I caught just the briefest glint of suspicion in his eyes as he stared at the man. "This is Constable Richard Avery. He, along with Commissioner Carruthers and a pair of other constables, helped us catch the Black Rose Ruffians two years ago, remember?"

I glanced at the man again and it all came back to me. The Black Rose Ruffians were a gang of kidnappers holding wives of the wealthy for huge ransoms. Constable Avery, his family going back seven generations in England, reported his wife kidnapped by them. It was only because of Holmes's brilliant deductions that Scotland Yard found them, broke the gang up and secured Avery's wife unharmed.

"And how is your wife... Camilla, is that correct?" Holmes asked, pretending for some reason to find it hard to remember her name.

Young Avery nodded, blinked his eyes quickly and answered. "Very well, sir." His answer didn't sound convincing to me at all, but apparently Holmes hadn't heard the answer, which was strange because I've seen him track a cricket down in a field from fifty yards away. He leaned in closely, his nose nearly touching Avery's neck and asked him to repeat his answer. In a louder voice, Avery said, "Very well, sir! Thank you!"

"Good, good," Holmes said. "Is she here tonight?"

"No, sir," Avery replied, he was sweating profusely now, his skin growing so pale it seemed transparent. That purple bruise on his chin was disappearing right before my eyes. I thought he was going to faint straight out. "She's visiting her cousin in Cornwall. But she sends her good wishes to you."

"That's very nice of her," Holmes said as he politely pulled away from Avery's neck and released his hand, but not without a quick look at his fingers. Then he flashed a glance down at Avery's boots. Something was going on right in front of me, but I didn't know what it was. Why was Holmes acting so strangely? What was all this suspicious inspection about?

Commissioner Carruthers looked as in the dark as I was.

"Tell me, Constable Avery," Holmes began. "When did your wife leave for Cornwall?"

"Uh... two days ago, sir. Wednesday. I put her on the steamer in Paddington Station two days ago. Y-yes, that's right."

"Hmmm. I would love to go up to Cornwall and visit her. See if she's completely recovered from that horrible event of two years ago. Do you think she'd mind?"

"Uh… not at all, sir. But she'll be back in three days. You could call on us then at Averyshire. I think that would be better."

"I see," Holmes said flatly. There was a long uncomfortable silence between the two men, most of which Avery spent refusing to make eye contact with Holmes. "As I recall, your wife has blond hair, does she not?"

"Yes-yes, sir. That's correct." Young Avery was trembling like a plucked violin string now.

Holmes reached out, fingered something on Avery's jacket, then pulled his hand back. In between his fingertips was a single strand of blond hair. Holmes brought it up to his nose and sniffed it. "Commissioner Carruthers," he said. "I think it proper that you arrest this man."

The Commissioner's face went red as a carpet burn. "Arrest him? Avery? For what?"

Holmes's eyes settled directly into Avery's and a slight, knowing grin creased his face.

"For the murder of his wife Camilla."

✗   ✗   ✗   ✗

"I say, Holmes," I began, flummoxed to the gills. "You never cease to amaze me."

"It was all very elementary, my dear Watson," Holmes said for the first time ever.

We were standing outside the confession box in Scotland Yard where through a window we could see Constable Avery sitting at a table weeping into his hands. He'd just confessed to strangling, then burying his wife in the forest outside the grounds of Averyshire, the castle that had been kept in his family for seven generations. It was a crime of passion. He'd been having an affair with a Lady from another well-to-do family and Camilla found out. She threatened to divorce him, make everything public at the fundraiser that night, destroy his family name and wreck his wealth. A wealth that was willed to him only if he promised to take a menial job, learn what the true importance of having money was all about—that's why he'd become a constable. While constables were digging up Avery's wife, Avery's father, approaching seventy years old, had been notified of his son's crime and was on the way with a barrister. Commissioner Carruthers was reading the confession Avery had written, shaking his head in disbelief, his face still red.

"But how did you know?" I asked Holmes, nearly delirious with curiosity.

"It all began with you, Watson."

"Me? What did I do, Holmes?"

"It was you who brought attention to Avery's ill countenance," Holmes explained. "You logically assumed his paleness was caused by yellow fever. But remembering that we're in late October now and it's too cold for mosquitos to live and breed and spread yellow fever, so his paleness had to be caused by another factor. He claimed it was by being caught out in the rain and he caught a slight chill, but if you remember, Watson, it hadn't rained last night—it rained yesterday morning."

"Yes, that's right! We went out to pick up our tuxedos for tonight. It was a clear and starry night!" I exclaimed.

"Proving Avery lied, and when someone lies, there has to be another logical solution. Leading me no other choice but to deduce that his paleness and clamminess were caused by exertion. But exertion from doing what? While shaking his hand I felt a number of fresh, thick calluses, the kind only brought on by digging with a heavy shovel. A quick look at his fingernails showed that there was fresh soil underneath them. Another quick look at his boots proved that they hadn't been shined, but were covered in a thick layer of dirt. So then I wondered; why was he digging as recently as an hour before arriving to the event hall? Which led me to the bruise on his chin, also fresh in every aspect. I'm sure when Commissioner Carruthers looks up Avery's work schedule, he'll find that Avery was off last night. The violent drunken labourer was an invention. I surmised that he received the bruise earlier tonight, but from who?"

"Who, indeed?" I asked incredulously.

"When I noticed that Avery's wife was absent from tonight's event, something no constable's wife would do unless under duress, I suspected it was his wife who had given him the bruise in a desperate fight for her life, so I started asking him questions about her."

"I remember."

"Then I'm sure you noticed how his nervousness increased, how he began stuttering and sweating. Every answer concerning his wife was a lie."

"But how could you know that?" I asked.

"Easily. Avery claimed that he hadn't seen his wife for two days—that would be Wednesday—yet when I leaned in, feigning deafness, I distinctly smelled her perfume on his jacket. It's called *Misty Mountain*, the same perfume she was wearing two years ago when we rescued her from the Black Rose Ruffians. So she and Avery had been in very close quarters very recently. Then, as you saw, I found a strand of Camilla's freshly washed hair on Avery's jacket. Upon closer inspection, I saw that it had been pulled out by the root during a violent process."

"Pure brilliance, Holmes!" I said, my head drowning with an overload of information.

"The kicker was that Avery claimed he'd put his wife on a Paddington Station steamer heading out for Cornwall on Wednesday, but I've memorized all the train schedules in London and know the Paddington Station steamer only goes to Cornwall on weekends."

"I'm—I'm fumble-gutted, Holmes," I said. "Only you could have pulled this off."

"On the contrary, Watson," Holmes countered. "All one has to do is remember to use all of his senses when investigating a crime. As I said before, it's all elementary."

✗

GC Rosenquist was born in Chicago and now resides in Lindenhurst, IL. His love for the mysteries of Sherlock Holmes began as a child when he saw Basil Rathbone in "The Hound of the Baskervilles." GC Rosenquist is also a huge fan of Sir Arthur Conan Doyle. For more information, go to gcrosenquist.com.

THE STRANGE CASE OF THE WRINKLED YETI OF THE CLUB FOOT AND HIS ABOMINABLE LIFE

by Gary Lovisi

We all know that Watson was often a somewhat less than accurate chronicler of the cases of Sherlock Holmes, whether intentional, or not. Being a Holmes fan and collector for some decades, as well as the author of some pastiches that continue the adventures of the Great Detective, I was amazed when I came upon this manuscript hidden in an old desk that I purchased in a dusty old New England antique mart. When I got the desk home, upon closer examination, I discovered secreted behind the top drawer a slim weather-proofed packet which held the following manuscript, which I have reproduced herein exactly as written. While I can not attest to the accuracy of this strange missive, I leave it to your good judgment as to the veracity of the words herein.

FROM THE REMINISCENCES OF
JOHN H WATSON, M D.

It is with a heavy hand that I take up my pen to write this particular narration of one of the most intriguing and yet embarrassing aspects of all my chronicles of the cases of my friend, the great detective, Sherlock Holmes. I write these words in the year 1894 to put truth to the tale as I have discovered it from Holmes's very own lips.

I have written previously how my dear friend Sherlock Holmes kept records of his early cases in a large tin box which he once shared with me before he put the box in storage. That box sadly went missing, a tragic loss to the ages. Whether it resides in some secret vault or even the dark dungeon beneath the Diogenes Club, I do not know. However, the great artist Sidney Paget did make a drawing of Holmes and myself looking through this box and that illustration even appeared in the May 1893 issue of *The Strand Magazine*. That issue, contained my chronicling of the Sherlock Holmes case "The Musgrave Ritual." It took place at the beginning of his career as a consulting detective on October 2, 1879. However, at the time when I was told the story of the Musgrave puzzle by Holmes, he also mentioned in passing even earlier cases that he had been involved in since the start of his career in 1877.

Holmes made mention to me of these early cases, which he said took place between 1877 and the time of "The Musgrave Ritual." The case in question here is the one generally known as that of "Ricoletti of the club foot, and his abominable wife." Holmes only mentioned that brief description of the case to me verbally and no more. It is a case unrecorded by me and one that certainly has become one of the most intriguing titles of any of my friend's adventures lo these many years—but it would become my most embarrassing and unforgivable of all errors.

It was in May, 1893, when *The Strand Magazine* hit the newsstands containing my chronicling of "The Musgrave Ritual." I was proud of that story, for not only did it recount one of Holmes's earliest adventures and appear in print at last, it formed the backdrop of his early career as a consulting detective illuminating his great genius and talents. Little did I realize at the time the turmoil the publication of that story would cause me.

At the time, I had not seen Holmes for some months. I no longer resided with him at our old Baker Street digs, but with my sweet wife in a small townhouse in Central London. Over the years I had been doing quite well chronicling the cases and having them published in *The Strand* through the kind devices of Doctor Doyle, who acted as my literary agent. I often did not receive reaction from Holmes on the publication of these stories—which were fictionalized accounts of his cases—most of the time they were of cases we shared together and so my notes were quite accurate— but "The Musgrave Ritual" was quite different. Even unique. That is because it was the one case that Holmes narrated to me verbally. It was in the winter of early 1888 when he had shown me the contents of his large tin box. A box full of his earliest cases. It was a veritable treasure trove, but he did not allow me to go through the contents (as I certainly wished to do so)—nor to read extracts or make notes. Nevertheless, at the time I was just overjoyed to know the material existed.

From inside that box, he suddenly withdrew a smaller wooden box and this he did show me, for the contents pertained to Reginald Musgrave's strange problem. Of the remainder of the material in the tin box, I noted many bundled sheets and papers—a mysterious gold mine of Holmes's work before I had ever met him! Sadly, I never actually read a word of any of that other material. My friend was usually very tight-lipped about his earliest cases. That box is gone now, lost to eternity. That one instance was the only time Holmes spoke to me concerning his long-time friend Reginald Musgrave. He told me the story speaking quickly in his usual rapid-fire bursts of frantic energy. I listened in rapt attention as I scrambled to quickly jot down what facts and notes I could glean from him as the words rapidly burst forth from his lips. It was difficult for me to keep up with Holmes's quick words, but I did my best to get the gist of the story. In the telling, he also mentioned some earlier cases he worked on in that early period. He did not go into detail on any of these, merely mentioning intriguing titles or a scant phrase that offered a mysterious tid-bit hint. I quickly scribbled these names down into my notes as well, just as I heard them at the time from Holmes's own lips. I realized these might make an intriguing addition to the main story I wanted to tell of Holmes's early days—one of these I had written down as the Ricoletti case.

Over the many years of our association Holmes rarely mentioned my chronicles of his cases. Oh, for sure he pooh-poohed them as being overly melodramatic and catering to the lowest aspect of popular taste. He even told me that I often played loose with the facts—but I stood firm on the notion that some fictionalization and dramatic license was necessary for popular publication. "That is the problem," he would reply, then drop the discussion. However, until now he never complained seriously about any of my chronicles of his adventures. In truth, I believe up until then he was rather flattered by them and he did mention I had a certain flair with the pen. But that day in May 1894, it all changed. I had a visit from Sherlock Holmes to my London apartment and he was not in the best of moods. I thank my lucky star that my sweet Mary was away for the week to her sister's house in Surrey, so she would not be there to witness my abject embarrassment. My partner, Dr. Philip K. Jones had taken over my practice for the day so that I was free and quite alone when my surprise guest arrived.

The door knocker boomed in anger that morning and, answering it, I was immediately surprised but delighted to see my old friend Sherlock Holmes framed in the doorway. He stood tall and firm in deerstalker and Inverness cape, just as I always pictured him in my mind and he looked well, hale and hearty—but severely troubled.

"Hello, Watson," was all he said.

"Holmes?" I asked, utterly surprised to see him. He was the last visitor I ever expected these days. We had not seen each other in months and our association had grown sparse, though I missed him dearly. "Holmes!" I shouted and took his hand, shaking it with a release of my pent-up enthusiasm. "It is so good to see you!"

"May I come in?" he asked rather tersely. I could see something was severely troubling him. "There is a matter I must speak to you about."

"Of course, of course," I stammered, leading him into my small parlour. "What can I do for you? You know you only need ask?"

Holmes looked at me sharply, fierce anger flowed from his eyes for a heartbeat, then it quickly died down and was replaced with a wan smile and a sad sigh.

It was that same exasperated look he often gave Lestrade whenever the inspector told him his theory upon some crime, showing his thinking process to be thick as a brick. He was not happy. I was most unsettled.

I quickly took my friend's coat and then led him to a comfortable seat. I asked if he required a drink and he briskly refused.

"It is so good to see you again, Holmes. So good!"

He gave me a stern look. "Whatever will I do with you?"

"What do you mean?" I was growing fearful now. "Have I done something to offend you?" I blurted, alarmed. Of course, nothing could be further from my wishes and while I did not say this verbally, Holmes knew all too well that it was true.

"Watson, Watson, Watson," he said shaking his head in abject dismay, "I have just read your *Strand* story, "The Musgrave Ritual.""

"Was something amiss?" I asked sheepishly, for Holmes always told me my flair for the melodramatic in my writings and fawning enthusiasm for his methods and talents would land me in trouble one day.

"Amiss! That is how you would put it? It is an unmitigated disaster!"

I looked downward, suitably chagrinned. I had obviously gotten some fact or date wrong. Holmes was a stickler for details. Often tiny and insignificant items—or so I often thought—meant so very much to him. And yet, I realized with a bit of trepidation that my notes of this particular case were not as full as others, for they had been scribbled in haste many years before, and only after Holmes narrated the particulars to me that winter in 1888. Truth be told, I often had trouble reading my own scrawl of a script. I hoped I had not made some error—or if so, that it was not anything significant—but Holmes's visit seemed to belie that wish. My mind was awhirl with worry. Perhaps the problem was that I had not let Holmes read the final version of the story before publication? While I knew he was reluctant to read any of my missives of his cases—I realized that offering to show him the manuscript beforehand would have been a wise decision.

"I am sorry, Holmes. Truly, if I have made some error in the Musgrave story…"

Holmes shook his head sadly. "It is not the Musgrave case, old man, it is what you added into the story."

"Added? Whatever do you mean?" I asked, truly perplexed.

"You mentioned my early cases… before Musgrave," he stated flatly.

I thought about that and what I had written about those cases in the story. It had been only the most cursory mentioning, just a few words or titles here and there. I often did this in my chronicles of his cases, which I felt lent credence with tantalizing hints to my stories. I looked over at Holmes. "Let me see. I only made mention of the cases you yourself mentioned to me. There was the Tarleton murders, that fellow Vamberry, an old woman, I believe Russian, the aluminium crutch, oh yes, and Ricolletti."

"Precisely!" Holmes positively barked out the word.

"Ricoletti?" I asked with a tremour, wondering just what I had done.

Holmes fairly shrieked at me in dismay now. "Ricoletti of the club foot and his abominable wife!"

"Yes? My God, what is it, Holmes?"

"Ricoletti of the club foot and his abominable wife! Where ever in heaven or hell did you get that, Watson?!"

I gulped nervously, "W-why from your own words. You mentioned them to me when we looked through your old tin box that day in 1888. I admit you mumbled a bit and my hearing was not quite up to par, but that is what I heard plainly."

"You heard it plainly?" Holmes shook his head in abject exasperation. "I am leaving…"

"B-but… Holmes… What is it? Please…"

Sherlock Holmes stood up to his full height and gave me a piercing look from those hawk eyes that froze me in my tracks. Then he sighed and said quite succinctly, "Watson, that day in 1888, I did *not* say, 'Ricolleti of the club foot and his abominable wife'—of all the damnable things—I *said*, 'the wrinkled Yeti of the club foot and his abominable life!' Do you see the difference?"

"W-what?" I stammered.

"What, indeed! You have bollixed up the facts as never before. It is quite unforgivable. You have created the greatest example of mis-hearing there ever was."

"Are you sure?" I blurted dumbfounded, immediately regretting the question.

"Really, Watson, do you ask me if I am sure of my own words?"

"No, of course not." I swallowed hard, nervous now. "My God, Holmes, I-I don't know what to say, I am sorry. I had no idea. I feel terrible. My hearing is not as it should be after my experiences in the war, but I swear to you, that is what I heard you say that day long ago—or at least that is what I *thought* you said."

Holmes was not moved.

I pleaded, "I admit I tend to the melodramatic in my recounting of your cases, but I do try to stick closely to the facts—or the main facts—except in those areas where you have advised me to change names, dates, or certain places. I am so sorry. This is most embarrassing. I do not know what to do about it."

"Do about it?" Holmes stated sharply. "You have done quite enough!"

I hung my head down in sad resignation. I failed my old friend.

Holmes must have felt the truth of my contrition. "Well, there is nothing you can do about it now. It is all out and in print. It will go down through the ages as one of my earliest unrecorded cases—and it shall remain unpublished."

"Of course," I agreed readily.

"Unpublished, but not unrecorded, dear Watson." Then Sherlock Holmes looked at me with a softness to his features he had not shown yet, obviously taking pity upon the poor wretch I was and his great heart opened up to me. He shook his head and then a slim smile escaped his thin lips. "Really, Watson, you are incorrigible! Ricoletti of the club foot and his abominable wife? Whatever were you thinking? You do need to have your hearing checked."

I nodded sadly.

Then Sherlock Holmes actually laughed, but it was of good nature and with a twinkle in his eyes.

"I am sorry," I said with a deep sigh.

Holmes merely waved his arm in vast dismissal. "It is done. There is nothing more we can do about it now."

I spoke up quickly. "I can write a retraction or perhaps a correction, in the next issue of the *Strand*."

"Yes, that would surely do it, bring more attention to the mistake and make yourself look more the fool—and me by implication. No, I think not."

"Then what can I do to make it up to you, Holmes? I apologize sincerely for this error and I am terribly embarrassed by it."

"As you should be, Watson, as you should be," Holmes chided me, but there was no anger or malice in his voice now. "However, you do need to make amends."

"Anything, Holmes!" I stammered eagerly.

"Good, then please bring me a glass of that fine brandy you possess and I shall tell you the true facts and details behind the strange case of the wrinkled Yeti of the club foot and his abominable life."

I quickly poured my friend a liberal dose of the liqueur and rushed to gather up my pen and writing pad.

"Take it down exactly as I give it to you."

"Of course, Holmes," I blurted eagerly, overjoyed that his anger had abated, astounded now that he was actually going to recount to me one of his rare early unknown cases. I would make sure to get it right this time.

"Are you ready, Watson?" Holmes asked, taking a sip of the brandy and laying his neck back upon the head-set of my large comfortable chair.

I sat across from him upon the settee, prone forward in rapt anticipation with pen and pad in hand.

"Good, then we shall begin." Holmes then closed his eyes, silent for a moment, obviously his vast mind reaching back through the years, collecting and collating the particulars of that early case, gathering every bit of fact and detail like some fantastic thinking machine.

Here then, is "The Strange Case of The Wrinkled Yeti of The Club Foot and His Abominable Life," just as Sherlock Holmes told it to me on that warm May morning in 1894.

✗   ✗   ✗   ✗

I have a restless mind, Watson, none should know that better than yourself, my old friend. I have always been interested in crime, of course, but that began early on with an interest in puzzles. Also the corollary questions. How do things work? Why do they work the way they do? I also confess an interest in the unusual, the strange, oddities, even freaks. And that is how I came upon the mysterious Yeti. Or, as he is termed by some persons: the Himalayan Monster. But he is called Yeti by the inhabitants of mountainous Nepal and very much feared. He is a legend, a myth, but one all too real to the people who live there. The story of it dates back to 1832. The Yeti is said to be a tall beast covered in dark hair walking on two feet, some type of pre-human or prehistoric man perhaps. A missing link? Who can say? Regardless, as an oddity it fascinated me back then in my youth for the simple reason that one of these creatures was said to be on display near London at the time. This was way back in 1878, before the Musgrave Affair, at a time when the Clyde & Barrows Carnival show was in town under tent outside London on the old fair grounds.

Well, I had to go and see this wonder for myself. I was young then and fascinated by such things. At the time, there was another such curiosity making all the rage throughout London—that of a horribly deformed young man, Joseph Carey Merrick, or John Merrick to some, who was called by others, The Elephant Man. Merrick back then was a mere sixteen-year-old boy, but even then he had massive and rather singular deformities. He earned his living by entertaining customers in what can only be termed a freak show. Merrick proved to be a most charming and shy young man. His "act" was a rather distasteful display of his horrendous deformities, but through it he was able to earn the money to support himself, afford a small room, and not go hungry. It was a grim Hobson's Choice, but one he was apparently willing to make. I assumed the Yeti at the Clyde & Barrows Carnival would be much the same situation. I was wrong.

On a cool summer morning in 1878, I traveled to the then rural environs outside Greater London where the fairground was then located. It was a massive area of some one hundred acres full of gaily-colored tents and painted wagons. It was a circus, gypsy camp, carnival, and country fair all rolled into one. It was exciting and also dangerous. Even back then, my criminal senses were well honed and I knew the area was home to many a cut purse, way layer, and scoundrel, but the worse of the lot were not those who preyed upon the unsuspecting thrill seekers who came there from the city such as myself to spend a few pence and view mysterious oddities and wonders. The worst of the lot were the men who ran the shows, specifically the sinister and vile exhibits down what was called "Freak Show Alley." This was a dark, dreary lane of ratty tents and broken wagons, yelling barkers, smoky rooms, muddy ground, and displays of the most extreme oddities and freaks ever seen—in some cases they crossed the line into utter depravity. There I saw women for sale, children in chains, people kept as cattle and… monsters. I had never seen more debased examples of the human condition. The various "shows"—a better term would be "horror shows"—and their masters did all they could to accentuate the ugliness and grotesquerie of their sad exhibitions and to debase their humanity as much as possible. It was in one of these horrid places that my eyes came upon the monstrous Yeti.

I paid my tuppence to a grim fellow at the entrance and with a large crowd I was quickly ushered into a dark tent where I found myself standing before a large dirt pit. In the pit, in chains and being driven forward to us to view, was the likes of something I had never seen before in my life. It was a man—and yet it was not a man. Could it be one of the fabled Yetis of Nepal, that pre-human creature of the land of snow and ice? I thought not, but it was certainly a reasonable facsimile and the crowd loved it. They positively ate it up. I watched and began to feel sick. The man—for surely he was a man and not some Yeti at all—was being horribly mistreated. He looked to be ill and he was surely someone of very limited mental abilities. I believe the carnival term is "geek." He was quite large, almost seven feet tall and rather massive, perhaps twenty stone in weight. A veritable monster—but not a monster. And yet his body was all wrinkled and ravaged with deep furrows. It appeared to me that the poor creature was being starved. His head and upper torso were overwhelmed with long, matted dark hair and his body, almost entirely naked but for a small dirty loincloth, was covered in dark hair, along with dirt, mud, bruises, welts, and horrible purple blotches. It was obvious the poor wretch had been mercilessly beaten. I stood there ashamed—ashamed that any human being, no matter how deficient in mental abilities— could be treated in such a horrendous manner. My heart broke for the man while the crowd roared their delight and approval with every punishment and cruelty the trainer inflicted upon the poor creature. I do not believe they saw him as a human being at all, but the monster he was made out to be—I could only turn away and in disgust walk towards the exit of the tent. I had seen enough. I was severely shaken by what I viewed and the roar of approval of the crowd filling my ears made the matter all that much more terrible. As I reached the exit, I felt as if tears would burst forth from my eyes, but instead a deep and pressing anger took hold of me. A rage grew within me.

"I will not allow this to stand!" I barked, then I stormed back towards the open pit area. I pushed aside the laughing, cheering crowd and walked up to the so-called Yeti beast-man and his malicious trainer. They both looked at me curiously. The "Yeti" growled fearfully, but I saw no real danger from him, only the fear of the terrified child in his sad eyes. I did not fear any attack from him. The trainer was another matter altogether.

"Wot's this 'ere! Get back, ye bloody wanker! We's dunna allow any blokes near the mysterious yeti."

He raised a large club at me threateningly, the same club he used to control the so-called Yeti to beat him into submission.

"I will not let this stand!" I shouted and, before the trainer's club could strike me down, I drove my fist into his face. Blood spurted, he screamed bloody rage, and then he charged me like a raving bull. I used a useful Judo trick I recently learned to trip him and when he rose to his feet I gave him another fist to the face. This time the man sank to the muddy floor unconscious. The crowd roared—they must have thought it all part of the show.

The Yeti shook and swayed back and forth, cried and sank into a fetal ball. The big, terrible monster was just a sad, sick man much abused. I stood there for a moment not knowing quite what to do. I had not planned this out, you see. I had never done such a thing before, it was against my nature to act so impetuously, but I was proud that I had done so I put it all down now to exuberant youth. Nonetheless, I was at a loss as to what to do next. I saw a commotion brewing at the opening at the far end of the tent. It seemed the trainer's mates were coming inside to see what happened. They were four burly fellows with clubs going hard at each person in the tent, pushing and knocking them out of the way in an effort to get to me. They would be at me soon. What to do? I quickly approached the Yeti—I call him that for lack of a more accurate word—but he was unable to hear me. I noticed the chain clasped to his ankle. That would surely have to go. I realized the trainer must have the key for the chains; I quickly found it and released the Yeti.

"You are free! You can leave now!" I stated as the trainer's mates drew closer, carefully inching forward. I had to make my escape soon or get my head bashed in—for I could not overcome all four attackers. Then I suddenly felt a pull on my sleeve and looked to see one of the most incredible sights I have ever seen in my life.

She was young and quite lovely, but upon her face was a full growth of dark long hair. A beard! A bearded lady!

"Quickly, you have to get out of here, but please help me save John. He doesn't deserve this!"

"John?" I asked quickly.

"The Yeti, now hurry, my friends will hold off the crew until we can get away."

Then I saw what she meant. Behind her were a group of the most amazing people I have ever seen. These were the so-called freaks from the various side shows and tents of Freak Alley. There was a muscle-bound strong man, a very tall and very thin "rubber man," four midgets dressed as police bobbies with, of all things, night sticks, a fierce "lion man" with a mane of thick blond hair, and a snake woman with a very large real snake. I believe it was a python.

"My name is Zelda," the bearded woman told me.

"Sherlock Holmes," I replied. It was surely one of my most precarious meetings under the circumstances.

"Come now, help me get John out of here. We're leaving this place, we've all had enough. A Freak Show is one thing, but slavery is another matter. Those men held John captive and kept all his money, they treated him terrible because he was so helpless. Now we will take him to safety. Will you help?"

"Of course."

Zelda turned to her cohort and shouted, "Here they come. Tear them up, boys!"

The melee that ensued was incredible, but it gave Zelda and me the time we needed to get the Yeti—John—out of the tent and to freedom. I was sure John did not know what was transpiring at all, but he did as Zelda told him to do. It was apparent he trusted her. We led him away as best we could. He had a terribly deformed club foot and he often stumbled, but he did not fall because Zelda and I held him up, one of us at each side of him as we made our way out.

We escaped through the back of the tent with the mad melee still going on inside. There were screams and running patrons who never expected such madness at a Freak Alley show. Soon, the alley was bursting with terror and chaos. Someone knocked over a wood-burning brazier and a fire started on one of the tents that soon leapt with the wind and spread to others. Before long, most of Freak Alley was ablaze with roaring flames and screaming, running people. The smoke covered our escape.

By then Zelda and I had taken John to the edge of the fairground, where I was able to procure a wagon and driver to take us to my Montague Street flat back in Central London.

Circus people and carny folk look out for each other and none more so than those possessing the unique talents and abilities that allow them to perform in the freak shows. Zelda and her cohort of fellow entertainers eventually formed their own show in another city, where they continued to exhibit their various talents to earn an honest living. They took good care of the mysterious Yeti—John—who turned out to be one John Anderson, late of the British Army, and a veteran of the Crimea. It was later learned that John Anderson had been a sergeant of sappers at the Battle of the Alma; where he exhibited heroic actions. He had been mentioned in dispatches, but was presumed lost in action. His club foot was the result of a broken foot in that battle that had never been set nor healed properly. However, far worse than his physical wounds were his mental ones. He lost his mind in the battle. John was later found on the battlefield and brought back to England and then quickly discharged where he became just another beggar upon the streets of London. He allowed himself to grow unkempt and dirty, with long matted hair and apparent mindless actions. That was when his "trainer" found him and in a brilliant blaze of morbid inspiration took him captive and created the Monstrous Yeti.

Now John Anderson was free. Many years later I heard tell of how he still thrilled the people of a northern city with his antics. Zelda and her troupe of entertainers took good care of him. He peacefully passed away in his sleep recently. And that, my good

Watson, is the true story of "The Wrinkled Yeti of the Club Foot and His Abominable Life."

⚔   ⚔   ⚔   ⚔

Sherlock Holmes smiled at me and said, "I believe I'll take another glass of that excellent brandy, if you please."

"Of course." I jumped up to pour him one more full glass as I thought about all he had just told me. I looked at him expectantly. "An amazing story, Holmes. Simply amazing! Thank you for relating it to me, and for setting the record straight."

"I have always told you, Watson, that you often play fast and loose with the facts, but this time it was an error of gigantic proportions, even for you. We are lucky there is no one but us who knows the truth behind your mistake. However, I do want you to do something for me now. You have written up this story just as I have told it to you and now I want you to hide it away. Then someday, perhaps after our deaths, it shall be discovered by some lucky soul and the true story of the case can then be told. We need to set this right, but it need not be set right in our lifetimes. I fear it would make us both look the fool otherwise."

"Of course, Holmes, I will do whatever you wish." Then I took the pad that contained my manuscript of the story, written exactly as Holmes told it to me and folded it into a tight little bundle and wrapped it inside a waterproof package. I looked over at Holmes, and he indicated the desk in the corner.

"That is my wife's desk, not mine," I explained.

Holmes only nodded with a slight smile, "Better yet—or perhaps, better *yeti*, eh, Watson?"

I nodded. Though not usually given to puns, it did show me a change for the better in my friend's disposition. I placed the manuscript package in the top desk drawer.

"No, Watson, take out the drawer. In the back of the opening you will find a small ledge. After I leave you, take a hammer and small nails and affix it there. Then replace the drawer. Do not tell your wife and we will erase this embarrassing matter from our minds forever. We will speak of it no more. Perhaps a hundred years from now, some sly fellow will come upon your hidden manuscript. I only hope he knows what to make of it."

"Thank you, Holmes."

"Good old Watson, I must say this turned out to be a pleasant visit, after all."

"I am always glad to see you, Holmes."

"And I you, Watson."

Then Sherlock Holmes left my home on his way back to the rooms that held so many memories for both of us, 221B Baker Street.

Before I affixed the manuscript package which I have now entitled "The Strange Case of the Wrinkled Yeti of the Club Foot and His Abominable Life," I added some additional introductory paragraphs as well as this brief addendum of explanation to the lucky fellow who may someday find this package. It is upon you now to see to it that my embarrassing error is corrected in the popular press and all is set right for eternity in this matter as per the wishes of my friend, the great detective Sherlock Holmes.

Yours most truly,

John H Watson, M D, late of the British Army

✗

One of the most intriguing hints of an unrecorded Sherlock Holmes case given to us by Watson in the canon is the snippet, "Ricoletti of the club foot and his abominable wife." What did it mean? What was it about? Watson and Holmes give us no facts, no details, just that brief phrase as hint. However, that intriguing passage has become fodder for much speculation by Sherlockians over the decades. It is estimated that there have been no less than seventeen published written records of this case by various authors in various pastiches. Unfortunately, all of them have proven wrong until now. In his book, A Sherlock Holmes Commentary *(David & Charles, UK, 1972), D. Martin Dakin on page 113 talks about how Watson misheard Holmes's words about the matter, after all he never saw the phrase written down, so the good doctor got it wrong when he mentioned this case in his retelling of "The Musgrave Ritual." Well, it wouldn't be the first time!*

Regarding The Himalayan Monster, also known as the Yeti, it would not be called The Abominable Snowman until 1921, when that term was first coined.

✗

Gary Lovisi is an MWA Edgar-nominated author for the Best Short Story of the year, for his Sherlock Holmes pastiche "The Adventure of The Missing Detective." He is a Holmes fan, collector, and writes various articles and short stories of, and about, The Great Detective, some of which have appeared in this magazine. He is the editor of *Paperback Parade* and *Hardboiled* magazines, and of the recent Sherlock Holmes anthology, *The Great Detective: His Further Adventures* (Wildside Press). You can find out more about him and his work at his website: www.gryphonbooks.com, or on Facebook.

THE WRONG DOCTOR

by Rafe McGregor

I

Baker Street, London

> *My dear Mr Langham – I am sure that you wish to forget the unfortunate circumstances of your meeting with Mr Holmes and I, but I nonetheless beg your indulgence. Holmes's intervention in the Windover Hill affair was motivated by the pursuit of justice and I suspect that your preference, as an agent of the law, was for the prevention of further offences. In this regard, I was pleased to discover that you have been living peacefully on the Yorkshire coast these last fifteen years. If you are able to accommodate a brief interruption of your retirement, I would esteem it a great kindness if you would favour me with your opinion on a criminal matter in which I am unable to consult Mr Holmes. I shall call upon you at 4 p.m. on Thursday. I shall try again at the same time on Friday. In the event that neither is convenient, I shall await you in the Royal Hotel, where I have reserved a room for the duration of the weekend.*
>
> > *Yours sincerely,*
> > *John H Watson*
> > *March 25th 1902*

I was surprised at the letter, but not at the skill with which Watson piqued my curiosity. He was, of course, something of a polymath— a doctor, a soldier, a detective, and lately a man of letters—and in this respect much more like Holmes than the self-deprecating tone of his memoirs revealed. He exemplified, in matter of fact, the ideal to which all gentlemen in the British Empire should aspire even if so many of us fall short of it.

My own fall had been administered by Holmes when he had discovered my homicidal somnambulism, an unfortunate symptom of a hitherto unknown kind of dementia which resulted in me investigating a crime I had myself committed. My health and fortune had both taken several turns since and I was now head of a modest household in Whitby. I supported myself, my housekeeper (the aptly-named Mrs Knaggs), and her young son with the anonymous scribbling of the implausible adventures of *the other Baker Street* detective, the fictional—and rather ridiculous—Sexton Blake.

Watson's letter was part of a parcel that arrived in the last post on Wednesday, the remainder of which was a thick octavo volume entitled *The Hound of the Baskervilles*. The latest of Holmes's adventures had begun in the *Strand* the previous summer and the penultimate instalment was still on my desk. I was grateful for the gift, which would allow me to finish the tale before the April issue of the magazine arrived, but it was a strange choice. My identity as a Sexton Blake author was known only to my editor and Watson could not have guessed that I was an enthusiastic member of his reading public when all the evidence—my status as a victim of Holmes's scientific method—pointed in the opposite direction.

I set the letter aside, opened the novel, and flipped through the pages. The book contained full-page plates of all of Mr Paget's wonderful illustrations, but I ceased my perusal as I neared the end. I reached for the March *Strand*, numbered 135 in volume xxiii, where the instalment ended in high dramatic style, part-way through chapter fourteen, with the emergence of the hound 'out of the wall of fog.' I noted that on the previous page I had underlined Holmes's comment to Watson on this meteorological phenomenon with a pencil: *Very serious indeed—the one thing upon earth which could have disarranged my plans.* By the time I finished Watson's novel, I knew precisely why he would be calling at No 10 Flowergate the following afternoon.

II

Watson knocked while the clock was striking four and I opened the door promptly. He had changed very little since our one and only meeting and was an altogether fine specimen of a man our age—for we were both close upon our half-centuries. He was still athletic in build, maintained a military bearing, and continued to wear his handkerchief in his sleeve. The only difference I could discern were the streaks of grey in his moustache and I reflected that while I was but a shadow of my former self, Watson had remained the quintessential English gentleman. As host, the overture was mine to make.

"Good day, Dr Watson, how do you do?"

He smiled, removed his right glove, and took my hand in a firm, honest grip. "Very well, thank you, Mr Langham. You too appear to be in excellent health."

"Pray come in. Allow me to take your stick and coat. The sideboard will support the weight of your hat and gloves admirably." I ushered him into my sitting-room, where the fire was keeping the cold at bay. "Do sit down and make yourself comfortable. I have asked Mrs Knaggs to make tea. May I offer you some?"

Watson's limp was slightly more pronounced than I remembered, though he walked quite steadily without his stick. "Yes, please, that's very kind of you." I rang the bell on the side-table, imagined rather than heard the corresponding grunt of disapproval in the kitchen, and sat down with less ease than Watson. He glanced at the copy of *The Hound*, which I had placed on a footstool. "May I also thank you for your kindness in receiving me today. I trust that my presence is not inconvenient."

"Not at all." Holmes impressed his clients by deducing facts about them from their appearance and mannerisms and I was determined to entertain Watson with an equivalent performance. I lifted the volume for effect. "Mr Holmes as represented in this gripping tale of yours is not quite the man I met in Sussex the previous year. He is, if I may say so, not at his best."

Watson betrayed no emotion, but asked, "What evidence leads you to that conclusion?"

"There are several points, but one is conclusive. I quoted without opening the book: *'The one thing upon earth which could have disarranged my plans.'* What native Briton would be surprised by the sudden appearance of fog on Dartmoor? Common sense aside, Mr Holmes had both visited the moor during the Straker investigation and spent several days and nights on the tor. Furthermore, he had motive to exercise extra care in making his final plans given his earlier failure to safeguard his client's life—I refer, of course, to Selden's death. In sum, Dr Watson, Sherlock Holmes was wrong!"

I let the volume fall on the footstool, but the drama in my *dénouement* was ruined by Mrs Knaggs, who waddled in with a wide tray loaded with tea, biscuits, and custard tartlets. She greeted Watson with enthusiasm—he was still, of course, a handsome man much-beloved by the fair sex—placed the tray on the table with uncharacteristic care, and even uttered a gracious 'thank you, sir' when I said I would serve my guest. Watson indicated his preferences for milk, no sugar, and biscuits, then waited for me to resume my seat.

"You are correct, Mr Langham. Holmes had not yet recovered from his physical breakdown in Lyon in eighty-seven and was on the verge of a mental one when I'm afraid to admit that I abandoned him for my late wife." Watson's face contorted with pain for a moment. "Eighty-eight was also the first occasion on which he crossed swords with Professor Moriarty, and whatever other work he was engaged upon, he was always also unravelling Moriarty's web."

I seized on the mention of Moriarty for my second *dénouement*: "It is no coincidence that you decided to consult me when I happen to reside some fifty miles from an assassin with whom I myself crossed swords during my police career." I leaned forward and picked up *The Hound* again. "Moriarty was the man behind the attacks on the Baskerville family and Moran was his agent. Colonel Sebastian Moran, lately retired to the Grange in the Yorkshire Dales, is the real killer of the Baskervilles!"

Watson shook his head. "No, not Moriarty or Moran, Mortimer."

My shock rapidly gave way to horror and I opened the novel to the first page of the final chapter: *Sir Henry and Dr Mortimer were, however, in London, on their way to that long voyage which had been recommended for the restoration of his shattered nerves.* "Sir Henry's voyage with Dr Mortimer!"

Watson continued to shake his head. "A sabbatical from which he never returned."

III

Now that I'd been told, it seemed not only the obvious, but the inevitable, conclusion to the narrative. "You left clues, didn't you? The adversarial nature of Mortimer's first meeting with Holmes, Holmes's recognition of his scientific acumen, Mortimer's position as executor of Sir Charles's estate, his defensiveness when questioned about the will, his apparent willingness to believe in the legend…"

"I wrote some drivel about an unseen force entangling us in an imperceptible net, but it was true. It was Mortimer. He was always *there*. Everywhere! It began with the ruse with the stick to put us off guard and finished with him dragging Sir Henry off to sea. Mortimer introduced us to first the legend and then Sir Henry, he never left Sir Henry's side in London, and he visited Sir Henry and I every day at Baskerville Hall. He shepherded the young baronet to his death and stage-managed Holmes, Stapleton, the whole damned case. I told Holmes of my suspicions, but he wouldn't believe it."

"The missing page from your letters!" I cried.

"Yes."

I knew I was caught up in the thrill of it all, so I forced myself to adopt an analytic approach, probing for weaknesses. "But what about Stapleton—and his wife's statement?"

"Rodger Baskerville was a bloody fool. Holmes couldn't account for his plan because he didn't have one. He disgraced himself as Baskerville in Costa Rica and Vandeleur in Pickering and I think his arrival in Dartmoor was a sign of desperation. He was the perfect foil for Stapleton."

"I thought it was odd that Holmes's description of *a foil as quick and supple as my own* ended up referring to such a bungler. Why did his wife implicate him if he wasn't guilty—good God, Mortimer was having an affair with her, wasn't he!"

"You are most perceptive, Mr Langham. Mortimer told us that his wife was an invalid, but he was in fact a widower. Mrs Beryl Baskerville was tired of being dragged around the world by her petty criminal of a husband and appears to have been easy prey for Mortimer. It's not enough to cover one's tracks, one needs to offer an alternate suspect to the authorities and who better than Stapleton? I don't know exactly what transpired at Merripit House after Sir Henry left, but I do know that Mortimer was waiting for Stapleton on the moor."

I wasn't convinced yet. "But the Baskerville case was about securing the fortune. Surely Sir Henry wasn't foolish enough to leave it to a gentleman he had just met?"

"I am not presenting my conjecture clearly. Mortimer was in league with Mr James Desmond, Sir Henry's cousin."

"Ah, I thought he was dismissed rather too quickly by Holmes. An elderly clergyman or some such?"

"The *late* Mr Desmond was retired from the pulpit, infirm, and reclusive. Holmes eliminated him as a suspect on the basis of a telegram from the Westmoreland constabulary and nothing else. He was, as you have said, far from his best."

"Mortimer killed Desmond?"

Watson enumerated Mortimer's crimes on his fingers. "Mortimer murdered Sir Charles, Stapleton, Sir Henry, and then Desmond. The first and last deaths were attributed to natural causes and the second and third involved disappearances in circumstances where it was impossible to recover the corpses. Mortimer was Desmond's sole beneficiary. He committed four perfect crimes and secured a fortune of close to three quarters of a million pounds."

A man with less charisma than Watson could have persuaded me to accept his theory: the re-solution concealed in the text of the novel was a great deal more plausible than the purported solution. "How may I be of assistance?" I asked.

"I am shortly to abandon Holmes for a second time and I should like to bring the matter to a close beforehand by way of compensation. I intend to confront Mortimer tomorrow morning and would very much appreciate your company."

"Then I'd better pack." I reached for the bell.

"There's no need. Mortimer used his ill-gotten gains to build himself a manor house on the North York Moors. Would you believe he lives on the edge of *Howl* Moor? If I put that in a memoir I'd be accused of writing fiction."

"What brought him here, the archaeology?"

"Possibly, but more likely his wife's bidding. The ghost of Mrs Vandeleur has returned to her old haunt disguised as Mrs Mortimer."

IV

Watson and I boarded the first train for York on Friday morning and arrived in the little village of Goathland fifteen minutes later. The station-master directed us to the inn-keeper, who offered us a sturdy wagonette, for although our destination was only a few miles hence, the road was poor. Watson declined the offer of a driver, took the reins himself, and moved over so that I could join him. He seemed to know where he was going and we set off into a bright but chilly morning, the surrounding mist gradually yielding to the combination of sunshine and a stiff breeze from the west. The track upon which we travelled traversed the gentle slope of the moorland, rising to our right and subsiding to our left. Both sides were dominated by the bright purple of the heather rather than the darker greens and browns of the grass and shrubs. Aside from the distant ridge from which the wind fell and a small forest a mile or more away, the horizontal expanse was punctuated only by a few black-faced sheep and the occasional dry-stone wall.

I had spent Thursday evening consulting the records of the Whitby Literary and Philosophical Society, of which I was a member, and committed a large-scale map of the north-eastern quarter of the moors to memory. Hunters Hall was located between Hazel Wood and Grey Earths Wood to the north and Wade's Causeway and Howl Moor to the south. Mortimer had already made his mark on the moors by clearing the causeway of vegetation and had published papers to the effect that the landmark was a Roman road. He was no doubt in search of skulls—skulls which he had apparently been depositing in, as well as removing from, the earth. Watson kept his own counsel throughout our journey and I was not altogether certain of the reason for my presence. My guess was that I was a deterrent in the event that Mortimer decided to add a fresh corpse to the Neolithic and Bronze Age skeletons beneath the causeway, but maybe there was more to it.

Shortly after passing Grey Earths Wood, we turned south onto a narrower track that curved around a rock-strewn rise before ending in a line of rowans, twisted and bent by centuries of storm and wind. A tall, narrow tower rose above the trees. Watson pointed with the whip. "Hunters Hall."

We approached an ugly ironstone lodge, squatting next to a pair of shiny wrought-iron gates. The gates were open and there was no sign of life in the lodge. The avenue beyond was deep in shadow, bending sharply out of sight after a few dozen yards. In the shade, hard and clear like an equestrian statue upon its pedestal, was a mounted man. He was sombre and stern, a penang-lawyer poised over his forearm as he watched the path of our approach.

"Watson," I whispered, but he was already halting the horses.

The rider emerged from the gloom. "Well, if it isn't Mr Sherlock Holmes and Dr Watson."

I recognised James Mortimer M.R.C.S. from Watson's thumbnail sketch in *The Hound*. His height, emaciation, protruding nose, and bowed back combined to give the impression of a human sickle perched precariously on a horse's back. He was wearing an expensive broad-brimmed hat, gold-rimmed spectacles, and a smart silk cravat, but his attire deteriorated as it descended: a shabby frock-coat, creased trousers, and muddy riding boots. He had not lost the air of peering benevolence with which Watson had characterised him and indeed he thrust his head at us as if to bring his close-set eyes nearer to their target.

"I've been expecting you gentlemen for a very long time. I thought I'd been granted a reprieve when Mr Holmes's demise was reported, but when I heard you'd survived I was sure you'd find your way here. When Beryl told me about the publication in the *Strand* in August, I awaited you each evening. Now, I must—hallo, you're not Mr Holmes! Who's this, Dr Watson?"

"My associate, Mr Roderick Langham. Mr Langham, Dr James Mortimer. Why were you expecting Holmes and I?"

"Because sooner or later it must have dawned on Mr Holmes that he was wrong. If Sir Henry's disappearance at sea wasn't obvious enough, the brevity of the period Mr Desmond's god granted him to enjoy his fortune must have made my position plain." Mortimer was neither fearful nor contemptuous as he all but admitted his guilt.

"You murdered both Baskervilles, Stapleton, and Desmond." There was ice in Watson's voice.

"Morally, I am responsible. Legally… I'm not going to insult your intelligence by pointing out the public facts of two deaths by natural causes, one by misadventure, and one by suicide."

"You gloat, sir."

"I am a man of science, Doctor, I deal solely in facts and leave others to pass judgement."

"I assure you I am here for that very purpose. I am well-acquainted with the facts and I intend to share every last detail of my judgement with you. I may not have proof that will stand in a court of law, but you will not sleep soundly from this day forward."

"No, sir, no, you are in error. Hiring Mr Holmes gave me a credibility with Sir Henry which I could never have gained otherwise, but it was always a calculated risk. The reappearance of Mr Holmes at some later date was a part of that risk so I have been prepared for this day for many years. To be perfectly frank, I am relieved that the moment has arrived at last and I feel that you have done me a service, even if that was not your intention. I should like to repay that service. You are seeking some sense of an ending, something akin to that with which you complete the stories my wife admires so? As long as this gentleman," he rotated his head towards me, "has no official standing, I shall be glad to receive you both tomorrow evening and answer any questions that lie between us. Say five o'clock? Very good. Now that's settled, would you be so kind as to remove your conveyance from my gateway. There is just enough room for you to manoeuvre without having to enter."

V

Watson asked if I would mind postponing discussion until we had returned to Whitby, so I spent the journey back by wagonette, train, and foot smoking my pipe in silent contemplation. I could not fathom Mortimer, who seemed as cool a customer as any criminal I had ever faced in my day. My main concern was Watson. What would he do? He had maintained a steely calm throughout the interview and an immobility and impenetrability of countenance worthy of Holmes since, but what could he hope to achieve? Mortimer had committed the most perfect series of murders imaginable. Even the circumstantial evidence was severely limited and if Mortimer was able to prove prior acquaintance with Desmond, then that too would evaporate like the mist. If Watson wasn't careful, he might find himself embroiled in a libel battle with an extremely wealthy man, in the process of which Holmes's reputation would be torn to shreds by the press. A glance at my acquaintance's fine, noble features nonetheless gave me confidence in his ability to find a solution to the problem.

Midday found us back in my sitting-room, drinking tea while Mrs Knaggs prepared luncheon upstairs.

"Now that we have both had sufficient time to mull this conundrum over, may I enquire as to your thoughts?"

I cleared my throat. "I must disappoint you, for I see only danger ahead."

"So do I. Holmes once said '*when a doctor goes wrong he is the first of criminals; he has nerve and he has knowledge.*' Mortimer's nerve enabled him to do away with the two younger gentlemen with the utmost efficacy; his knowledge enabled him to take advantage of the older gentlemen's respective medical conditions. I have seen many cases with a great deal more evidence fail to reach the courtroom."

"Were I still a detective, I would not embarrass myself by presenting the case to the Director of Public Prosecutions as-is. The only way I can see that changing is if Mortimer's wife can be persuaded to testify against him and now that we're discussing the matter, I wonder if we placed her in danger this morning."

Watson's brow furrowed and he scratched his head. "I think that you're right about Mrs Mortimer being the only witness, but then again, how much has she actually witnessed? She will have known something of Mortimer's machinations on the moor, but I doubt she was privy to much more. He would only have confided in her completely if his trust was total, in which case she will not stand witness. If, on the other hand, she knows as little as I suspect, she would be no good on the witness stand. Either way, I think Mrs Mortimer safe."

I nodded. "And we mustn't let chivalry or prejudice against the weaker sex blind us to the fact that Beryl Garcia has chosen to spend all of her adult life with criminal husbands. Furthermore, the performance you describe at the end of *The Hound* was quite obviously just that, a performance. What do you intend to do?"

"I am afraid that I cannot answer that question, but I would be very grateful for your company tomorrow evening."

"You may count on it."

"I am indebted, sir, thank you."

"If Mrs Mortimer doesn't join us, perhaps you could slip away and seek a private interview with her. I could always distract Mortimer with talk of Bertillon or Lombroso."

Watson fixed me with a grave stare, the meaning of which was far from clear. Eventually, he said, "I think Lombroso would be more to his taste."

"I don't read Italian, but I have several of his papers from *The Monist* in my library. I shall spend tomorrow brushing up on them!"

Once again, I had predicted Watson's intentions. He was going to turn that gentlemanly charm which had so impressed ladies on three continents to a lady from a fourth. I wondered if he had perhaps been more intimate with the then-Beryl Stapleton than he had revealed in the memoir. It mattered little. I was convinced that Watson would succeed and determined to assist him in any way possible.

VI

Watson and I crossed the threshold of Hunters Hall at a few minutes after five on Saturday evening. He had opted to hire a driver this time, so we were both sitting comfortably in the back as the wagonette clattered along the avenue. Though the sun was far from setting, the day was overcast and the canopy formed by the trees clutching at each other low over our heads contributed to the gloom. The dark tunnel soon opened onto a broad turf lawn and we saw the hall for the first time. The building was a huge basalt block, with a porch projecting to the front and a single steeple rising high above us. The steeple was surrounded by four great chimneys, three of which puffed grey smoke into a greyer sky. The antique style, augmented with mullioned windows and copious amounts of ivy, was at odds with the pristine stone, but the cheerful freshness made a welcome change from the sinister gateway. We were met by a smartly-dressed footman, who led us up the stairs into a modern entrance hall raftered with baulks of timber and decorated with innocuous paintings of rural and pastoral scenes. Watson appeared to pay the hall careful attention as the butler took our hats, coats, sticks, and gloves. I suspected he was familiarising himself with the floor-plan in the event that he found himself alone. We were directed from the hall to a parlour with cream and blue décor, a high vault, and fashionable clutter.

Mortimer was warming his hands by the fire, dressed much the same as the previous day. He turned to us. "Good evening, gentlemen. May I offer you some refreshment... tea, coffee, something a little stronger?"

"Just privacy, Dr Mortimer—unless Mrs Mortimer is joining us, of course."

"No, Doctor, Mrs Mortimer has no desire to renew your acquaintance. That will be all, Soames, please make sure I am not disturbed."

The butler left, closing the door behind him.

"Now, you must excuse my attire, but I've only just returned from the moors. I'm rather busy at present, with two excavations in addition to the work on what I can safely call Wheeldale Road. Please make yourselves at home."

There were four armchairs and a settle arranged around a long, low table atop which sat a large silver tray and cloche, a battered old cigarette case, and a leather tobacco pouch. Mortimer favoured the settle and Watson and I sat facing him. There was a second door behind Mortimer, which would be useful if Watson had to slip out undetected.

Mortimer peered over the table at us. "I hope you don't mind, but I've invited Stapleton to join us."

Watson kept his cool, but I couldn't help myself. "*Stapleton?*"

"Well, no, 'Stapleton' was one of his many aliases; Rodger Baskerville is his real name."

I turned to Watson, then back to Mortimer. "If Baskerville is alive, then your marriage to his wife is null and void."

Mortimer smiled. "I didn't say he was alive." He leaned forward, removed the cloche, and revealed a perfectly preserved skull.

I gasped. Not because of the skull or the surgical implications of its presence on the tray, but because of the legal use to which it could be put. It was all we needed. If Watson had brought his service revolver along we could simply seize it at gunpoint and make good our escape. I turned to him again, but he was staring at Mortimer.

Mortimer laughed. "Do forgive my little jest, but I admit it was worth it. If you could have seen your faces! This is the skull of the man you knew as Jack Stapleton, Dr Watson. You may note that it bears a remarkably similar supra-orbital development to that of Mr Holmes. Unfortunately in Baskerville's case it was not an indication of intellect, for the man blundered from one disaster to the next like one of his hapless butterflies. There were two scandals in South America, not one, then the school in Pickering and finally the fiasco on Dartmoor. I allowed him to flit about in my net until Mr Holmes skewered him with the blame and then I with something more substantial. Let me remove my *memento mori* so we are not distracted." Mortimer returned the cloche to its place, stood, picked up the tray, and stepped over to the sideboard. "As I am acquainted with the nature of your quest let me say that I shall be telling you that which I have not and will not confide to anyone else."

Watson flashed a glance at the windows flanking the sideboard, then at both doors, and then at me. He raised his left hand, indicating I should stay seated.

I nodded.

Watson rose, and moved in behind Mortimer.

I knew he was capable of dealing with our host, so I decided to grab the skull and make for the wagonette if a struggle ensued.

Mortimer set down the tray. "But where is Mr Holmes?" The low clang of metal on wood was muffled by a sharp click, a sound that I hadn't heard in a while, but recognised instantly. Mortimer turned as Watson raised his right hand from his pocket.

Mortimer's mouth dropped open and Watson shot him through the forehead; flesh, blood, and brain matter spattering sideboard, curtains, and window.

Watson turned, clutching the smoking revolver in his fist, and I jumped up, grabbing hold of my chair.

He marched towards me, kicked his chair over, reached down to edge of the table, and flung it on its side. Then he faced me, cocked the revolver again, and lifted it.

He was going to kill me too, blame Mortimer's murder on me.

In the fraction of a second I hesitated, Watson pressed the barrel to his left thigh and fired.

There was more smoke and more blood.

He cried out, dropped the weapon, and fell to the floor.

"I'm sorry, Langham, but this has always been my intention. I couldn't let Mortimer escape unpunished any more than I could let Holmes's good name be destroyed. We are all in your hands now."

VII

I do not know if my decision to bear false witness for Watson has redeemed my past or damned my future, but I do know that I could not let him throw his life away for the likes of Mortimer. Watson committed murder to defend his friend's reputation and I committed perjury to defend his, and the reputation of the English gentleman which he epitomised for me and so many others. He had nerve and he had knowledge.

✗

Rafe McGregor has published over one hundred and twenty short stories, novellas, magazine articles, journal papers, and review essays. His work includes crime fiction, weird tales, military history, literary criticism, and academic philosophy. Find out more on Google+.

THE CASE OF THE MISSING ARCHAEOLOGIST

by Carla Coupe

After making my way down the stair from my bedroom, I opened the door to our sitting room, then reeled back, coughing.

Thick clouds of evil-smelling smoke rolled through the door.

"Holmes? What on earth?"

Upon receiving no reply and by now thoroughly alarmed, I held my handkerchief over my mouth and dashed across the chamber, pulling the curtains wide and throwing open the window. Sunlight streamed a few feet into the room and disappeared into the swirling murk. A gust of wind gained entry and parted the cloud, revealing Sherlock Holmes stretched indolently upon the settee. Shag tobacco liberally sprinkled the front of his dressing-gown and his slipper-clad feet were propped on the arm. He opened his eyes and gazed at me.

"Ah, Watson. Is there a problem?"

"Have you been up all night?" I crossed the room and opened the door, sending smoke billowing onto the landing.

Holmes waved a hand. "Due to the absolute dearth of any cases that would challenge my abilities, I decided to compare the rate of combustion of a variety of tobaccos and did not notice the hour or the state of the atmosphere. And you might find it of some interest to know that I deduced the whereabouts of Lady Milford's cat."

I hesitated, but curiousity overcame my reluctance to humour Holmes. "Where is it?"

He stood in one fluid motion and moved toward his chamber. "Ask her to show you the new wrap His Lordship presented to her..." The door closed behind him.

I stared after him, hoping he was mistaken. However, remembering Her Ladyship's penchant for furs, I feared not.

"Goodness me, Doctor!" Burdened by our breakfast tray, Mrs Hudson paused at the threshold and coughed. "Another of Mr Holmes's experiments?"

I quickly cleared a space on the table. "As well as a night of cogitation, I believe."

She shook her head and set out the plates. "Another night without sleep cannot be good for him."

"On the contrary, Mrs Hudson." Holmes emerged from his room fully dressed. "My body responds to nothing so well as mental exercise."

"If you say so." She set a rack of toast on the table. "I shall leave the door open until this foul haze has dispersed."

Like the smoke in our chambers, my own mental fog faded by the time I finished my first cup of coffee and poured my second. Mrs Hudson reappeared with a fresh pot and the morning's post. Holmes shuffled through a handful of envelopes before plucking one from the pile and ripping it open. A small crease formed between his brows as he read.

"An intriguing missive, Watson. What are your thoughts?" He tossed the letter across the table.

I swallowed my last bite of kipper before picking up the paper.

"Dear Mr Holmes," it read. "I have consulted the police in vain regarding my brother's disappearance three days ago. I shall call upon you this morning at ten to obtain your advice.

"Sincerely, Rose Longridge."

I laid the letter on the table. "My thoughts? Why, there is little enough to analyze: a scant two sentences."

"Exactly!" Holmes sprang to his feet and crossed to the fire. He began to fill his pipe. "The young lady—and she is indeed young, I would say no more than five-and-twenty—is quite masculine in her concision. Yet you know my methods: there is much to be learned from paper and ink. In this case, the paper is of good, but not exceptional quality. One could purchase similar sheets at any reputable stationers. I draw your attention to the ink, however. I have seldom encountered ink of such opacity and texture in Europe. Indeed, I have only seen it used to create images of complex and sinuous design, the hallmark of Oriental scripts."

I studied the letter again. "It appears plain black ink to me."

Holmes paused to draw on his pipe. "As it would to everyone who had not displayed curiousity regarding the subject. There might be something of interest in this after all. Finish your breakfast and then we shall await the arrival of Miss Rose Longridge."

With a small smile, Holmes settled in his favourite chair, burying himself in that morning's *Times*.

✗　✗　✗　✗

Mrs Hudson was clearing the breakfast dishes when the bell rang. She bustled out with the crockery and returned with a young lady—Holmes had been quite correct regarding her age—dressed in a severely-tailored suit of moss green. She glanced from Holmes to me, then returned her gaze to him.

"Mr Holmes." She held out her hand and after a momentary hesitation he took it. With a brisk motion she shook his hand then turned to me. "I am afraid I have not had the pleasure of your acquaintance, sir."

"Miss Longridge." A smile flitted across Holmes's face. "May I present my friend and colleague, Dr John Watson."

"Doctor." We also shook hands; her grip was strong and entirely business-like.

"Please be seated Miss Longridge and tell me about your brother's disappearance. Was it after your return from Egypt?" Holmes asked.

She did not attempt to conceal her look of surprise as she sat. "How did you know I have been in Egypt, Mr Holmes?"

He shrugged and leaned against the hearth. "You are naturally fair-skinned, despite your dark hair and eyes. Your face and hands are deeply tanned and the colour has not had time to fade. Although England enjoyed a mild spring, you could not have achieved that colour on these shores; therefore, you have been abroad. You are wearing a necklace of faience beads, masterfully crafted, which can most easily be purchased in Egypt. And there is sand so deeply embedded in the hem of your travelling dress that even a thorough cleaning did not remove it completely, indicating a prolonged stay."

Her expression transformed from surprise to amusement as Holmes listed his observations. When he finished, she clapped her hands together.

"Bravo, Mr Holmes. You are correct on all counts." Then she sobered. "Including the fact that Alston disappeared after our return from Cairo."

"You were visiting the ancient monuments?" I asked, taking a seat on the settee.

"I rather think Miss Longridge participated in an Egyptological excavation," said Holmes before she could reply. "And judging from the paint stains on her hands, she acted as the expedition artist."

She nodded. "For the past twenty years my uncle, Professor Preston Longridge, has mounted yearly expeditions. For five years my brother has acted as our uncle's secretary and maintained the records. This was my second year as artist. It is taxing work, but I love it, as does my brother. We finished for the winter and returned from Egypt on the *Lancaster* three days ago."

"That was when your brother disappeared?"

She stared at the fire, surreptitiously blinking away her tears. "Yes. The voyage had been uneventful, but I could sense that something was bothering Alston. He appeared unusually nervous, constantly glancing over his shoulder, starting at the least sound. I began to grow concerned about his health and he admitted to me he hardly slept during the voyage.

"When we prepared to disembark, Alston asked me to take charge of his baggage, for he had to see to the expedition's artifacts. I thought it odd, for generally Hussein, my uncle's manservant, was responsible for transporting any items we brought back. Then Alston took me by the shoulders. I thought he might speak, but he only kissed me on the brow and hurried away. That was the last I saw him."

Her voice wavered on the final words. She took a deep breath and turned to Holmes.

"My uncle and I informed the police of his absence, but there is little they can do. We have also made enquiries at hospitals."

Holmes studied her for a moment. "Do you believe your brother might have sought medical advice?"

She slowly shook her head. "I do not know why he would. He has always been healthy."

I coughed gently. "Three days is not an undue period of time for a young man to absent himself. Perhaps your brother required an interlude of solitary recuperation from his efforts or decided to stay with friends."

"Without informing me first? He would anticipate my concern." She clasped her hands tightly. "Yet I would have waited before seeking your advice but for the discovery I made this morning."

Holmes narrowed his eyes, all his attention fixed on Miss Longridge. "A discovery?"

"Yes. I went to Alston's room. I decided to search his cases in hopes that he might have left a clue regarding the reason for his behaviour during the voyage."

"Were they not already unpacked by one of the servants?" asked Holmes.

"No. Alston often places delicate objects in with his clothing so he might study them during the return voyage and the servants know better than to touch his traps. As I said, I went to his room, but when I opened the door, I found his cases open, his clothing and other effects strewn about. I questioned all of the servants, but none admitted to knowing anything of this matter."

"One of them could be lying," I said.

"It is possible, I suppose. But the window was open and there is a ledge beneath, affording a means of entry."

"This is a serious matter," said Holmes. "You did not notify the police?"

"Mr Holmes, the police already believe me to be an overwrought sister. I am certain they would dismiss this merely as a matter of lax housekeeping."

Holmes stood and crossed to the window. "I am afraid—" he began. His gaze fixed on the street below and his frame suddenly suffused with a vibrant energy I recognized from other cases. I rose from my chair.

"Tell me, Miss Longridge," Holmes said. "Did anyone accompany you here today?"

"No. Why do you ask?"

I started toward the door, already anticipating his next move.

"Stay here, Watson. I shall—"

The remainder of his comment was lost as he dashed into the hall, the sound of his footsteps fading as he rapidly descended the stair. I ran to the window, where I was joined by Miss Longridge. On the pavement below, Holmes emerged precipitously from the front of the house. His head turned like that of a hound coursing for the scent of the fox. I threw open the sash and leant out, hoping that my higher vantage might provide a glimpse of whatever—or whomever—caught Holmes's eye. The scene before me was remarkable only for its lack of noteworthy activity. A cab, a delivery wagon, and a few pedestrians were all that greeted my scrutiny.

"What is Mr Holmes doing?" Miss Longridge asked as she stood beside me, leaning out the aperture. One hand clutched the frame, the other held the crown of her hat firmly to her head.

Below us, Holmes knelt on the pavement, his dark head close to the ground. He pulled an envelope from his pocket, laid it on the pavement and brushed something inside. Then he stood, dusting off his knees. Mrs Hudson would have something to say about the state of his trousers, I was certain.

"No doubt he will explain when he returns," I said.

We watched from the window until Holmes rejoined us.

"I assume you saw a passerby who appeared Egyptian," I said, feeling rather pleased with my deduction. "Perhaps sporting a fez? And what did you discover?"

Holmes smiled briefly before tipping the contents of the envelope onto a clean glass slide. It appeared to be dust, or perhaps ash.

"A moment, please." He nodded to Miss Longridge. Then he slipped the slide into his microscope and after adjusting the eyepiece, studied it. With a pleased hum, he withdrew the slide and held it beneath his nostrils, his eyes closed, sniffing delicately. Finally, opening his eyes and moistening his finger, he gathered some of the substance onto the tip and touched it to his tongue.

"Well?" I asked.

"To answer your earlier question, Watson, no, the man in question did not wear a fez, but a broad-brimmed hat that shaded his features." He set down the slide and turned to Miss Longridge. "Yet he smoked Egyptian tobacco while waiting outside our door for approximately a quarter hour and when he observed my attention, he quickly retreated."

"That was tobacco ash?" she asked. "But how can you possibly know it is from Egyptian tobacco?"

"Holmes can identify dozens of varieties of tobacco," I replied and turned to him. "The more important question is why this unknown man was waiting outside our rooms. Was he following Miss Longridge?"

"That is what we shall endeavour to find out." Holmes rubbed his hands together. "Come, Miss Longridge! Watson and I shall accompany you home and we shall see if your brother's things can shed some light on this mystery."

✗   ✗   ✗   ✗

The Professor's home was a sprawling structure situated near Hampstead Heath. Screened from the road by tall brick walls and densely planted shrubs, the building itself was a curious amalgam of styles. We were greeted in the half-timbered entry by a dark-skinned servant whom Miss Longridge called by the name Hussein. The man's lean countenance displayed the impassivity of a well-trained butler, but his black eyes glittered beneath heavy brows.

Despite the day's bright sunshine, shadows filled the hall. Oak paneling and patterned wallpaper combined with thickly leaded windows reduced the sun's effect and the pierced metal lamps did little to augment the general illumination. Rich furnishings failed to mitigate an air of oppression.

"Where is Uncle Preston?" she asked Hussein as she removed her gloves and hat.

"The master is not at home, Miss." He took our hats and coats. "He did not say when he would return."

"Very well. Mr Holmes, Doctor. My brother's room is this way." She started up the sweeping stairway on the right. Glancing back at Hussein, she continued. "If Uncle returns, ask him to join us in Alston's room."

He bowed. "Yes, Miss."

I spared him a look as I passed. His body was still inclined slightly, but his face... rarely have I seen an expression of such intensity on a human countenance. I could not identify the emotion displayed: fear, perhaps, or anger? Or was it desire that sparked such an upwelling? Before I could study it further, his expression returned to well-schooled aloofness.

I hurried up the stair, my footsteps muffled by the Oriental carpeting. Miss Longridge, followed by Holmes, turned into a short corridor.

"Here we are, gentlemen." Miss Longridge stopped at a door approximately half-way down the corridor. "I instructed the servants to leave the room as I found it," she continued, unlocking the door and entering the room.

Following close behind, Holmes strode to the center of the room and paused, his keen eyes moving over the disorder.

The chamber was large and airy with two tall windows, walls papered with Eastern designs, and modern furniture of polished mahogany. A chest of drawers and a writing desk stood against the right wall with the bed on the left. An upholstered chair was positioned between the windows, a small table at its side. In front of the bed, two large cases stood open and the clothing, notebooks, toiletry articles and other items of a personal nature that had previously been packed inside were strewn across the bed and floor.

Holmes knelt and closely examined the first case, his forefinger resting on his lips as his keen eyes studied the battered leather sides and stained cloth interior. He retrieved something from the case, what appeared to be a small piece of dried grass or straw, and let it flutter to the floor. Moving to the next case, Holmes frowned and bent so low that his head was practically inside. To my surprise, he did not remove the small pile of clothing still in place, instead merely studying it from several angles.

I reached down into a pile of shirts and picked up a small figure made of a material akin to glass.

"A *shawabti*," said Miss Longridge, carefully taking the figure. "A funerary statue, crafted of faience." She held it up to the light and frowned. "How unfortunate. It has cracked."

An exclamation from Holmes drew our attention. He lay on the carpet, his nose almost pressed into the pile, his hand hovering a hair's-breadth over the wool.

"What is it?" I cried, stepping over a pair of trousers to join him.

"Stay back!" He held up an admonitory hand. "Do not disturb the tale that this carpet has to tell."

I stopped. "And what tale is that?"

"A bare foot, small, narrow..." He crawled to the partially open window, then stood and examined the casement. "You were quite correct, Miss Longridge. Your intruder entered the room from here. There is a clear footprint on the sill." Throwing wide the sash, he leant out. "And the ledge is quite spacious and convenient. It would not be difficult to gain admittance."

After asking permission and following the path he pointed out, I joined him at the window and studied the print on the sill.

To her credit, Miss Longridge appeared more puzzled than frightened.

"A small, bare foot? Do you mean a child did this, Mr Holmes?"

"It is one possibility." His gaze fixed on her face. "Do you know a reason for the presence of a child here?"

She hesitated and he continued: "Even a fact that appears insignificant could be of vital importance to solving the mystery of your brother's disappearance."

"Very well," she replied. "It is only that I thought I heard a child crying last night."

"When was this?"

"I don't know. I did not sleep soundly and during one of my periods of wakefulness I heard sobbing and assumed it was from a neighbouring house. The sounds did not last long; I fell asleep shortly thereafter."

"It may not have been a child," I said. "A woman's foot may be as small and an agile woman could have entered this way."

"As an agile man may exit." Holmes suited action to words and stepped out onto the ledge.

"Mr Holmes!" cried Miss Longridge, rushing to the window despite Holmes's injunction. "Have a care, please!"

As is his custom when on the scent, Holmes paid her no heed. He crouched on the ledge, studying the stonework, then gazed intently to the left. With a sharp exclamation, he stepped carefully along the ledge until he reached the roof of a conservatory or garden room jutting from the house proper. He bent low and grasped a broad drainpipe, swinging himself off the ledge and landing easily on a small wooden access hatch on the conservatory's roof.

Holmes paused and looked up at us as we leaned out the window, then turned his attention to the drainpipe he had just descended. He pulled his handkerchief from his pocket and gave it a shake. He draped it across one hand then removed something from beside the drainpipe and placed it in the handkerchief.

"He has found a clue," I said, turning to Miss Longridge.

Eyes bright, lips parted, she followed Holmes's activity.

Folding his handkerchief carefully, Holmes thrust it into his coat pocket and by means of a conveniently-placed water barrel, descended to the gravel path. Once there, he immediately dropped to his knees and cast about for a moment. He must have discovered the trail, for he crawled along the path, disappearing around the side of the conservatory.

"Should we meet him outside?" she asked.

"We will wait here. No doubt he will wish to examine the rest of the room."

After several minutes, Holmes appeared, striding briskly along the path. He quickly climbed onto the water barrel and, retracing his earlier path, returned to the room.

As he smoothed his hair, Miss Longridge asked, "What did you discover?"

"That you have commendable servants," said Holmes. "Who rake the gravel path daily, thereby obliterating any tracks until one reaches the lawn."

"And the clue?" I gestured at his pocket.

"Our housebreaker is indeed female, as we suspected," replied Holmes, withdrawing the handkerchief and opening it slowly. Three long pale yellow strands lay on the silk. "She looked down when she reached the drainpipe and her hair tangled in a bracket." He refolded the handkerchief and slid it back into his pocket.

"But how did she gain entrance?" I asked as Holmes drew down the sash. "Was the window locked or latched?"

Miss Longridge nodded. "Yes, it was latched."

"You are certain?" Holmes examined the latches. "These were not forced."

"I am certain, for I checked the latches myself when Alston's belongings were brought in."

I opened my mouth to speak, but Holmes quickly placed a finger to his lips and I let my comment die. Did the young house-breaker have a confederate in the household? And if so, who had access to the locked room?

"No doubt there is a reasonable explanation," said Holmes dismissively.

Miss Longridge frowned, but did not pursue the matter.

"And now to this room," he said, rubbing his hands together as he surveyed the disorder. "Is anything missing?"

Miss Longridge glanced around and her mouth twisted in a rueful smile. "Unless my brother left an inventory, I would have no idea."

"What of the artifacts he packed in his clothing?"

"Again, without a list, I would not know if an object had been taken. But do continue your search his possessions, Mr Holmes, if you believe it would be useful."

With deft fingers, Holmes began to sort through the belongings on the bed. A soft cough drew our attention to where Hussein stood at the door. He made a small bow to Miss Longridge.

"Excuse me, Miss. You have a visitor." The final word was said with such thinly-veiled contempt that Holmes looked up from his inspection of a small black-leather-bound notebook.

Miss Longridge stiffened. "Who is it?" she asked.

"Dr Rashad." There was no mistaking Hussein's disapproval. I wondered if it was of the man himself, or that he would call upon Miss Longridge. Holmes bent again to the notebook.

With a small sigh, she frowned. "Show him to the library. We will join him there." She waited until Hussein left before turning to us. "Hussein is quite devoted to our family and distrusts all outsiders."

"Quite understandable," I replied, when it became clear that Holmes's attention was elsewhere.

"Mr Holmes?" Pausing until his gaze returned to her, she gestured toward the door. "Dr Rashad traveled with us from Egypt. You may wish to question him about the journey."

"Of course," said Holmes, rising. "I am finished here. Come, Watson."

I do not believe she observed him slip the notebook into his pocket before he crossed the room. We waited in the corridor while she locked the door, then followed her down the stair.

The library was located at the rear of the house. Shelves of leather-bound books stretched from floor to ceiling, while dark carved paneling added to the general gloom. A man stood facing the unlit hearth and he turned toward us as we entered. He wore a suit of impeccable cut and the whiteness of his shirt contrasted with his dark colouring. High cheekbones in his thin face and a prominent hawk-like nose hinted at an aristocratic lineage.

He bowed. "Miss Longridge. I take it you have not heard from your brother yet?" His English was as pure as Holmes's or mine.

"No, I have not," she said with an underlying warmth that brought a soft smile to his austere features. She introduced us. "I know Uncle wished to wait a few more days before taking action," she added, taking a seat in front of the window, "but I could not bear it any longer. This morning I asked Mr Holmes and Dr Watson if they could shed any light on this mystery."

"Do you believe you will be able to help Miss Longridge find her brother?" Rashad asked, claiming a chair beside Miss Longridge while Holmes and I sat across from them.

"I hope that we may be of service," Holmes replied, crossing his legs. "You traveled from Egypt on the same ship as the Longridges."

"Yes." He settled back in his chair and studied Holmes.

"Miss Longridge says her brother appeared distressed and preoccupied during the journey. What is your assessment of his behaviour?" asked Holmes.

Rashad hesitated, as if deliberating. "I believe Mr Longridge felt the burden of his duties during the voyage and—"

"For pity's sake, Abdul!" she said, reaching a hand to him. "You have known Alston since you were both up at Oxford, yet you speak as if he were a stranger. Please, if you..." Colour tinted her cheeks as he took her hand for a moment, releasing it gently. "Please answer Mr Holmes's questions honestly and completely."

Rashad nodded. "Of course. I want to discover what happened to Alston as much as you do."

"We understand the difficulty of confiding in strangers," I said. "We will honor your confidences."

"Unless a life hangs on them, as has happened before," interrupted Holmes.

Rashad drew a deep breath before replying. "A sensible caveat. Then I must tell you that Alston was not himself during the voyage. He appeared distracted and in the grip of a powerful nervous complaint, which only grew stronger as the journey progressed."

"Do you know of any reason for this behaviour?" asked Holmes.

Rashad's dark, assessing gaze held that of Holmes for a long moment. Suddenly he closed his eyes and bowed his head as if he had released some great burden.

"Mr Holmes," he began as the door to the hall was thrown open.

"Rose!" boomed a deep, hearty voice. A broad-shouldered man, deeply tanned and with a full head of greying hair, seemed to fill the entire room, such was his presence. His bright blue eyes traveled around the assembled company. "Ah, you are entertaining! Hullo, Rashad. I trust you are well."

Before Rashad could reply, Miss Longridge rose and crossed the room. "Uncle, I know you wished to wait a little longer before consulting Mr Holmes..."

"So this is the famous detective." The Professor leaned down and dropped a kiss on Miss Longridge's brow, then turned to us. He thrust out his hand to Holmes. "How d'you do?"

"And his colleague, Dr Watson," said Miss Longridge.

"Delighted!" he said, giving my hand a vigourous shake. "Rose's been in quite a state since Alston disappeared. But I'm afraid she called you out unnecessarily." He smiled at her and held up a sheet of foolscap. "I have just this moment received a letter from Alston."

"A letter!" Miss Longridge snatched the paper from his fingers and quickly scanned it. "He says a friend from Oxford met him as he was disembarking and urgently requested his assistance..." Her brow creased as she read aloud: "'It was imperative that I immediately accompany him to Yorkshire, where I found his difficulty even more complex than he originally indicated. Please forgive me, dear sister, for neglecting to write to you earlier. I am certain you have been worried on my behalf, but know that I am well and will return once circumstances permit. Your loving brother, Alston.'"

"You see?" The Professor smiled. "All your worry has been for naught."

"But..." Miss Longridge re-read the letter. "But who is this friend? He mentions no name."

"Perhaps Alston felt discretion was necessary," said Professor Longridge, patting her on the shoulder. "Whatever the case, my dear, you have no need to worry."

Holmes stepped forward. "If I may, Miss Longridge?" He held out his hand.

The Professor's smile faded. "A private correspondence—"

"Don't be ridiculous, Uncle. After almost setting Mr Holmes on a wild goose chase, I am happy to share this." She handed Holmes the page.

"And the envelope, please." Holmes studied the letter and the envelope for a long moment, then returned both to her with a little bow. "Thank you. We will trouble you no further."

"But what of my brother's belongings?" asked Miss Longridge. "Who could have entered this house and rifled through them?"

A smile flitted across Holmes's face. "That is indeed a mystery."

Miss Longridge frowned. "Well, then, if you have no solution to the problem, should we consult the police?"

The Professor started, raising his hands. "The police? Good gad, my girl, what an idea!"

"I did not say I have no solution," said Holmes calmly, "simply that it is currently a mystery."

"Really, Holmes, you are being quite annoyingly inscrutable," I murmured as Miss Longridge glared at him.

"I hope to have news for you soon," he said. Then he nodded to Rashad and the Professor and turned to me. "Well, Watson, shall we go?"

We made our farewells, well-thanked by Miss Longridge, whose ire abated upon Holmes's assurances, and we left the house.

"That was certainly rum," I said as we made our way down the long drive to the road. "What are the odds that a letter from her brother would arrive immediately after you were consulted?"

Holmes lifted a brow. "You did not believe in the friend and his difficulty?"

"I don't know," I said slowly. "There was something... not quite right about the entire business. Still, Miss Longridge appears satisfied with her brother's current situation, as well as your efforts to discover the culprit who disturbed her brother's things."

"And that is enough to allay your concerns?"

"It appears the letter did not convince you, at any rate."

"Not only the letter, my dear fellow. I bring to your attention the state of the servant's cuffs, the matter of the footprint on the sill, and the question of the letter's delivery."

Before I could ask Holmes to explain himself, we were hailed from behind. We paused and Dr Rashad hurried up to us.

"Mr Holmes, Doctor, a moment of your time, please."

Holmes glanced back at the house. I followed the direction of his gaze; Hussein stood in the open door watching us.

"Of course," said Holmes. "Let us converse out of sight of the house, however."

We gained the main road before Holmes stopped and turned to Rashad. "I take it you can shed some light on this business. For you do not believe in the friend in need any more than Watson or I do."

"It is very puzzling, Mr Holmes."

A nursemaid passed us pushing her charge in a perambulator and her curious stare silenced Rashad.

"Gentlemen," said Holmes, glancing about. "There is an inn across the road. Shall we continue our conversation over luncheon?"

Rashad hesitated, brow furrowed as he glanced at the building. "There is another more congenial public house not far from here..."

"And yet I am intrigued by the name of this one—'The Queen of Sheba,'" said Holmes, leading the way across the street.

Rashad and I followed. We entered a pleasant brick building, where we were warmly greeted by the landlord, a tall sandy-haired man. To my surprise, Holmes responded by admiring the building and engaged George Byrnes, for such was the landlord's name, in an animated conversation regarding the improvements he made, how many rooms the inn boasted, the typical number of guests and today's luncheon offerings. The interior was quite modern with large windows and gas lighting, although it still afforded the private nooks and quiet corners so beloved by the English diner.

Once we were seated in the back where we would not be disturbed, we ordered our meal and at the landlord's behest, three pints of "the best bitter in the country." After the landlord left, Rashad turned to us.

"It will not take long to tell. Alston and I attended Oxford together. We fancied ourselves men of the world and ran with a fast crowd. As is often the case, our quest for pleasure quite overcame the moral lessons of our upbringing and we developed several... unfortunate propensities during our years of scholarship.

"I do not wish to condemn Alston for his youthful mistakes, for I shared most of them. Yet once we left the confines of Oxford, Rose... Miss Longridge took it upon herself to bring us to task and we both saw our behaviour for what it was: the dissipation and decadence of young men of promise. We had too much money, too much time, and far too good an opinion of ourselves."

I glanced at Holmes, who was sitting with his eyes closed, his fingers steepled before his face. "This is not an uncommon occurrence," I said. "Many a sober judge and solemn legislator ran wild in his youth."

Rashad nodded. "Very true. And yet if Miss Longridge had not spoken, we might still be enmeshed in vice. As it was, however, we vowed to correct our behaviour, to put aside the activities that could bring shame upon our families and ourselves. In this we succeeded, with a single exception: Alston found it difficult to break one habit."

"And that is?" Holmes's eyes were still closed.

Our mutton and bitter arrived, served by the landlord and a long-limbed, coltish young woman, obviously his daughter. She was perhaps sixteen and wore her flaxen hair pinned up, yet lacked a more mature woman's poise and grace. As she placed the cutlery before Holmes, she fumbled and his knife clattered to the wide oak boards. With a flash of movement at odds with his earlier lethargy, Holmes bent and retrieved the knife from the floor, handing it to her with a nod.

Waving away the landlord's apologies, Holmes declared the fault his and was rewarded with the girl's shy smile and murmured thanks.

"You may go, Susan," her father said once our food was on the table, but he waited until we tasted our mutton and pronounced it good before leaving.

Holmes tilted his head and looked at Rashad. "You were saying?"

Rashad put down his rapidly-diminishing pint. Had he converted to Christianity? He was certainly not an observant Mohammedan if he imbibed.

"Alston's unfortunate weakness is one that is both embraced and condemned by Society. He is an inveterate gambler."

"You believe his disappearance is somehow connected to his gambling."

"I do."

"In what way?"

Rashad took a deep breath, as if steeling himself. "Over the winter, Alston confided in me that he amassed a number of debts before he left for Egypt."

"Gambling debts?" asked Holmes.

"No doubt. His salary, though perfectly adequate for a bachelor in his situation, would not cover a quarter of the total and he admitted he had little or no hope of collecting the sum necessary to settle them all."

"Not an uncommon situation, unfortunately," I said. "Could he not apply to the Professor for assistance?"

"When I suggested that, he merely shook his head and said that all of the Professor's resources go to financing further expeditions."

"What of his sister?" asked Holmes.

"Miss Longridge does possess a small income, but she knows nothing of the matter and Alston is adamant that she remain ignorant of his weakness. I tell you, gentlemen, he was absolutely distraught on the journey back. I offered what I could—my income is adequate for my needs, but little more—and he refused. 'I have placed myself in a damnable position,' he said, 'and I must accept the consequences.'" Rashad pushed away his plate and leaned forward. "Then he turned his back to me and spoke quickly and low, as if to himself. 'I will break her heart,' he said. 'What do you mean?' I asked, but he denied saying anything and would not discuss the matter further."

"'I will break her heart,'" I repeated. "Undoubtedly he dreaded Miss Longridge learning of his weakness."

Rashad nodded, his expression grim.

"And yet his sister just received a letter from Mr Longridge, which provided an explanation for his absence," said Holmes. "She is content. Why should we still be concerned about him?"

"You do not believe that letter is genuine, Mr Holmes," said Rashad.

"The letter was in the same hand as the papers Miss Longridge said were his," Holmes replied.

"So why do you doubt its authenticity?"

"Oh, I have no doubt that Alston Longridge wrote that letter. However, I do not believe in the friend-in-need and an unexpected journey to Yorkshire."

Rashad frowned. "Then what *do* you believe, Mr Holmes?"

Holmes leaned back, his eyes heavy-lidded, lending him a secretive air. "It is too early for me to formulate a theory. I am, as yet, still gathering facts."

"I hope to God you reach a conclusion soon," Rashad said, his quiet words at odds with the intensity of his emotions.

"Have faith, Dr Rashad," I said, placing a comforting hand on his arm. "Holmes does not waste time in his investigations."

"Is there a particular reason you are anxious for your friend?" asked Holmes.

Rashad hesitated, one long finger tracing the rings of moisture on the table before him. "You would share my alarm if you witnessed the panic and desperation in his eyes."

"That is not an answer to my question. Let me phrase it another way: do you believe he is in danger of taking his own life?"

Rashad passed his hand over his face, then met Holmes's gaze. "That, Mr Holmes, is why I am so afraid."

✗   ✗   ✗   ✗

Upon finishing luncheon, we all shared a cab, letting off Dr Rashad at his lodgings near the British Museum before continuing on to Baker Street. Once in our chambers, Holmes spent some little time reading through the small notebook he purloined from Longridge's room. After a quarter-hour, he set it aside and turned to me.

"If I were to ask you, Watson, about private collectors of ancient Egyptian artifacts, what names come to mind?"

"Goodness." I frowned, marshalling my thoughts. "I only know what I read in the newspapers, but there's Lord Worsley—I believe he has two mummies in his collection, as well as a number of Greek and Roman statues, but of course, they're not Egyptian..." I paused for a moment. "The Earl of ------ has an extensive collection of papyri, which he has lent to the Bodleian, and there is that manufacturer—Loveless, Lovert... Lovage, that was the name— who bought up a number of smaller collections from under the nose of the British Museum."

"Well done," said Holmes. "Do not forget the American ambassador, who has one of the finest collections of cartonnage funerary masks in existence."

"This is all very interesting, I'm sure, but does this have anything to do with the disappearance of Miss Longridge's brother?"

"Possibly, possibly. We shall see."

Holmes then penned several notes and dispatched them via messenger and proceeded to ignore me for an hour as he sat in abstracted silence, perched in his chair with his long legs drawn up, his arms wrapped around his shins, his chin resting on his knees as he gazed into the fire. When he finally roused himself, he disappeared without a word for half-an-hour, returning with a heavy tome tucked under his arm. Sitting at the table, he studied the book intently. I caught a glimpse of illustrative plates on one page, but could not see clearly enough to identify the subject and since Holmes was in one of his uncommunicative moods, I did not inquire further.

I spent the time catching up on my medical journals, the ticking of the clock the only sound in our chambers, apart from the muted sound of traffic outside our windows and the quiet rustle of my journal pages.

At half-five Holmes closed the book, blinked twice and bounded to his feet with a smile. I set down my journal and rose, stretching.

A knock sounded. Holmes rubbed his hands together. "Here is Mrs Hudson with a cold supper."

We dined lightly as Holmes discoursed on the art of the ancient Egyptians; to my surprise, a subject upon which he appeared knowledgeable and informed. I pushed back my plate and was sipping my coffee when Holmes lifted his head and raised an eyebrow.

"Ah. A response to one of my queries."

Then I heard the light steps of the maid, who knocked and entered, holding an envelope.

Holmes snatched it up along with his knife, glancing at the direction before slitting the envelope and removing the folded sheet.

After a quick perusal he rose, a gleam of excitement sparking in his cool grey eyes.

"What news?" I asked, springing to my feet.

"You are finished? Good. Join me and we shall call upon Sir Richard Lovage." Holmes started down the stair.

I dashed after him. "Lovage? Now?"

Holmes tossed me my coat and donned his own. In a few moments, we were out the door and in a cab, hurrying toward an address in Kensington.

"Why are we calling on Sir Richard?" I asked, sitting back against the creaking leather seat. "Unless... Is it possible that young Longridge clandestinely sold an artifact in order to raise the money to pay off his gambling debts?"

Holmes nodded. "It is certainly one possibility."

"If he sold it to Sir Richard, surely the man would not be foolish enough to confess that." Holmes shrugged and I continued. "Although if Longridge sold it to another collector, jealousy or spite might loosen Sir Richard's tongue."

"Bravo, my dear Watson!" cried Holmes, clapping his hands together. "Your insight into the human heart rings true. No doubt that between the two of us, we shall winkle out any knowledge Sir Richard might possess regarding this matter."

✗   ✗   ✗   ✗

We alighted on a broad pavement before a stately, if uninspired, Georgian residence. A servant answered the door and took our hats, then led us through thickly carpeted corridors to a well-appointed library. Despite the warmth of the evening, a cheery blaze crackled in the Adam fireplace and shelves of leather-bound volumes filled the four walls. What space was not occupied by books displayed a wide variety of Egyptian artifacts, including statues, fragments of wall paintings, carved panels and standing upright in one corner, a magnificently decorated coffin.

Sir Richard sat at a gleaming mahogany desk covered with sheets of foolscap and several heavy volumes that lay open as if for ready reference. He looked up and jumped to his feet as we entered, his round face breaking into a smile.

"Mr Sherlock Holmes and Dr Watson!" he cried, hurrying forward, both hands extended. "What an honor to be asked to assist the man who has brought justice to so many, as well as his chronicler!" He grabbed Holmes's hand and shook it vigourously, then darted to me and repeated his actions while continuing his encomiums. When he released my fingers, I rubbed my crushed hand surreptitiously, studying this scion of business enterprise. Short and rotund in stature, a fringe of curly mouse-brown hair haloed his face and gave him the look of a teacher beloved by his students more for his humour and good nature than for his learning. His clothing was smart and unexceptional, save for the golden image of a woman's face he wore on his stick-pin. Fine features and a remote beauty lent it an exotic air. Another artifact, perhaps?

Breaking into Sir Richard's monologue with a laugh, Holmes stepped over to the coffin, his long, sensitive fingers gently trailing down the gilded surface. "You are too kind. But we did not impose upon your time to hear our praises sung."

"No, of course not! Indeed not!" Sir Richard joined Holmes beside the coffin, patting and stroking it as if it were a favourite pet. "In your note you mentioned that I could assist you, which I am delighted to do! What knowledge I have is at your disposal."

Holmes moved to a vitrine laden with a multitude of small artifacts, mainly pottery and faience *shawabtis* similar to the one we found in Alston Longridge's room. "I believe there is some controversy amongst experts regarding the images of the Pharaoh Khuenaten—"

"Ah! A most intriguing issue," interrupted Sir Richard, bounding over to join Holmes. For the next ten minutes he lectured on the topic, scarcely pausing for breath as he followed Holmes. Holmes, for his part, murmured and nodded and continued to move about the room, gently touching objects with his forefinger.

I contented myself with sitting beside the fire, watching the interplay between the two men. Their physical differences lent the scene an almost comical air. Holmes, tall, ascetic, intelligent eyes half-veiled by lowered lids, would have looked at home in a monk's simple habit, while Sir Richard exemplified his polar opposite, round and jolly and ebullient, his rosy cheeks bunched with laughter. Only one time did his smile briefly fade: when Holmes leant to examine a pair of small stone statues, his finger gently brushing one seated figure, then the other. Sir Richard resumed his smile as Holmes turned, however; obviously a momentary abstraction.

After a while Sir Richard wound down, his words slowing until he finally ground to a halt.

"Most informative," murmured Holmes. "A rare opportunity to learn from an expert in the field."

With a deprecating cough and wave of his hand Sir Richard disavowed the title of expert. "I have some small knowledge of Egyptology," he said, returning to his seat behind the desk. "It is seldom that I have the chance to display it. But surely you did not call on me to listen to my views on Khuenaten."

"You are correct," said Holmes, taking another chair. "Professor Longridge's nephew, Alston, disappeared when their party arrived in England and his sister has asked me to look into the matter. I believe you know the young man?"

"Disappeared?" Sir Richard's habitual smile faded. "Goodness me, how distressing. I'm slightly acquainted with him—the field is a small one and we all do know each other to some degree—but I'm afraid I cannot help you. I haven't set eyes on him since..." He paused with a frown. "Since last autumn."

"What of Professor Longridge?" I asked. "Has he assisted you in acquiring this excellent collection?"

Sir Richard laughed. "Heavens, no! Longridge despises all private collectors, most especially me, and would rather see every artifact in a museum than in private hands."

"Surely not every Egyptologist holds the same views," said Holmes. "For if that was the case, you would have collected something quite different: Chinese porcelain, or Japanese armour, perhaps."

Sir Richard raised one brow with a smirk. "Ah, but where there is a will, there is a way."

"Even if the way is rather less than legal?" asked Holmes.

The clock on the mantel struck the half hour and Sir Richard glanced at it with a frown. "Excuse me, gentlemen. I'm afraid I have another appointment." He rose and stepped around the desk, one hand extended to Holmes. "Thank you for indulging my enthusiasms and I hope you locate young Longridge."

We murmured our thanks. After shaking both our hands, he tugged on a bell-pull located beside the hearth. "Braeburn will see you out."

✗   ✗   ✗   ✗

The servant hailed a cab and we climbed in. Holmes gave our address, but as soon as we had rounded the corner, shouted "Stop!" After a hurried consultation with the driver and an exchange of coin, we waited in the hansom in a spot where we could see the front of Sir Richard's house, but where, I hoped, we could not be seen.

"I take it that we are waiting for Sir Richard to lead us... to Alston Longridge, perhaps?"

Holmes's mouth quirked in a half-smile. "That is one possibility, Watson."

"Is he in league with Longridge?"

Before Holmes could answer, the butler exited the house and signaled for another hansom.

"So he won't use his own carriage," said Holmes with satisfaction. "He prefers the anonymity of a cab."

Sir Richard's portly form appeared on the step and hurried into the cab. As soon as he was settled, it drew from the curb and headed toward the river at a brisk pace. Fortunately it kept to the main roads, where there was sufficient traffic to mask our pursuit.

As we traveled, I turned to Holmes, who stared at the passing scenery with a frown. Before I could repeat my question, however, he held up his hand and I subsided into silence. Following his example, I contemplated the passing buildings. What had Holmes deduced from Sir Richard and the items in his study? Sir Richard's interest in Egyptology was clear, but what else had Holmes seen? Try as I might, I could not trace the connection between him and Longridge, yet it appeared there must be one.

Our cab continued to shadow Sir Richard's down the Strand and when we turned onto Whitehall, Holmes leaned forward, eyes narrowed. The other hansom came to a halt at the corner of Downing Street and Sir Richard clambered out and hurried down the street toward that most august address.

"Holmes?"

"Return home, Watson," he said as he opened the door and dashed after Sir Richard.

Thoroughly bewildered, I gave the driver the new instructions. Was Sir Richard calling upon the Prime Minister? If so, why? And what did Holmes believe he could do by following him?

I laid aside my journal and consulted my pocket watch. Half past eleven and no sign of Holmes since he abandoned me in the cab. I sighed. Time for bed. Perhaps I would see Holmes in the morning, when I would tax him for answers.

I set my foot upon the stair to my chamber when a familiar figure burst into the room and flung himself into his chair with a groan, his head cradled in his hands.

"Good heavens, Holmes!" I hurried to his side. "What on earth is the matter? Are you injured?"

"Only my pride, Watson," he said, his long fingers carding through his hair. "Only my damnable pride."

I resumed my seat. "Well, I cannot mend that, but do tell me what happened! Was Sir Richard admitted to Number 10? Did you follow him and speak with Lord Salisbury?"

With a bitter laugh he raised his head, smoothing back his ruffled locks. "Allow me a moment, my good fellow. A glass of port would not come amiss after my labours." He rose and poured himself a measure.

"Sir Richard," he began, after sitting and quaffing half the glass, "is rather more well-connected than I expected. He had no more than to walk up to the prime minister's door to be admitted." He paused to take another sip.

"And you? Did you seek entrance?"

He chuckled. "I am afraid that my notoriety, while useful in certain circumstances, would not impress Lord Salisbury's secretaries. No, I did not even make the attempt. Instead, I lounged in a convenient doorway, a City clerk enjoying a smoke and a moment's respite after a hard day's work. Sir Richard emerged from the prime minister's after a quarter hour and hailed another cab."

"Surely he did not return home, or I would have seen you hours ago."

"No, he attended a concert, had a light supper alone and only then took a cab to his house. I watched him enter his house and waited another half an hour in case he ventured out again. Only when all the lights in the house were extinguished did I hurry back to you. At no point did I see him speak with anyone more than in passing—save, of course, when he was at the prime minister's."

I shook my head. "So we are no further ahead in finding Alston Longridge than before."

"No, I am afraid not." Holmes finished his wine and stretched his legs out toward the fire. "Go to bed, Watson. I shall stay up for a while longer."

✗ ✗ ✗ ✗

The following morning I entered our sitting room to discover Holmes at the breakfast table staring into a cup of coffee. He ignored my greeting and only roused himself when Billy brought the morning's post.

Two letters caught his attention. "Miss Longridge writes that she will call upon us later this morning. Apparently she has discovered something 'of great concern.'"

"That sounds ominous," I said. "Should we call on her?"

"I think not. She is not one prone to hysterics and yet..." He pondered her missive for a moment, then put it aside and picked up the other letter.

"Well, Watson, what do you make of this? Brother Mycroft begs us to call upon him first thing this morning at his office."

I swallowed the last bite of my toast. "Does he say why?"

"Knowing Mycroft, it could be almost anything, from the mundane to grave matters of state." Holmes flung the note onto the table and rose. "Shall we see what he has to say?"

"Certainly." I drained my coffee cup and joined Holmes at the door. "I wonder what Miss Longridge could have discovered that was of such great concern?"

Holmes clattered down the stair and snatched up his hat and stick. "It could be one of a number of things, but since she did not deign to explain herself, I could not venture to say what prompted her to write."

"Perhaps looking into your brother's difficulty will allow you to view Miss Longridge's matter from another angle." I followed him out to the street and into the cab he hailed.

His response was an inelegant snort.

Within a quarter hour we exited the cab at an anonymous government building and followed a soft-footed clerk through winding passages. Half-way along a lengthy corridor he stopped before one door of many and gave a single knock. Then he opened the door and ushered us inside.

"Sherlock, Dr Watson, come in." Mycroft did not rise from behind his mahogany desk, but simply gestured to two comfortable, leather-covered chairs placed before it. A filled bookcase lined one wall and a portrait of Her Majesty hung on another. Light spilled through windows that faced the street, picking out dust motes hanging in the air.

As I sat, Holmes clasped the back of the other chair and leaned against it, studying his brother with a pensive air.

"No," Holmes said, cocking his head to one side. "It is not a mundane matter, is it?"

Mycroft sighed and shook his head. "No, unfortunately not."

Holmes sat, resting his elbows on his knees, his gaze fixed on his brother. "Then please tell us everything."

"All?" Mycroft raised one brow. "That is not possible, for there are some matters of state that cannot be shared. However, I *can* tell you that we have recently become privy to information that a group of radicals from a country in which Britain has certain... interests, plans to assassinate the prime minister in the next day or two."

"Is that all?" Holmes said, sitting back with a grimace. "How many times has Lord Salisbury's life been threatened in the past year alone—five, or is it six times?"

"Great heavens, Holmes!" I cried. "Surely not! There has been nothing in the papers...."

"Even so," said Mycroft, his eyes fixed on his brother. "As a member of the general public, Sherlock is not supposed to know that."

"And yet you are taking this threat uncommonly seriously. Why? What is different about this one?" His eyes narrowed and he leapt from his seat, pacing the limited confines of the office. "Perhaps the radicals have support from monied interests, or from those with power and influence, which would make them a more serious threat."

"Perhaps." Mycroft pressed his lips together and stared out the window. "And perhaps the radicals have corrupted the minds and loyalties of our young men, those who are exposed to their view of the world."

Holmes stopped pacing. "Are we speaking of young men in general, or one in particular?"

Mycroft turned to his brother. "What do you know of the disappearance of Alston Longridge?"

"Alston Longridge?" I stared at Mycroft. Surely he did not know of Holmes's commission to search for the young man. Or did he?

Holmes did not appear surprised by his brother's knowledge. "Ah. So Rashad's story about Longridge's gambling debts was... not false, but a misdirection."

"You have already met Dr Abdul Rashad, have you?" Mycroft leaned back in his chair, clasping his hands over his rotund midsection. "Miss Longridge asked you to find her brother and Rashad conveniently appeared, confided in you, sending you off to search in another direction while Longridge himself is involved up to his neck."

"Surely not," I said. "Why would he act so traitorously?"

"Longridge's debts are real enough," said Holmes. "And his creditors are growing anxious. Is that how the radicals gained traction with him, Mycroft?"

"Very likely. In the meantime, we would speak with this young man, for I suspect he knows a great deal about the plot. Unfortunately," he said with a frown, "we cannot locate him at the moment."

Holmes smiled. "Hence your invitation to me. Well, do not despair, brother mine. Take up your coat and hat and we shall beard Alston Longridge in his den."

"You know where he is?" I rose and glared at Holmes. "Why did you not tell Miss Longridge? She has been worried sick about her brother's disappearance."

"Alston Longridge is playing a deadly game, Watson. I needed to find out more before exposing him. Now that I know his goal,

I agree with Mycroft that it is time to gather him in and discover what he knows."

Mycroft provided a sleek brougham for our errand. As we entered, Holmes spoke softly to the groom, probably giving him directions.

At times Holmes's penchant for secrecy drove me to distraction and this was one such time. After we settled in the carriage, I taxed him for not trusting me or his brother with this knowledge and he smiled briefly. "You must allow me my little peculiarities, Watson. I admit that I am fond of a dramatic revelation or two."

Mycroft coughed, as if in agreement. During our journey, both the Holmes brothers would speak only of inconsequential matters and I slumped in the corner, staring out the window and attempting to discern our direction and ultimate goal.

As we approached Hampstead Heath, I turned to Holmes. "No, Holmes, it cannot be! Longridge cannot be hiding in his uncle's home."

"Never fear, Watson, he is not."

"Then where..." My voice trailed off.

The carriage stopped before The Queen of Sheba, where we had lunched previously, and Holmes bustled us out of the brougham and into the building. We came upon the landlord still tying on his apron.

"Ah, Mr Byrnes!" cried Holmes as he headed up the stair. "Forgive us, we will only be a moment!" I followed close on his heels.

"Sir! Wait! You cannot—"

"I rather think we can," said Mycroft, taking the landlord's arm and preventing him from following us.

Holmes did not hesitate at the top of the stair, but turned left and dashed down a dim corridor.

At the far end a pale form moved, emitting a shriek. "What are you doing here? What do you want?"

Putting on a burst of speed, Holmes ran past a young woman—the landlord's daughter—and crashed through a door at the end of the hall. I was just behind him, in time to see a dark head disappear over the window-sill. Holmes leapt for the window while I, without prompting, turned on my heel and hastened back the way we had come, dodging the girl who shrieked and followed me.

Mycroft was soothing the landlord as I passed and in a moment I was out the door and calling to the groom to assist us. I rounded the building as a wild-eyed and wild-haired young man—presumably Alston Longridge—dropped from the window ledge to the ground and hared off in the direction of his uncle's house. Holmes was a scarce breath behind him.

Longridge made it to the shrubbery, but fortunately slipped on a slick patch of ground and landed, face-first, in a magnificent rhododendron. It was the work of a moment for the three of us—Holmes, the groom, and myself—to extricate him and escort the begrimed young man, muttering and swearing, back to the inn. The groom returned to his horses, richer by half a crown as a reward for his efforts, while Holmes and I saw Longridge inside.

Mycroft greeted our arrival with an ill-concealed sigh, for he and Mr Byrnes had been joined by Mr Byrnes's daughter, Susan. No longer the shy and retiring girl of yesterday, she harangued Mycroft with a practiced air. As soon as she noticed us, she ran to Longridge and threw her arms around him.

"What have they done to you?" she cried, releasing him only to brush away the loam and leafy bits that clung to his shirt and hair.

"Nothing that he did not do to himself," said Holmes. He glanced at his brother, who raised a single brow and nodded once. "Mr Byrnes, may we beg the use of a private room? I would prefer to handle this matter quietly, at least initially."

We were shown into a snug room. Miss Susan only agreed to wait outside after Longridge and Holmes promised that her *paramour* would not leave without informing her. Once Longridge extricated himself from Susan's clasp, he stalked into the room and stood, arms crossed, looking into the fire.

Mycroft sat on a horsehair settee, whilst Holmes leaned against the mantelpiece, his gaze fixed on the young man. I took a place before the door, my back to the polished oak boards. If I could not help with the interrogation, at least I could act as guard.

Longridge turned to face us. Before his present troubles he would have been considered a handsome man, but now his countenance showed the ravages of sleeplessness and perhaps guilt, for purpled bruises stained the thin skin beneath his eyes and his pasty complexion was bedewed with perspiration. With a shaking hand he pushed heavy locks from his forehead.

"I suppose introductions are in order," said Holmes. "Although since you followed your sister to our doorstep and smoked a cigarette made of Egyptian tobacco until I spotted you and you fled, you surely know that I am Sherlock Holmes and this is my colleague, Dr Watson. The other gentleman is my brother Mycroft."

"Well done, Mr Sherlock Holmes," he said, his voice a hoarse rasp. "I know of you and Dr Watson, of course." He nodded at Mycroft with a frayed air of insouciance. "And Mr Holmes. What can I do for you, gentlemen?"

Holmes barked a laugh. "I'll give you credit for nerve, Mr Longridge. Our errand here is two-fold. I was initially tasked by your sister to find you, for she was concerned by your disappearance, despite the letter you wrote to assuage her worry."

Longridge drew a deep breath and met Holmes's gaze. "Well, you have succeeded in finding me. I'm certain Rose will be relieved to know that I am well and living almost next door to her." He threw himself into a nearby chair, leaned back and closed his eyes. "Now go away."

"It is not as simple as that," said Holmes. "I said that our errand was two-fold. The other matter with which we are concerned is far more serious." He sat in the chair across from Longridge, hands clasped before him. "I have come into possession of information regarding a threat to the Government...." He paused, his piercing gaze fixed on the young man.

Longridge did not open his eyes, but his hand quivered.

"If it is a matter of money," began Mycroft.

Before he could continue, Longridge opened his eyes and leapt to his feet, his face contorted. "Money? So that's what this is about? You think you can simply buy my cooperation?"

"No," replied Holmes quietly. "But we could settle your debts."

Longridge hesitated, brow furrowed, breathing heavily. "And what would you expect in exchange?"

Mycroft spread his hands. "It's quite simple. Merely answer our questions honestly and completely."

"No."

Cocking his head to one side, Mycroft regarded him steadily. "I see."

"I doubt that very much."

"Then please do explain it to me."

"No," Longridge said, thrusting his hands in his trouser pockets in a vain attempt at nonchalance. "No, I'm not saying another word."

Mycroft glanced at his brother, but Holmes looked at me and rose. Then I heard loud voices in the corridor outside our room.

I turned and opened the door, intending to slip through and see who was causing such a commotion, but stopped on the threshold, staring. Mr Byrnes struggled with a disheveled Dr Rashad, who was clutching a piece of paper. Miss Susan grasped her father's sleeve, tugging ineffectually.

Upon seeing me, Mr Byrnes gasped, "Sorry, sir. He says it's important."

Holmes came up beside me. "What is it, Rashad?"

"They have her, Mr Holmes!" he cried, waving the paper. "Those bastards have taken Rose!"

"What?" Longridge tried to push between Holmes and me, but we both grabbed his arms and stopped his progress. "Abdul?" His voice cracked.

Rashad's snarl softened when he looked at Longridge and he stilled, holding out the paper. "This was slipped under my door less than an hour ago." His gaze turned to Holmes. "Mr Holmes, you must help us!"

Holmes released Longridge and plucked the letter from Rashad's hands. He quickly scanned the document, then indicated the room we had just occupied. "If you will."

Longridge twisted in my grasp. "Let me go! I must find her!"

"We will," said Holmes, his face set, implacable. "But we must first discuss the matter and you must tell us everything you know."

"I cannot!"

Byrnes released Rashad, who crossed the room and stood before his friend. "Alston, we *must* cooperate with Mr Holmes," he said quietly, practically vibrating with tension. "If we don't find her by tonight...." He raised his hand and covered his eyes.

"But..." Longridge took a long shaky breath, then nodded. "Very well."

In a trice, Holmes herded us back into the small room, thanking Mr Byrnes for his assistance and closing the door on the attentive faces of both father and daughter.

Rashad and Longridge, wide-eyed and abashed, looking far younger and more frightened than they had a few minutes ago, sat in the chairs on either side of the fireplace. Mycroft had not moved from his seat on the settee, but sat in stolid imperturbability. I resumed my place before the door; it was possible that either or both of the young men would tire of Holmes's questions and rush headlong into the search.

"What can you tell us about the paper and author of the message?" asked Mycroft.

Holmes took his place by the fire and examined the paper. "It is cheap enough, readily bought at any stationers. Written with a worn nib. The author uses block letters, but cannot disguise his innately elegant penmanship. Apart from that, it is uninformative."

"And the threat?"

"'We have Rose, your flower of womanhood. Tell no one and she will be returned unharmed once the task is done. Otherwise, she will make an amusing plaything for those who support our cause.'"

With an inarticulate cry, Longridge leapt to his feet. "No! He promised—"

"Who is *he*?" Mycroft snapped. "The threat stands clear before you, Mr Longridge. Will you cooperate and allow us a chance to find and rescue your sister, or will you continue your foolish silence and condemn her to a horrifying fate?"

Rashad stood and faced his friend. He reached out and laid a quivering hand on Longridge's shoulder. "We must speak. Even if I did not love her as I do, I could not live, knowing what my silence would mean to her."

Longridge's gaze moved from Rashad to Holmes to me and thence to the narrow window.

"Even if you managed to break free," said Mycroft gently, "do you not think we have the resources to quickly track you? You *cannot* complete your mission."

Longridge's shoulders slumped. "Then either Rose or I will be ruined."

"If we can discover your sister's whereabouts and return her to safety," said Mycroft, "we can take steps to mitigate your fate."

The young man struggled with himself for a long moment, but eventually gave in to the inevitable. "I will tell you what I can. I fear it isn't much."

He collapsed into a chair, his hands shaking. I slipped out the door and requested a glass of brandy from Mr Byrnes, which was immediately provided. Returning to the room, I insisted Longridge drink before beginning his story. After a few sips his colour improved and he appeared to gain strength.

His tale was a familiar one and coincided with Rashad's account: a young man with more money than sense who fell in with a dubious crowd and who soon saw his debts mounting far beyond his means to pay.

"I was desperate, Mr Holmes, when I received a letter asking me to meet a man in a Cairo coffee shop to discuss 'relieving me of my burden.' I agreed and that night I drank coffee with an educated Egyptian."

"Can you describe this man?" asked Holmes.

"Only generally," said Longridge. "He sat in the shadows and much of his face was concealed with a *kaffiyah*, that is, a head-cloth. I could tell that he was bearded, of middle age, thin and spoke English well, with only a slight accent."

"And what of his proposal?" said Mycroft.

Longridge drew a deep breath. "In exchange for paying off my debts, I would secret several unique and valuable artifacts in my personal luggage and remove all documentation relating to their discovery. I would, in essence, be violating every principle of scientific excavation my uncle instilled in me. When I returned to England I would leave them at a tobacconist's on Wimpole Street. I have no idea what happened to them after that."

"That was all?" Mycroft raised one eyebrow.

Longridge glanced at Rashad. "No."

"Alston, you said that was all you were asked to do!" Rashad stared at his friend, brow furrowed. "What else did they demand of you?"

"It is ridiculous," said Longridge. "Absurd! I am to go to Downing Street this evening and when the prime minister emerges to attend a state dinner, I will set off a string of firecrackers, shout in support of Egyptian independence, jostle passersby and generally create a scene."

"You would certainly do that," I said with a laugh. "Not to mention drawing the attention of any constables in the area."

"Thereby affording a diversion," added Holmes. "We can hazard a guess as to the reason."

Mycroft nodded. "Indeed."

"What reason is that?" asked Rashad. "Apart from Alston making a public laughing-stock of himself."

Longridge shrugged and a maidenly blush tinted his cheeks. "I would do more in order to be free from my debts."

"I'm afraid there is nothing amusing about this matter, Doctor, Mr Longridge." Holmes's voice was icy. "You have become involved in nothing less than an attempt to assassinate the prime minister."

Both young men gaped at Holmes. The colour drained from Longridge's face and Rashad gasped; their reactions were a testament to their lack of fore-knowledge regarding the plot.

"No," breathed Longridge. "No, that can't be."

"Impossible! Alston would never consider such a thing!" cried Rashad.

"Of course I would not!"

Holmes narrowed his eyes. "Then prove your loyalty to crown and country by helping us discover the leaders."

"Very well," said Longridge, wilting beneath Holmes's stern regard. "We will do what we can to help."

"Excellent!" cried Holmes, rubbing his hands together. "Now, I know Miss Susan climbed the wall to your room and retrieved the artifacts you were tasked to acquire. Was it your uncle's servant Hussein who unlatched the window for her?"

"Yes, but how did you know that?"

Holmes waved away Longridge's question. "It was obvious to one who can read the clues. How did you communicate your request to Hussein?"

"I wrote him a note, which was delivered by the bootboy."

"You were confident he would do as you asked?"

"Hussein would never question an order from any of us."

"How convenient," said Mycroft, rising from the settee in the manner of a whale breeching. "Sherlock, it is growing late...."

"Yes. Yes, you are right." Holmes paused for a moment, his forefinger tapping lightly on his lips. "I believe, Mr Longridge, that you placed in your luggage two stone statuettes from Egypt, each about eight inches tall with heavy rectangular bases."

"Good God, Mr Holmes!" Longridge leapt to his feet. "Are you a wizard? How on earth did you know that?"

Holmes waved his hand negligently. "I also know that your statuettes went to Sir Richard Lovage."

"Lovage?" Brow furrowed, Longridge glanced at Rashad. "The collector?"

"Do you know him?"

Longridge chuckled dryly. "Only as a thorn in my uncle's side. My uncle disapproves of private collectors."

Rashad frowned. "I beg your pardon, but what does this have to do with finding Rose... Miss Longridge"

Immediately sobering, Longridge took a step toward Holmes. "Rose! We must find her, Mr Holmes!" He turned to me, his expression that of a bewildered child. "But where do we start?"

Mycroft consulted his pocket watch and gave a gentle cough. "Sherlock, time presses. I will accompany Mr Longridge while he completes his task and shall entrust Dr Rashad to your care."

"'Complete my task?'" cried Longridge. "Of course I won't—"

"But you will, Mr Longridge," said my friend. "You will be under observation, as will those whom Mycroft suspects of being involved."

"But Lord Salisbury..."

"Will not be in any danger, I assure you," said Mycroft, taking Longridge's arm. "Your involvement is critical, however. It will allow us to identify and shine light upon those lurking in the shadows."

Longridge hesitated, then nodded.

Holmes turned to his brother. "You will call in the police?"

"Of a sort."

"Ah."

"Gentlemen," said Mycroft, a note of authority in his voice that brooked no further discussion. "We shall confer on this matter later, once Lord Salisbury and the young lady are safe."

I opened the door for Mycroft and Longridge. They passed me, Mycroft with beefy fingers wrapped tightly around the young man's upper arm, Longridge with imploring gaze and lagging steps, and I closed the door behind them.

"Well, Holmes," I said. "How are we to find Miss Longridge? She could be anywhere."

Holmes picked up the letter Rashad received and contemplated it for a moment. "No, I think not. In his haste, the kidnapper has given himself away, Watson." He turned to Rashad. "I doubt they have injured Miss Longridge, but she is no doubt uncomfortable and frightened and we should free her as soon as possible."

Rashad started toward the door. "Then why are we waiting, Mr Holmes?"

⚔ ⚔ ⚔ ⚔

We squeezed into a cab and Holmes was unexpectedly forthcoming as we set out.

"The handwriting in the letter is that of Sir Richard Lovage," he said, smiling briefly at my expression of outrage at the news. "Yes, even so, Watson."

"Why would he do such a thing?" I asked.

"That is a question Sir Richard can more properly answer," he said. "I am certain that Mycroft and his colleagues will be inquiring into his motivations once this day is done."

"But what of Rose?" Rashad's brow was furrowed.

"I will be able to answer that more fully once we reach our destination."

Rashad heaved a great breath and slumped against the seat. "How could he have captured her in the first place? And where?"

That I could answer. "She sent a note that she would call upon us today. I expect Sir Richard's men were watching the Professor's house and when she left, waylaid her along her route."

"She is not a timid woman and would have fought back," said Rashad. "They must have struck her unconscious."

"Speculation without facts is unproductive," said Holmes, who then proceeded to ignore our further questions and stare thoughtfully out the window.

⚔ ⚔ ⚔ ⚔

Holmes directed the driver to the head of an alley behind Sir Richard's house, where we disembarked. A stable yard stood before us, somnolent in the afternoon light, its quiet only broken by the buzz of flies around filth.

With a quick look around, Holmes chivvied us to an alcove interrupting a blank brick wall, where we would be sheltered from prying eyes. He then raised his hand to his lips and blew a piercing whistle.

A small dark head appeared over a water barrel. "Mr 'olmes!" The head was followed by a thin form clad in a most bizarre collection of rags, including a much-mended nightshirt with the lower portion unevenly cut off to fashion a shirt, and a waistcoat several sizes too large. The child scrambled over the barrel and dashed to Holmes, where he executed a peculiar salute.

"Report," said Holmes, nodding gravely at the small figure.

The boy gave a cheeky grin and saluted again. "Well, Mr 'olmes, I followed 'im, like you asked. 'Opped on behind the carriage, neat as a pin. 'E an' two of 'is grooms went to 'Empstead 'Eath, where 'e waited outside the 'ouse you described until a carriage carryin' a young lady came out. 'Is nibs stopped it an' 'ad words wif 'er, sommat about 'er brovver."

Rashad groaned and covered his face with his hands. Brows raised, the boy glanced at him, shrugged, then turned back to Holmes.

"She 'opped out of 'er carriage and into 'is and we drove to a ware'ouse down by the docks. One of the grooms climbed out, went inside the ware'ouse and comes right back wif the watchman, who 'eads to the pub at the corner. Then the two grooms carry a big bundle between 'em and into the ware'ouse they go. We drove back, 'e saunters inside and 'e 'asn't stirred an hinch since."

"Very good, Jenkins. Where is this warehouse?"

Jenkins gave a detailed description of the location and exterior of the building where Miss Longridge was being held. Holmes appeared to recognize the area and asked a few questions regarding the building's situation relative to others. Finally satisfied, he handed the child a shilling, with instructions to remain on duty and not to let Sir Richard leave without following.

We returned to our cab and once inside with directions given, I turned to Rashad.

"From Jenkins's report, I am certain they did not harm her. They probably used chloroform or a similar compound to render her unconscious."

My words did not appear to provide much comfort to the young man, for his fingers whitened in his clasped hands and his tightly-pressed lips were bloodless.

"Holmes," I tried. "What is the plan once we reach the warehouse? I did not bring my revolver with me and unless you have secreted one in your pocket, I fear we are weaponless."

"My pockets are quite without firearms, Watson," said Holmes with a careless wave of his hand. "Our actions once we reach our destination will depend on a number of factors, none of which I can speak of with any certainty until I view the field of battle, as it were."

✗　✗　✗　✗

As we traveled closer to the docks, the character of the buildings, not to mention the denizens of the areas, changed. Dressed stone gave way to brick, which gave way to timber. Shadows lengthened and deepened, damp crawled up the walls from mud and cobbles. The very air was miasmic, redolent with the smell of the river.

Our cab finally drew to a halt at a nondescript intersection and Holmes roused himself.

"We are around the corner from the warehouse where Miss Longridge is being held. Stay here while I reconnoiter." He stepped from the cab to pay the driver.

"Don't be ridiculous, Holmes," I said, clambering out to the muddy street. "The task will go faster if we both go."

Rashad joined us. "I will not be left."

Holmes glanced at us and gestured for us to follow as the cab clattered away. He pointed out the warehouse, but led us to the front of a public house on a nearby corner.

He motioned us to a dank, unused doorway in the building adjacent to the pub. "You both must wait while I see if the watchman is still here. If he is and we all try to question him, he will undoubtedly refuse to speak." He turned up the collar of his coat and by merely altering his stance and expression, became a rough character in keeping with the locale. With a nod, he rounded the corner and was gone.

Rashad sighed and lowered his head, apparently deep in thought. After several minutes, he turned to me. "Is there any hope that we can rescue Miss Longridge, Doctor?"

"I have seen Holmes triumph over greater odds," I replied. "If it can be done, Holmes will prevail."

"I wish I shared your optimism."

A voice came from the street. "Have faith, Dr Rashad!"

I gave a start. "Holmes?"

"Who else should it be?" Holmes rounded the brick wall that formed a portion of our hiding place and clapped Rashad on the shoulder. "Take heart. Cunningham, the watchman, was in the midst of drowning his sorrows in the pub's best bitter, but was still sober enough and angry enough at his unwarranted dismissal to provide information about the interior of the warehouse—for a price, of course."

"Well?" Rashad quivered with suppressed energy. "What are we to do?"

"Come."

Holmes led us down an alleyway and around the back of the warehouse, where a small door was set into a set of large double doors. He extracted a key from his pocket and raised it with a smile.

"Courtesy of Cunningham?" I asked.

"Indeed." His smile disappeared. "Once we are inside, we must tread lightly and not speak save in an emergency, for sound carries well in such a cavernous space. Cunningham reckons they will be holding her in a small staging area to the right of the front doors."

"Surely there's an upper office," I said. "Would they not prefer that to being on the warehouse floor?"

"Perhaps so," said Holmes. "But I have been reliably informed that the upper office is cramped and airless and that the only door is locked with a Chubb lock, to which Cunningham does not have the key. While is it possible they have taken her to the office, it is not probable."

Rashad paced as Holmes spoke, his movements growing increasingly erratic. Finally he rounded on Holmes, eyes blazing. "Enough! We must act now!"

Holmes gazed at him, one brow raised. "We *are* acting now, Doctor. If you would be so kind as to collect a few of those broken bricks lying next to the building, I will open the door. Once we are close to Sir Richard's men, we will lob one or two of the bricks away from us. While they go to investigate, you will assist Miss Longridge while Watson and I stand guard and fend them off, if necessary. We will attempt to exit from the front, but if that's not possible, we shall return here. Is that clear?"

Rashad and I nodded and I picked up an abandoned Stillson spanner that lay beside a stack of barrels. I hefted it, smacking it into my palm several times. It would make an admirable cosh, if necessary.

We entered in Holmes's wake, moving as silently as possible through a dim maze of crates and barrels; most were covered in a thick layer of dust and had obviously not been disturbed for some time. What could they contain?

Holmes raised his hand and we halted, Rashad quivering like a hound straining at a lead. A rumble of male laughter echoed in the rafters, dying away to a mumble. After a moment, Holmes nodded and we proceeded.

At last we reached a vantage point. We crouched behind two large crates and peered through the narrow gap between them. In a clearing of perhaps ten feet by ten, two men sat on small crates, a barrel acting as a table, all their attention on the playing cards in their hands. I searched for Miss Longridge in vain, my heart sinking when I did not see her.

Holmes bent and murmured in my ear. "She is wrapped in the tartan travelling rug."

I nodded. Only the soles of her boots were visible as she lay on a rough pallet of straw, her captors between us.

Beside me, Rashad stiffened and whispered, "Rose." No doubt he spotted her as well.

Holmes tapped on his shoulder and Rashad startled. With a gesture, Holmes indicated the direction for him to toss one of the brick halves he carried.

Jaw set, Rashad lobbed the brick into the maze of crates and it landed with a thud. The two guards stared at each other for a moment, then dropped their playing cards and leapt to their feet. After exchanging a glance and a nod, one grabbed a piece of pipe from where it lay on the floor and moved over to the bundle that was Miss Longridge. The other pulled a pistol from his coat pocket and walked in the direction of the noise.

I waited until the second man disappeared into the crates before tapping Rashad's shoulder and pointing a little to the right of where his original throw landed. He bared his teeth and heaved the brick; this time it landed with a crash.

The remaining guard started, but remained at his station and did not take the bait. I grimaced at Holmes, who merely shrugged. Hefting the spanner, I leaned toward him.

"You and Rashad take on this one; I'll flush out the other," I murmured.

He nodded and I turned away, listening intently to the sound of movement among the crates. The man I followed, a great, hulking brute, obviously felt no reason to tread softly, for a child could have followed his winding path through the crates and barrels.

We were some way from where Miss Longridge lay when I heard a sharp cry from that direction.

"Bert!" And then a series of grunts and thuds, as Holmes and Rashad attacked.

My man let out a ripe curse. "Alf?" he shouted to no response.

Ahead of me, I glimpsed him retracing his steps by heading down a narrow passage bordered on both sides by stacked crates; I ran to ambush him at the end closest to me. When he emerged from the passage, his hand wielding his gun slightly in the lead, I leapt out and collided with him, swinging the spanner. The length of metal caught his wrist, sending the gun flying. He screamed and we caromed into a barrel as he collapsed to his knees, his wrist cradled to his chest.

I scrambled to my feet, but before I could wield the spanner again, he let out a bellow and launched himself at me. His broad, bullish head struck my midsection, winding me, and I crashed against a crate. Thick fingers found my throat as he pressed forward, his red-rimmed eyes mad with fury. My head swam, my sight grew dim as his grip squeezed, an iron band around my trachea.

Desperate for oxygen, I brought the spanner down on his lower back. He yelped but did not loosen his hold; indeed, it felt as if his fingers dug deeper. With a final, Herculean effort, I willed my numbed fingers to tighten on the spanner and smashed it into the back of his skull.

With a groan, he fell to the ground, insensible. I drew in huge gulps of air, my head clearing slowly. As soon as I could walk without danger of collapsing, I knelt and checked my assailant's pulse. It was strong beneath my fingers and I breathed a small sigh of relief. I have no objection to killing one who has attacked me, but would prefer to bring him and his colleague before the law. I palpated the back of his bruised and bleeding head, but his skull was thick and despite my blow, remained intact. He would not regain consciousness anytime soon, so I hurried to assist Holmes and Rashad.

I need not have worried, for I arrived to find a disheveled Holmes securely binding the bruised and bloodied guard with a length of rope, while Rashad freed Miss Longridge from the travelling rug. She lay limp in his arms, only the shallow movement of her breast showing she yet lived.

"The brutes!" I cried—croaked, rather—when I saw the remains of the chloroform-soaked cloth that had been bound over her nose and mouth and the bruises forming on her face and throat.

"I take it you have disabled the other one," said Holmes, frowning as his gaze traveled over my abused throat. "Does he need to be bound as well?"

I nodded and we soon collected Bert, tying his hands and feet together firmly. Once that was done I tended to Miss Longridge, who was reviving slowly after her ordeal.

"Thank you, Doctor," she murmured. "I am not seriously injured."

"I shall kill them." Rashad's words were quiet, but I did not doubt their sincerity.

"I share your anger at Miss Longridge's treatment, but let the law deal with these two," said Holmes. "Our aim is to catch those who have engineered this outrage, as well as the threat to Lord Salisbury. I am safe in saying that once they are tangled in our snare, Mycroft will ensure there is neither escape nor pity for the perpetrators."

Within the hour, a constable had been located and dispatched for assistance and our two captives, now fully conscious, had become exceedingly vocal in their protestations of innocence and demands to see Sir Robert blamed for the kidnapping.

Holmes stared down at the two, trussed like Christmas geese on the filthy straw, and quietly promised that if they did not hold their tongues, he would leave them alone with Rashad. The immediate silence was blissful.

Miss Longridge, her dark eyes clear and bright again, pulled from Rashad's protective embrace and stood facing Holmes. "I am most grateful for your help, gentlemen, and am sorry that you have been injured whilst rescuing me, but how did you find me?"

Holmes briefly explained the events of the past several hours.

When he had finished, Miss Longridge frowned at Rashad. "Although I love him dearly, I can believe Alston would be so naïve and foolish, but you, Abdul!"

To his credit, Rashad did not waste our time with flimsy protestations. He bowed his head, meekly accepting Miss Longridge's censure.

"Do not judge Dr Rashad too harshly," said Holmes, ignoring her lifted brow and skeptical gaze. "He was not privy to the majority of the plot."

At that moment, several uniformed officers arrived, along with three men dressed in mufti, whom I took to be detectives. Holmes took them aside and after a brief conversation he returned with the news that we were free to leave.

"Mycroft will undoubtedly have questions for us later," he said. "But his men will take charge of our prisoners."

"And what of Sir Richard?" I asked, my throat still tender. "Will they arrest him?"

"He is being watched discreetly, but we do not want him to get the wind up. There are others involved in this affair, possibly at high levels within the Government, and Mycroft means to smoke them out. Mr Longridge will play his part—"

"No!" cried Miss Longridge. "You must not ask this of him!"

"I am afraid we must." Holmes turned to watch as our two prisoners were removed from the warehouse. "It is essential that the plot proceed as planned."

"But what of Lord Salisbury?" said Rashad. "Surely your brother would not agree to actions that could endanger the life of the Prime Minister!"

"That is well in hand, Doctor." Holmes consulted his pocket watch. "Watson and I must hurry to Downing Street. Dr Rashad, please escort Miss Longridge back to Baker Street, where she can rest and recover—"

"I do not need to rest and recover." Miss Longridge lifted her chin in challenge. "I am perfectly recovered, and insist on joining you."

"My dear Miss Longridge," I began.

"That is out of the question," said Holmes, while Rashad shook his head.

"Someone must watch over Alston's interests," she said, "if for no other reason than to ensure he does not become the cats-paw of anyone else."

I opened my mouth to protest as Holmes burst into laughter. Miss Longridge scowled at him and he held up his hands as he struggled to control his smile.

"Forgive me." He clapped his hands together. "Yes, yes, you shall join us and keep an eye on your brother's interests. And you, Dr Rashad, will come and keep an eye on Miss Longridge."

✗   ✗   ✗   ✗

We drove to an anonymous building near Downing Street, where we were closely scrutinized before being conducted to an office as bland and nondescript as a blanc mange. A tall, thin man as characterless as his office rose from behind his cluttered desk. "Ah, Mr Holmes. I am Barrington-Smythe," he said.

As Holmes performed the necessary introductions, he returned Barrington-Smythe's bow. Then he murmured "so plain Mr Smith was not good enough any more."

If Barrington-Smythe heard Holmes, he gave no indication. "Mr Holmes, your brother requests that you and Dr Watson join him. Your... companions may wait here."

"I will do nothing of the sort," said Miss Longridge. "My brother is—"

"An exceedingly foolish young man," said Barrington-Smythe, a touch of anger warming his voice. "Who would be wise to leave these matters to his betters."

"Only to be manipulated by those so-called betters," she retorted. "I shall ensure that he will not become your dupe." Miss Longridge turned and stepped toward the door.

Holmes intercepted her, shaking his head. "Come, Miss Longridge. I agreed to bring you along to keep watch over your brother's interests, but there is much to be done before the evening is over. Please sit down." He glanced at Barrington-Smythe. "Perhaps tea would be possible?"

While Barrington-Smythe summoned a young man and sent him for tea, Holmes drew me aside. "I must consult with Mycroft, Watson. Keep an eye on the young lady."

"And what of Rashad?"

Holmes chuckled. "He is Ruth to Miss Longridge's Naomi. By watching her you will, perforce, watch him." With a final glance at the young couple, he slipped through the door.

A tedious quarter-hour ensued. Another young man brought in a covered tray and dispensed tea, which was indeed soothing to my poor abused throat. Once our tea was drunk and a few rather stale pieces of bread and butter were consumed, we sat in silence until Holmes reappeared in the doorway.

"Well, Miss Longridge," he snapped, settling his cuffs, "your brother refuses to cooperate unless he is allowed to see you and ensure for himself that you are none the worse for your ordeal."

"I cannot allow," began Barrington-Smythe, but he subsided at a sharp gesture from Holmes.

With a triumphant smile Miss Longridge rose, her movements mirrored by Rashad and Barrington-Smythe. "How fortunate that I am here and can immediately reassure him, Mr Holmes."

"Indeed." Holmes's frown softened and he appeared to regain his *sang-froid*. "Yes, Dr Rashad, you may accompany her." He gestured to the door.

We were escorted through a labyrinthine series of corridors, eventually debouching through a small side door onto Derby Gate. Alston Longridge stood on the pavement near the Whitehall corner, his grim expression melting into a broad smile as he beheld his sister.

She threw herself into his arms with a cry of joy and he held her close for a long moment. Finally he drew away and studied her, his smile fading as he beheld her bruises. With a gentle finger he traced a purpling spot on her cheek.

She shook her head. "It is nothing," she said. "They will fade soon and all will be well."

"I wish I could believe that," he replied, stepping away. She clung to him, but did not object when he withdrew his hands from hers. "Mr Mycroft Holmes has promised to intercede on my behalf once this is over. Pray that he can sort out this mess."

She grew solemn. "And I pray that it stays sorted."

"Now," said Holmes, "Mr Longridge must prepare for his part. This way, Miss Longridge."

We turned onto Whitehall, joining the jostling crowd on the pavement. Holmes led us past the Red Lion and I gazed longingly into the dim interior. A pint and a pork pie would have filled the empty cavern inside me, which was now making itself felt and unfortunately, heard.

There was no respite, however, and we continued down the pavement, Holmes and Rashad in an animated conversation about the seemingly magical properties of Roentgen's discovery. Holmes waxed eloquent about its investigative assistance, while Dr Rashad argued for its help in diagnoses. Miss Longridge, arm in arm with Dr Rashad, appeared to ignore their conversation and like a robin in a winter garden, looked about curiously as we walked.

Suddenly Miss Longridge checked her progress and stared across the street.

"Uncle Preston?" With scarcely a pause, she caught up her skirts and darted through a gap in the traffic. "Uncle Preston!"

Holmes was the first to regain his wits and follow her, while Rashad and I trailed close behind. Dodging wagons, cabs, and carriages, I scanned the pavement as I ran. Professor Longridge did indeed stand gaping at his niece on the opposite pavement. He wore a broad-brimmed hat that shaded his face and a shapeless coat of an indeterminate colour, but there was no hiding that sturdy form and those chiseled features.

As Miss Longridge approached, he lifted his hands and cried out. "No!" Seldom have I heard such a cry of anguish, and with a flare of his coat he turned and ran. Miss Longridge and Holmes pelted after him, but another familiar form caught my eye.

Head bowed, the servant Hussein strode along in the opposite direction. He clutched a large paper-wrapped parcel to his breast and appeared to match his stride to the crowd, neither lagging behind nor forging ahead, in an effort, perhaps, to avoid notice. He did not appear to see me and I checked my mad dash as I made it safely across the street, turning to shadow his footsteps.

We covered several hundred feet when, without warning, Hussein turned on his heel and strode back up the pavement toward me. I had no time to conceal myself, or even to avert my face—his gaze met mine and the expression of shock and surprise on his visage would have been comical if the stakes were not so serious.

With a shout he barreled past me, shoving unwary pedestrians and toppling several to the ground. I leapt after him, bounding over a woman's skirts as she lay stunned, and cried out "Stop! Thief!" I hoped that timeless plea for help might garner the necessary assistance.

I moved as quickly as I could, yet he outdistanced me easily. He wove between the unwary, his path clearly delineated by jostled pedestrians.

"Thief! Stop him!" I cried again.

Suddenly his head disappeared and a cry went up from the crowd that immediately formed. A deep voice bellowed and another, familiar voice rang out above the hubbub.

"Back! All of you!"

"Holmes!" I forced my way through a sea of coats and dresses, emerging into a clearing where Rashad pinned Hussein to the pavement, Miss Longridge stood near the Professor, who was held fast by two large constables, and Holmes cradled the parcel in his arms.

"Ah, there you are, Watson," said Holmes. "And unless I am much mistaken—yes, Mr Longridge, Mycroft, please join us."

Longridge hurried to his sister, while Mycroft Holmes, looking as solid and respectable as a banker, calmly regarded the scene, a raised eyebrow his only concession to the drama of the moment.

"Well done, Sherlock," he said. "I take it that the bomb is not in imminent danger of exploding?"

"I doubt it, but just in case..." Holmes turned to the Professor. "Are we likely to be blown to bits, Professor? No, do not struggle, sir. Please do not move, Mr Longridge. I ask again, Professor: are your niece and nephew in danger of dying by your hand?"

The Professor suddenly sagged in the arms of the constables. "No. I have not set the timer."

"Excellent!" cried Holmes. He handed the parcel to another constable, who received it gingerly. "Take it away. Carefully, mind!"

The constable was shepherded away by two of Mycroft's men and I must say that I breathed a sigh of relief once that deadly parcel was out of sight.

"And now," continued Holmes, rubbing his hands together and looking altogether delighted, "shall we allow the constables to perform their duties, Mycroft? Or would you prefer to take charge of the matter?"

Mycroft heaved a sigh and waved a hand toward the building behind us. "We may as well conclude this annoying and ridiculous episode, Sherlock. Dr Rashad, please allow your captive to rise... No, Hussein, there is no point in attempting to escape. Surely you can see that you will not run far before you are recaptured. Now, let us all repair to my office, where you, Professor, will explain the reasons behind this act of treason. If you will not, Sherlock will do so."

✗　✗　✗　✗

There were too many participants to fit comfortably in Mycroft's office, so we reconvened in an office used for larger meetings. A large dining table was surrounded by a dozen chairs and a tea service adorned the sideboard, steam wafting from the silver pot, a selection of cakes spread out on the three tiers of the cake stand.

After settling Miss Longridge in her seat I raided the sideboard, for I was quite ravenous. Mycroft took his place at the head of the table, while the Professor and Hussein were bustled into seats on opposite sides, with a burly constable standing behind each of their chairs. Frowning, head bowed, Holmes stood behind the chair at the foot of the table, his gaze focused on polished mahogany. Miss Longridge and Rashad sat between the Professor and Mycroft, while Longridge and I took our places beside Hussein. Once seated, we all turned to Holmes with expectant expressions.

After a few moments, Holmes raised his head. "Professor, when did Sir Richard initially approach you regarding his plan to assassinate Lord Salisbury?"

A murmur passed around the table as the Professor stared at his clasped hands. "I received his letter the day we returned from Egypt."

Miss Longridge turned to him. "You did not know of this until after Alston disappeared?"

Holmes held up his hand. "Please reserve your questions and comments until the Professor has finished. Continue, if you will."

Professor Longridge sighed. "Lovage asked me to meet him regarding a matter of some importance to my nephew. Alston had not been himself for the past several weeks but we were closing up the excavation and preparing to leave Egypt for the season and I... I put my own concerns ahead of my nephew's well-being and never enquired into the reason for his abstraction." He looked at Longridge. "I am sorry, my boy. I failed you."

"No! It is I who brought disgrace to our family," cried Longridge and was immediately hushed by Holmes.

The Professor continued. "When Alston disappeared I chastised myself for my inaction and agreed to meet Lovage in the hopes I would receive more information on the source of Alston's troubles." He bowed his head, his throat working.

"At which point," Holmes said, "Sir Richard informed you that he had bought up your nephew's gambling debts and that he expected Mr Longridge to perform a service... How did he phrase it?"

"'To rid the country of a perfidious demagogue and release those unjustly enslaved.'"

Mycroft leaned back in his chair. "We suspected Sir Richard is in league with the radicals who are willing to use violence to achieve Egyptian independence, and now we have proof."

"I suspect that he takes a rather practical view of the matter," said Holmes, turning to the Professor. "Did Sir Richard mention what he receives in exchange for supporting their cause?"

"Artifacts," snarled the Professor, his eyes flashing. "He crowed to me—me!—that once the English and French were tossed out he would receive the pick of the artifacts discovered, allowing him to amass an unparalleled collection! When I objected, he told me that if I crossed him he would ruin Alston and ensure I would never excavate in Egypt again. I..." He covered his face with his hands for a moment, then raised his head, his clenched fists thudding on the table top. "I asked that... that *blackguard* what he asked of Alston in return for forgiving his debts. When he told me, I could not, *would* not allow it!"

"So Mr Longridge was to throw the bomb at Lord Salisbury," said Holmes.

"What?" Longridge half-rose from his seat. "Untrue! He never asked me—"

"Sit down. He did not ask you because the Professor agreed to perform that act instead." Holmes regarded Longridge gravely.

"Before she died," said the Professor, "I promised my sister that I would care for her children as my own. I did what any father would do."

Miss Longridge reached out, resting her hand on the Professor's. His expression softened as he gazed at her and he covered her hand with his own.

With a cough, he continued. "Lovage insisted that Alston be there, however; I could not sway him."

"And he provided the ingredients for the bomb," said Holmes.

"Yes," agreed the Professor. "From his work on our expeditions, Hussein has some experience with explosives and assumed the task of making the infernal thing—"

"Hence your mention regarding the state of his cuffs the day we visited!" I said, my gaze fixed on Holmes.

He smiled. "Exactly. Given the Professor's recent stay in Egypt and the rumours of unrest in that country, the traces of the ingredients for an incendiary device on his servant's cuff gave rise to concern. My research into who might be involved led me directly to Sir Richard and when Watson and I called upon him that day, I identified two statues of a size and shape that matched the impressions in the clothing packed in Mr Longridge's case. The statues were obviously recent acquisitions and it was no great difficulty to identify them as ones brought from Egypt by Mr Longridge."

I nodded, then a thought struck. "But Sir Richard visited Lord Salisbury after we left."

"No," said Holmes. "He entered the Prime Minister's residence, but there are others who live and work there in addition to Lord Salisbury."

Mycroft waved a negligent hand. "We have identified the interested party—a secretary Sir Richard had been blackmailing for over a year—and have quietly removed him from the premises."

"But Alston, why did you disappear from the ship and take refuge in The Queen of Sheba?" asked Miss Longridge.

"I was told not to return to the house with you and Uncle Preston," said the young man, his expression rueful. "I knew that Byrnes and Susan would keep my secret and I would still be close by in case you needed me."

Miss Longridge nodded. "Yes, Susan has grown into quite the woman." When her brother opened his mouth to reply, she held up her hand. "We shall discuss this further when we return home."

Longridge returned her steady gaze for a moment, then glanced at Rashad. "We shall discuss a number of things when we return home."

Miss Longridge's cheeks grew pink, but she met her brother's look without flinching.

Rashad, sitting on Miss Longridge's other side, took her free hand then turned to Holmes. "And what of Sir Richard? He is the instigator of all this; is he to simply walk away without censure?"

Holmes gestured to Mycroft, who answered Rashad's question. "Do not fret, Doctor. My men are in the process of... encouraging Sir Richard to meet with me in..." He consulted his pocket watch. "...a quarter-hour. I believe our discussion will be very interesting and that Sir Richard will find it expedient to surrender the whole of his current Egyptological collection to the British Museum and retire from public life. Otherwise he might find himself in a rather difficult legal situation."

"That is all?" exclaimed Rashad. "After brutally kidnapping Rose and threatening to disgrace Alston, that is the extent of his punishment?"

Mycroft rose ponderously. "Alas, Dr Rashad, it is the best I can do under the circumstances. Sir Richard has champions in Parliament and the Government and we must learn to accept the possible. Believe me, he will find the next several years neither comfortable nor pleasant."

⚔   ⚔   ⚔   ⚔

Sir Richard did indeed lose his collection to the British Museum, although he was allowed to 'present' it to the Museum as a gift. Miss Longridge and Dr Rashad married the following year and eventually Hussein abandoned his dislike of the good doctor. Her brother and Susan's wedding followed the year after.

Professor Longridge and his family and servants continued to excavate in Egypt and made several remarkable finds. Holmes recently pointed out an article in the *Times* describing their latest discovery, which apparently was due to the new Mrs Longridge's fearless exploration of certain sheer cliffs. Beautiful illustrations of the tomb and its contents were ascribed to a Mrs Rashad.

"Well," I said after I finished the article. "Who would have thought that awkward, tow-headed girl would be responsible for discovering a three-thousand-year-old tomb."

Holmes leaned back and chuckled. "After seeing how she scaled the walls of Professor Longridge's house, I am not surprised. It was quite a remarkable feat for a girl her age."

"Yes, she was quite intrepid. And Mrs Rashad—Miss Longridge as was—has a positive talent for drawing. The Professor appears to have two excellent female staff members."

"Quite," said Holmes with a yawn. "And now, Watson, if you would hand me that Bradford, I suspect our current client will telegraph a request that we meet him in York. We might as well be prepared."

✗

Carla Coupe fell into writing short stories almost without noticing. Two of her short stories—"Rear View Murder" in *Chesapeake Crimes II* and "Dangerous Crossing" in *Chesapeake Crimes 3*—were nominated for Agatha Awards. She has written a number of Sherlock Holmes pastiches, which have appeared in *Sherlock Holmes Mystery Magazine, Sherlock's Home: The Empty House*, and *Irene's Cabinet*. Her story "The Book of Tobit" was included in *The Best American Mystery Stories of 2012*.

THE ADVENTURE OF THE STOCKBROKER'S CLERK

by Sir Arthur Conan Doyle

Shortly after my marriage I had bought a connection in the Paddington district. Old Mr Farquhar, from whom I purchased it, had at one time an excellent general practice; but his age, and an affliction of the nature of St Vitus's dance from which he suffered, had very much thinned it. The public not unnaturally goes on the principle that he who would heal others must himself be whole, and looks askance at the curative powers of the man whose own case is beyond the reach of his drugs. Thus as my predecessor weakened his practice declined, until when I purchased it from him it had sunk from twelve hundred to little more than three hundred a year. I had confidence, however, in my own youth and energy and was convinced that in a very few years the concern would be as flourishing as ever.

For three months after taking over the practice I was kept very closely at work and saw little of my friend Sherlock Holmes, for I was too busy to visit Baker Street, and he seldom went anywhere himself save upon professional business. I was surprised, therefore, when, one morning in June, as I sat reading the British Medical Journal after breakfast, I heard a ring at the bell, followed by the high, somewhat strident tones of my old companion's voice.

"Ah, my dear Watson," said he, striding into the room, "I am very delighted to see you! I trust that Mrs Watson has entirely recovered from all the little excitements connected with our adventure of *The Sign of the Four*."

"Thank you, we are both very well," said I, shaking him warmly by the hand.

"And I hope, also," he continued, sitting down in the rocking-chair, "that the cares of medical practice have not entirely obliterated the interest which you used to take in our little deductive problems."

"On the contrary," I answered, "it was only last night that I was looking over my old notes, and classifying some of our past results."

"I trust that you don't consider your collection closed."

"Not at all. I should wish nothing better than to have some more of such experiences."

"To-day, for example?"

"Yes, to-day, if you like."

"And as far off as Birmingham?"

"Certainly, if you wish it."

"And the practice?"

"I do my neighbour's when he goes. He is always ready to work off the debt."

"Ha! nothing could be better," said Holmes, leaning back in his chair and looking keenly at me from under his half-closed lids. "I perceive that you have been unwell lately. Summer colds are always a little trying."

"I was confined to the house by a severe chill for three days last week. I thought, however, that I had cast off every trace of it."

"So you have. You look remarkably robust."

"How, then, did you know of it?"

"My dear fellow, you know my methods."

"You deduced it, then?"

"Certainly."

"And from what?"

"From your slippers."

I glanced down at the new patent-leathers which I was wearing. "How on earth—" I began, but Holmes answered my question before it was asked.

"Your slippers are new," he said. "You could not have had them more than a few weeks. The soles which you are at this moment presenting to me are slightly scorched. For a moment I thought they might have got wet and been burned in the drying. But near the instep there is a small circular wafer of paper with the shopman's hieroglyphics upon it. Damp would of course have removed this. You had, then, been sitting with your feet outstretched to the fire, which a man would hardly do even in so wet a June as this if he were in his full health."

Like all Holmes's reasoning the thing seemed simplicity itself when it was once explained. He read the thought upon my features, and his smile had a tinge of bitterness.

"I am afraid that I rather give myself away when I explain," said he. "Results without causes are much more impressive. You are ready to come to Birmingham, then?"

"Certainly. What is the case?"

"You shall hear it all in the train. My client is outside in a four-wheeler. Can you come at once?"

"In an instant." I scribbled a note to my neighbour, rushed up-stairs to explain the matter to my wife, and joined Holmes upon the doorstep.

"Your neighbour is a doctor," said he, nodding at the brass plate.

"Yes, he bought a practice as I did."

"An old-established one?"

"Just the same as mine. Both have been ever since the houses were built."

"Ah! then you got hold of the best of the two."

"I think I did. But how do you know?"

"By the steps, my boy. Yours are worn three inches deeper than his. But this gentleman in the cab is my client, Mr Hall Pycroft. Allow me to introduce you to him. Whip your horse up, cabby, for we have only just time to catch our train."

The man whom I found myself facing was a well-built, fresh-complexioned young fellow, with a frank, honest face and a slight, crisp, yellow moustache. He wore a very shiny top-hat and a neat suit of sober black, which made him look what he was—a smart young City man, of the class who have been labelled cockneys, but who give us our crack volunteer regiments, and who turn out more fine athletes and sportsmen than any body of men in these islands. His round, ruddy face was naturally full of cheeriness, but the corners of his mouth seemed to me to be pulled down in a half-comical distress. It was not, however, until we were in a first-class carriage and well started upon our journey to Birmingham that I was able to learn what the trouble was which had driven him to Sherlock Holmes.

"We have a clear run here of seventy minutes," Holmes re-marked. "I want you, Mr Hall Pycroft, to tell my friend your very interesting experience exactly as you have told it to me, or with more detail if possible. It will be of use to me to hear the succession of events again. It is a case, Watson, which may prove to have something in it, or may prove to have nothing, but which, at least, presents those unusual and outré features which are as dear to you as they are to me. Now, Mr Pycroft. I shall not interrupt you again."

Our young companion looked at me with a twinkle in his eye.

"The worst of the story is," said he, "that I show myself up as such a confounded fool. Of course it may work out all right, and I don't see that I could have done otherwise; but if I have lost my crib and get nothing in exchange I shall feel what a soft Johnny I have been. I'm not very good at telling a story, Dr Watson, but it is like this with me.

"I used to have a billet at Coxon & Woodhouse's, of Draper Gardens, but they were let in early in the spring through the Venezuelan loan, as no doubt you remember, and came a nasty cropper. I have been with them five years, and old Coxon gave me a ripping good testimonial when the smash came, but of course we clerks were all turned adrift, the twenty-seven of us. I tried here and tried there, but there were lots of other chaps on the same lay as myself, and it was a perfect frost for a long time. I had been taking three pounds a week at Coxon's, and I had saved about seventy of them, but I soon worked my way through that and out at the other end. I was fairly at the end of my tether at last, and could hardly find the stamps to answer the advertisements or the envelopes to stick them to. I had worn out my boots paddling up office stairs, and I seemed just as far from getting a billet as ever.

"At last I saw a vacancy at Mawson & Williams's, the great stock-broking firm in Lombard Street. I dare say E. C. is not much in your line, but I can tell you that this is about the richest house in London. The advertisement was to be answered by letter only. I sent in my testimonial and application, but without the least hope of getting it. Back came an answer by return, saying that if I would appear next Monday I might take over my new duties at once, provided that my appearance was satisfactory. No one knows how these things are worked. Some people say that the manager just plunges his hand into the heap and takes the first that comes. Anyhow it was my innings that time, and I don't ever wish to feel better pleased. The screw was a pound a week rise, and the duties just about the same as at Coxon's.

"And now I come to the queer part of the business. I was in diggings out Hampstead way, 17 Potter's Terrace. Well, I was sitting doing a smoke that very evening after I had been promised the appointment, when up came my landlady with a card which had 'Arthur Pinner, Financial Agent,' printed upon it. I had never heard the name before and could not imagine what he wanted with me, but of course I asked her to show him up. In he walked, a middle-sized dark-haired, dark-eyed, black-bearded man, with a touch of the sheeny about his nose. He had a brisk kind of way with him and spoke sharply, like a man who knew the value of time.

"'Mr Hall Pycroft, I believe?' said he.

"'Yes, sir,' I answered, pushing a chair towards him.

"'Lately engaged at Coxon & Woodhouse's?'

"'Yes, sir.'

"'And now on the staff of Mawson's.'

"'Quite so.'

"'Well,' said he, 'the fact is that I have heard some really extraordinary stories about your financial ability. You remember Parker, who used to be Coxon's manager. He can never say enough about it.'

"Of course I was pleased to hear this. I had always been pretty sharp in the office, but I had never dreamed that I was talked about in the City in this fashion.

"'You have a good memory?' said he.

"'Pretty fair,' I answered modestly.

"'Have you kept in touch with the market while you have been out of work?' he asked.

"'Yes. I read the stock-exchange list every morning.'

"'Now that shows real application!' he cried. 'That is the way to prosper! You won't mind my testing you, will you? Let me see. How are Ayrshires?'

"'A hundred and six and a quarter to a hundred and five and seven-eighths.'

"'And New Zealand consolidated?'

"'A hundred and four.'

"'And British Broken Hills?'

"'Seven to seven-and-six.'

"'Wonderful!' he cried with his hands up. 'This quite fits in with all that I had heard. My boy, my boy, you are very much too good to be a clerk at Mawson's!'

"This outburst rather astonished me, as you can think. 'Well,' said I, 'other people don't think quite so much of me as you seem to do, Mr Pinner. I had a hard enough fight to get this berth, and I am very glad to have it.'

"'Pooh, man; you should soar above it. You are not in your true sphere. Now, I'll tell you how it stands with me. What I have to offer is little enough when measured by your ability, but when compared with Mawson's it's light to dark. Let me see. When do you go to Mawson's?'

"'On Monday.'

"'Ha, ha! I think I would risk a little sporting flutter that you don't go there at all.'

"'Not go to Mawson's?'

"'No, sir. By that day you will be the business manager of the Franco-Midland Hardware Company, Limited, with a hundred and thirty-four branches in the towns and villages of France, not counting one in Brussels and one in San Remo.'

"This took my breath away. 'I never heard of it,' said I.

"'Very likely not. It has been kept very quiet, for the capital was all privately subscribed, and it's too good a thing to let the public into. My brother, Harry Pinner, is promoter, and joins the board after allotment as managing director. He knew I was in the swim down here and asked me to pick up a good man cheap. A young, pushing man with plenty of snap about him. Parker spoke of you, and that brought me here to-night. We can only offer you a beggarly five hundred to start with.'

"'Five hundred a year!' I shouted.

"'Only that at the beginning; but you are to have an overriding commission of one per cent on all business done by your agents, and you may take my word for it that this will come to more than your salary.'

"'But I know nothing about hardware.'

"'Tut, my boy, you know about figures.'

"My head buzzed, and I could hardly sit still in my chair. But suddenly a little chill of doubt came upon me.

"'I must be frank with you,' said I. 'Mawson only gives me two hundred, but Mawson is safe. Now, really, I know so little about your company that—'

"'Ah, smart, smart!' he cried in a kind of ecstasy of delight. 'You are the very man for us. You are not to be talked over, and quite right, too. Now, here's a note for a hundred pounds, and if you think that we can do business you may just slip it into your pocket as an advance upon your salary.'

"'That is very handsome,' said I. 'When should I take over my new duties?'

"'Be in Birmingham to-morrow at one,' said he. 'I have a note in my pocket here which you will take to my brother. You will find him at 126B Corporation Street, where the temporary offices of the company are situated. Of course he must confirm your engagement, but between ourselves it will be all right.'

"'Really, I hardly know how to express my gratitude, Mr Pinner,' said I.

"'Not at all, my boy. You have only got your deserts. There are one or two small things—mere formalities—which I must arrange with you. You have a bit of paper beside you there. Kindly write upon it "I am perfectly willing to act as business manager to the Franco-Midland Hardware Company, Limited, at a minimum salary of 500 pounds."'

"I did as he asked, and he put the paper in his pocket.

"'There is one other detail,' said he. 'What do you intend to do about Mawson's?'

"I had forgotten all about Mawson's in my joy. 'I'll write and resign,' said I.

"'Precisely what I don't want you to do. I had a row over you with Mawson's manager. I had gone up to ask him about you, and he was very offensive; accused me of coaxing you away from the service of the firm, and that sort of thing. At last I fairly lost my temper. "If you want good men you should pay them a good price," said I.

"'"He would rather have our small price than your big one," said he.'

"'"I'll lay you a fiver," said I, "that when he has my offer you'll never so much as hear from him again."'

""'Done!" said he. "We picked him out of the gutter, and he won't leave us so easily." Those were his very words.'

"'The impudent scoundrel!' I cried. 'I've never so much as seen him in my life. Why should I consider him in any way? I shall certainly not write if you would rather I didn't.'

"'Good! That's a promise,' said he, rising from his chair. 'Well, I'm delighted to have got so good a man for my brother. Here's your advance of a hundred pounds, and here is the letter. Make a note of the address. 126B Corporation Street, and remember that one o'clock to-morrow is your appointment. Goodnight, and may you have all the fortune that you deserve!'

"That's just about all that passed between us, as near as I can remember. You can imagine, Dr Watson, how pleased I was at such an extraordinary bit of good fortune. I sat up half the night hugging myself over it, and next day I was off to Birmingham in a train that would take me in plenty time for my appointment. I took my things to a hotel in New Street, and then I made my way to the address which had been given me.

"It was a quarter of an hour before my time, but I thought that would make no difference. 126B was a passage between two large shops, which led to a winding stone stair, from which there were many flats, let as offices to companies or professional men. The names of the occupants were painted at the bottom on the wall, but there was no such name as the Franco-Midland Hardware Company, Limited. I stood for a few minutes with my heart in my boots, wondering whether the whole thing was an elabourate hoax or not, when up came a man and addressed me. He was very like the chap I had seen the night before, the same figure and voice, but he was clean-shaven and his hair was lighter.

"'Are you Mr Hall Pycroft?' he asked.

"'Yes,' said I.

"'Oh! I was expecting you, but you are a trifle before your time. I had a note from my brother this morning in which he sang your praises very loudly.'

"'I was just looking for the offices when you came.'

"'We have not got our name up yet, for we only secured these temporary premises last week. Come up with me, and we will talk the matter over.'

"I followed him to the top of a very lofty stair, and there, right under the slates, were a couple of empty, dusty little rooms, uncarpeted and uncurtained, into which he led me. I had thought of a great office with shining tables and rows of clerks, such as I was used to, and I daresay I stared rather straight at the two deal chairs and one little table, which with a ledger and a waste-paper basket, made up the whole furniture.

"'Don't be disheartened, Mr Pycroft,' said my new acquaintance, seeing the length of my face. 'Rome was not built in a day, and we have lots of money at our backs, though we don't cut much dash yet in offices. Pray sit down, and let me have your letter.'

"I gave it to him, and he read it over very carefully.

"'You seem to have made a vast impression upon my brother Arthur,' said he, 'and I know that he is a pretty shrewd judge. He swears by London, you know; and I by Birmingham; but this time I shall follow his advice. Pray consider yourself definitely engaged.'

"'What are my duties?' I asked.

"'You will eventually manage the great depot in Paris, which will pour a flood of English crockery into the shops of a hundred and thirty-four agents in France. The purchase will be completed in a week, and meanwhile you will remain in Birmingham and make yourself useful.'

"'How?'

"For answer, he took a big red book out of a drawer.

"'This is a directory of Paris,' said he, 'with the trades after the names of the people. I want you to take it home with you and to mark off all the hardware-sellers, with their addresses. It would be of the greatest use to me to have them.'

"'Surely, there are classified lists?' I suggested.

"'Not reliable ones. Their system is different from ours. Stick at it, and let me have the lists by Monday, at twelve. Good-day, Mr Pycroft. If you continue to show zeal and intelligence you will find the company a good master.'

"I went back to the hotel with the big book under my arm, and with very conflicting feelings in my breast. On the one hand, I was definitely engaged and had a hundred pounds in my pocket; on the other, the look of the offices, the absence of name on the wall, and other of the points which would strike a business man had left a bad impression as to the position of my employers. However, come what might, I had my money, so I settled down to my task. All Sunday I was kept hard at work, and yet by Monday I had only got as far as H. I went round to my employer, found him in the same dismantled kind of room, and was told to keep at it until Wednesday, and then come again. On Wednesday it was still unfinished, so I hammered away until Friday— that is, yesterday. Then I brought it round to Mr Harry Pinner.

"'Thank you very much,' said he, 'I fear that I underrated the difficulty of the task. This list will be of very material assistance to me.'

"'It took some time,' said I.

"'And now,' said he, 'I want you to make a list of the furniture shops, for they all sell crockery.'

"'Very good.'

"'And you can come up to-morrow evening at seven and let me know how you are getting on. Don't overwork yourself. A couple of hours at Day's Music Hall in the evening would do you no harm after your labours.' He laughed as he spoke, and I saw with a thrill that his second tooth upon the left-hand side had been very badly stuffed with gold."

Sherlock Holmes rubbed his hands with delight, and I stared with astonishment at our client.

"You may well look surprised, Dr Watson, but it is this way," said he: "When I was speaking to the other chap in London, at the time that he laughed at my not going to Mawson's, I happened to notice that his tooth was stuffed in this very identical fashion. The glint of the gold in each case caught my eye, you see. When I put that with the voice and figure being the same, and only those things altered which might be changed by a razor or a wig, I could not doubt that it was the same man. Of course you expect two brothers to be alike, but not that they should have the same tooth stuffed in the same way. He bowed me out, and I found myself in the street, hardly knowing whether I was on my head or my heels. Back I went to my hotel, put my head in a basin of cold water, and tried to think it out. Why had he sent me from London to Birmingham? Why had he got there before me? And why had he written a letter from himself to himself? It was altogether too much for me, and I could make no sense of it. And then suddenly it struck me that what was dark to me might be very light to Mr Sherlock Holmes.

I had just time to get up to town by the night train to see him this morning, and to bring you both back with me to Birmingham."

There was a pause after the stock-broker's clerk had concluded his surprising experience. Then Sherlock Holmes cocked his eye at me, leaning back on the cushions with a pleased and yet critical face, like a connoisseur who has just taken his first sip of a comet vintage.

"Rather fine, Watson, is it not?" said he. "There are points in it which please me. I think that you will agree with me that an interview with Mr Arthur Harry Pinner in the temporary offices of the Franco-Midland Hardware Company, Limited, would be a rather interesting experience for both of us."

"But how can we do it?" I asked.

"Oh, easily enough," said Hall Pycroft cheerily. "You are two friends of mine who are in want of a billet, and what could be more natural than that I should bring you both round to the managing director?"

"Quite so, of course," said Holmes. "I should like to have a look at the gentleman and see if I can make anything of his little game. What qualities have you, my friend, which would make your services so valuable? Or is it possible that—" He began biting his nails and staring blankly out of the window, and we hardly drew another word from him until we were in New Street.

✗   ✗   ✗   ✗

At seven o'clock that evening we were walking, the three of us, down Corporation Street to the company's offices.

"It is no use our being at all before our time," said our client. "He only comes there to see me, apparently, for the place is deserted up to the very hour he names."

"That is suggestive," remarked Holmes.

"By Jove, I told you so!" cried the clerk. "That's he walking ahead of us there."

He pointed to a smallish, dark, well-dressed man who was bustling along the other side of the road. As we watched him he looked across at a boy who was bawling out the latest edition of the evening paper, and, running over among the cabs and busses, he bought one from him. Then, clutching it in his hand, he vanished through a doorway.

"There he goes!" cried Hall Pycroft. "These are the company's offices into which he has gone. Come with me, and I'll fix it up as easily as possible."

Following his lead, we ascended five stories, until we found ourselves outside a half-opened door, at which our client tapped. A voice within bade us enter, and we entered a bare, unfurnished room such as Hall Pycroft had described. At the single table sat the man whom we had seen in the street, with his evening paper spread out in front of him, and as he looked up at us it seemed to me that I had never looked upon a face which bore such marks of grief, and of something beyond grief—of a horror such as comes to few men in a lifetime. His brow glistened with perspiration, his cheeks were of the dull, dead white of a fish's belly, and his eyes were wild and staring. He looked at his clerk as though he failed to recognize him, and I could see by the astonishment depicted upon our conductor's face that this was by no means the usual appearance of his employer.

"You look ill, Mr Pinner!" he exclaimed.

"Yes, I am not very well," answered the other, making obvious efforts to pull himself together and licking his dry lips before he spoke. "Who are these gentlemen whom you have brought with you?"

"One is Mr Harris, of Bermondsey, and the other is Mr Price, of this town," said our clerk glibly. "They are friends of mine and gentlemen of experience, but they have been out of a place for some little time, and they hoped that perhaps you might find an opening for them in the company's employment."

"Very possibly! very possibly!" cried Mr Pinner with a ghastly smile. "Yes, I have no doubt that we shall be able to do something for you. What is your particular line, Mr Harris?"

"I am an accountant," said Holmes.

"Ah, yes, we shall want something of the sort. And you, Mr Price?"

"A clerk," said I.

"I have every hope that the company may accommodate you. I will let you know about it as soon as we come to any conclusion.

And now I beg that you will go. For God's sake leave me to my-self!"

These last words were shot out of him, as though the constraint which he was evidently setting upon himself had suddenly and utterly burst asunder. Holmes and I glanced at each other, and Hall Pycroft took a step towards the table.

"You forget, Mr Pinner, that I am here by appointment to receive some directions from you," said he.

"Certainly, Mr Pycroft, certainly," the other resumed in a calmer tone. "You may wait here a moment and there is no reason why your friends should not wait with you. I will be entirely at your service in three minutes, if I might trespass upon your patience so far." He rose with a very courteous air, and, bowing to us, he passed out through a door at the farther end of the room, which he closed behind him.

"What now?" whispered Holmes. "Is he giving us the slip?"

"Impossible," answered Pycroft.

"Why so?"

"That door leads into an inner room."

"There is no exit?"

"None."

"Is it furnished?"

"It was empty yesterday."

"Then what on earth can he be doing? There is something which I don't understand in this matter. If ever a man was three parts mad with terror, that man's name is Pinner. What can have put the shivers on him?"

"He suspects that we are detectives," I suggested.

"That's it," cried Pycroft.

Holmes shook his head. "He did not turn pale. He was pale when we entered the room," said he. "It is just possible that—"

His words were interrupted by a sharp rat-tat from the direction of the inner door.

"What the deuce is he knocking at his own door for?" cried the clerk.

Again and much louder came the rat-tat-tat. We all gazed expectantly at the closed door. Glancing at Holmes, I saw his face turn rigid, and he leaned forward in intense excitement. Then suddenly came a low guggling, gargling sound, and a brisk drumming upon woodwork. Holmes sprang frantically across the room and pushed at the door. It was fastened on the inner side. Following his example, we threw ourselves upon it with all our weight. One hinge snapped, then the other, and down came the door with a crash. Rushing over it, we found ourselves in the inner room. It was empty.

But it was only for a moment that we were at fault. At one corner, the corner nearest the room which we had left, there was a second door. Holmes sprang to it and pulled it open. A coat and waistcoat were lying on the floor, and from a hook behind the door, with his own braces round his neck, was hanging the managing director of the Franco-Midland Hardware Company. His knees were drawn up, his head hung at a dreadful angle to his body, and the clatter of his heels against the door made the noise which had broken in upon our conversation. In an instant I had caught him round the waist, and held him up while Holmes and Pycroft untied the elastic bands which had disappeared between the livid creases of skin. Then we carried him into the other room, where he lay with a clay-coloured face, puffing his purple lips in and out with every breath—a dreadful wreck of all that he had been but five minutes before.

"What do you think of him, Watson?" asked Holmes.

I stooped over him and examined him. His pulse was feeble and intermittent, but his breathing grew longer, and there was a little shivering of his eyelids, which showed a thin white slit of ball beneath.

"It has been touch and go with him," said I, "but he'll live now. Just open that window, and hand me the water carafe." I undid his collar, poured the cold water over his face, and raised and sank his arms until he drew a long, natural breath. "It's only a question of time now," said I as I turned away from him.

Holmes stood by the table, with his hands deep in his trousers pockets and his chin upon his breast.

"I suppose we ought to call the police in now," said he; "and yet I confess that I'd like to give them a complete case when they come."

"It's a blessed mystery to me," cried Pycroft, scratching his head. "Whatever they wanted to bring me all the way up here for, and then—"

"Pooh! All that is clear enough," said Holmes impatiently. "It is this last sudden move."

"You understand the rest, then?"

"I think that it is fairly obvious. What do you say, Watson?"

I shrugged my shoulders. "I must confess that I am out of my depths," said I.

"Oh, surely if you consider the events at first they can only point to one conclusion."

"What do you make of them?"

"Well, the whole thing hinges upon two points. The first is the making of Pycroft write a declaration by which he entered the service of this preposterous company. Do you not see how very suggestive that is?"

"I am afraid I miss the point."

"Well, why did they want him to do it? Not as a business matter, for these arrangements are usually verbal, and there was no earthly business reason why this should be an exception. Don't you see, my young friend, that they were very anxious to obtain a specimen of your handwriting, and had no other way of doing it?"

"And why?"

"Quite so. Why? When we answer that we have made some progress with our little problem. Why? There can be only one adequate reason. Someone wanted to learn to imitate your writing and had to procure a specimen of it first. And now if we pass on to the second point we find that each throws light upon the other. That point is the request made by Pinner that you should not resign your place, but should leave the manager of this important business in the full expectation that a Mr Hall Pycroft, whom he had never seen, was about to enter the office upon the Monday morning."

"My God!" cried our client, "what a blind beetle I have been!"

"Now you see the point about the handwriting. Suppose that someone turned up in your place who wrote a completely different hand from that in which you had applied for the vacancy, of course the game would have been up. But in the interval the rogue had learned to imitate you, and his position was therefore secure, as I presume that nobody in the office had ever set eyes upon you."

"Not a soul," groaned Hall Pycroft.

"Very good. Of course it was of the utmost importance to prevent you from thinking better of it, and also to keep you from coming into contact with anyone who might tell you that your double was at work in Mawson's office. Therefore they gave you a handsome advance on your salary, and ran you off to the Midlands, where they gave you enough work to do to prevent your going to London, where you might have burst their little game up. That is all plain enough."

"But why should this man pretend to be his own brother?"

"Well, that is pretty clear also. There are evidently only two of them in it. The other is impersonating you at the office. This one acted as your engager, and then found that he could not find you an employer without admitting a third person into his plot. That he was most unwilling to do. He changed his appearance as far as he could, and trusted that the likeness, which you could not fail to observe, would be put down to a family resemblance. But for the happy chance of the gold stuffing, your suspicions would probably never have been aroused."

Hall Pycroft shook his clenched hands in the air.

"Good Lord!" he cried, "while I have been fooled in this way, what has this other Hall Pycroft been doing at Mawson's? What should we do, Mr Holmes? Tell me what to do."

"We must wire to Mawson's."

"They shut at twelve on Saturdays."

"Never mind. There may be some door-keeper or attendant—"

"Ah, yes, they keep a permanent guard there on account of the value of the securities that they hold. I remember hearing it talked of in the City."

"Very good, we shall wire to him and see if all is well, and if a clerk of your name is working there. That is clear enough, but what is not so clear is why at sight of us one of the rogues should instantly walk out of the room and hang himself."

"The paper!" croaked a voice behind us. The man was sitting up, blanched and ghastly, with returning reason in his eyes, and hands which rubbed nervously at the broad red band which still encircled his throat.

"The paper! Of course!" yelled Holmes in a paroxysm of excitement. "Idiot that I was! I thought so much of our visit that the paper never entered my head for an instant. To be sure, the secret must lie there." He flattened it out upon the table, and a cry of triumph burst from his lips.

"Look at this, Watson," he cried. "It is a London paper, an early edition of the *Evening Standard*. Here is what we want. Look at the headlines: 'Crime in the City. Murder at Mawson & Williams's. Gigantic Attempted Robbery. Capture of the Criminal.' Here, Watson, we are all equally anxious to hear it, so kindly read it aloud to us."

It appeared from its position in the paper to have been the one event of importance in town, and the account of it ran in this way:

"A desperate attempt at robbery, culminating in the death of one man and the capture of the criminal, occurred this afternoon in the City. For some time back Mawson & Williams, the famous financial house, have been the guardians of securities which amount in the aggregate to a sum of considerably over a million sterling. So conscious was the manager of the responsibility which devolved upon him in consequence of the great interests at stake that safes of the very latest construction have been employed, and an armed watchman has been left day and night in the building. It appears that last week a new clerk named Hall Pycroft was engaged by the firm. This person appears to have been none other than Beddington, the famous forger and cracksman, who, with his brother, has only recently emerged from a five years' spell of penal servitude. By some means, which are not yet clear, he succeeded in winning, under a false name, this official position in the office, which he utilized in order to obtain mouldings of various locks, and a thorough knowledge of the position of the strongroom and the safes.

"It is customary at Mawson's for the clerks to leave at midday on Saturday. Sergeant Tuson, of the City police, was somewhat surprised, therefore, to see a gentleman with a carpet-bag come down the steps at twenty minutes past one. His suspicions being aroused, the sergeant followed the man, and with the aid of Constable Pollock succeeded, after a most desperate resistance, in arresting him. It was at once clear that a daring and gigantic robbery had been committed. Nearly a hundred thousand pounds' worth of American railway bonds, with a large amount of scrip in mines and other companies, was discovered in the bag. On examining the premises the body of the unfortunate watchman was found doubled up and thrust into the largest of the safes, where it would not have been discovered until Monday morning had it not been for the prompt action of Sergeant Tuson. The man's skull had been shattered by a blow from a poker delivered from behind. There could be no doubt that Beddington had obtained entrance by pretending that he had left something behind him, and having murdered the watchman, rapidly rifled the large safe, and then made off with his booty. His brother, who usually works with him, has not appeared in this job as far as can at present be ascertained, although the police are making energetic inquiries as to his whereabouts."

"Well, we may save the police some little trouble in that direction," said Holmes, glancing at the haggard figure huddled up by the window. "Human nature is a strange mixture, Watson. You see that even a villain and murderer can inspire such affection that his brother turns to suicide when he learns that his neck is forfeited. However, we have no choice as to our action. The doctor and I will remain on guard, Mr Pycroft, if you will have the kindness to step out for the police."

Lightning Source UK Ltd.
Milton Keynes UK
UKHW040011111120
373160UK00003B/296